BOOKED
FOR
MURDER

BOOKED
FOR
MURDER

An Old Juniper Bookstore Mystery

P. J. NELSON

MINOTAUR BOOKS
NEW YORK

First published in the United States by Minotaur Books, an imprint of St. Martin's Publishing Group

BOOKED FOR MURDER. Copyright © 2024 by P. J. Nelson. All rights reserved. Printed in the United States of America. For information, address St. Martin's Publishing Group, 120 Broadway, New York, NY 10271.

www.minotaurbooks.com

Design by Meryl Sussman Levavi

The Library of Congress Cataloging-in-Publication Data is available upon request.

ISBN 978-1-250-90995-4 (hardcover)
ISBN 978-1-250-90996-1 (ebook)

Our books may be purchased in bulk for promotional, educational, or business use. Please contact your local bookseller or the Macmillan Corporate and Premium Sales Department at 1-800-221-7945, extension 5442, or by email at MacmillanSpecialMarkets@macmillan.com.

First Edition: 2024

10 9 8 7 6 5 4 3 2 1

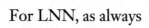

For LNN, as always

BOOKED
FOR
MURDER

1

OCTOBER CAN BE a summer month in South Georgia. Temperatures in the nineties, leaves still green and locked onto the trees; humidity so thick that a small fish could swim in it. And the gnats were everywhere. I'd forgotten about the gnats.

I left my bags in the beat-up old Fiat I sometimes referred to as Igor owing to several unfortunate accidents that had left it misshapen.

The steps up to the porch creaked out a warning, but I didn't pay any attention. If I'd paid attention to warnings, I'd never have followed Aunt Rose into the ridiculous world of the theatre.

Now I was too old for the ingenue, too young for the character parts, and you can only go to so many auditions for parts you don't get before you start considering that job in catering. Inheriting a bookstore felt like a rescue plan.

The front porch was the same as it had always been. Dried leaves from other autumns, dust from a thousand summer nights, five bentwood rocking chairs, two with broken cane seats.

I couldn't have said why my hand hesitated, holding the

old-fashioned brass key at the front door lock, but I stood there frozen for a moment, hearing Rose singing softly to herself just inside the door. Sometimes, apparently, the memory of melody lingers long after the song is gone.

I grew up in Enigma, Georgia. It's near Mystic and not far from Omega, and if you don't believe that, look at a map. We trust in the arcane in this part of Georgia. We existed first for turpentine, then for lumber. There was no reason for a private liberal arts college to be anywhere near us, but Barnsley College was thriving in the wilderness. And there was even less explanation for my aunt Rose, born in Enigma, raised near the railroad tracks, and then inexplicably bathed in the bright lights of Broadway for most of her life. She founded the Old Juniper Bookshop when she retired from the stage and returned to Enigma.

And when she died, she left it to me.

Down from Atlanta, what should have been a three-hour drive took nearly five thanks to a disagreement between a refrigerated eighteen-wheeler and a pretty blue Volvo. I arrived exhausted. Driving down the lonely main street I was a little surprised by all the empty buildings, places I used to go when I was a kid, now out of business. And at the end of that road, I pulled into the gravel driveway of the old Victorian mansion just at sunset.

And there it was: the castle of my childhood, with all its foreboding shadows.

Three stories tall, gingerbread trim, peeling paint, wraparound porch, balconies, gables, and ripple-glass windows, the house itself was a character from some lost Hawthorne novel. The burgundy and dark green color palette had been an effort to restore its look to something like the original, but the final result was more Boo Radley than Southern Belle.

I grew up here more than in my parents' house. I'd idolized my aunt Rose. She'd run away from home at seventeen and landed a job on Broadway the first week she was in New York, an understudy in *Anyone Can Whistle*. It opened April 4, 1964, and closed after nine performances, one of Sondheim's less-than-successful efforts according to the critics at the time. But Rose kept getting work, mostly in the chorus or as an understudy. Still, it was a life in the theatre, and she filled my head with her stories.

Those stories buzzing in my brain, I opened the door, and there it was: dust motes, musty air, the smell of old books, and I was in heaven. In that compendium of smells, I found my childhood, and all the long hours spent reading in the shop, talking with Aunt Rose, making plans and dreaming dreams.

I loved the ramshackle disorder of the place. It made me think of Colin Lamb's observation, "Inside, it was clear that the books owned the shop rather than the other way about," which was my aunt's organizational philosophy. The books, she always said, had told her where they wanted to be. So finding anything in the entire place was more an adventure than a destination.

In the last beam of gold from the setting sun, as the dust motes danced in the air, the smallest ballerinas in the universe, I had a deep sense of *home*.

Then the silence set in. I stood still there in the doorway and thought I'd gone deaf. The house was alone at the end of the block on the edge of town, with nearly an acre of land for the backyard garden.

Suddenly the song of a brown thrasher shot through the air. It was so loud that it startled me, and I was worried that the bird might be in the house, an omen.

I stepped inside and realized that someone had opened all the windows, at least on the first floor of the house. It hadn't done anything for the faint smell of mildew, but it had allowed the thrasher's music to come in, a better welcome than creaking stairs or stale air.

The foyer hadn't been swept in a while; it was difficult to see the other rooms in the failing light. I reached for the button switch beside the door, but when I pushed it, nothing happened. So first job in the morning: have the electricity turned on.

I remembered that Rose always kept candles in the desk that she used as her cash register. The desk was in the parlor to the left, and that room was especially dark. But I knew it well enough to get to the desk and find several long tapers and a large box of kitchen matches. Two of the candles were already in their own pewter holders. I lit one and set it on the desk, the other I carried with me. Sunlight was fading fast, and the candle in my hand gave the parlor a distinct luster of melancholy, made the room more recollection than reality.

I almost saw Rose sitting at her desk.

And there I was, at sixteen, reclined on the antique French sofa and arguing with Rose about FSU.

"It's the best theatre school in the south!" I'd told her.

She'd shook her head. "That's like saying 'the best bagel in Wyoming.' You need to study in New York."

Still, when I got a scholarship to FSU, Rose had paid all the rest of my expenses to go there. Would she have been proud of my so-called acting career in Atlanta?

The thrasher cried out again, and I suddenly had the impression that the noise was panic, not song. I battled a moment of horror-film fear—the proverbial dark, empty, haunted house with no electricity and a taper in my hand—and went to fetch a few of my things from Igor. I only got my suitcases. The rest of it would be safe in the car. I hadn't brought that much with me. I'd left most of my stuff in a storage place in Atlanta. I didn't know what else to do with it.

Back inside, I considered calling Rusty Thompson, Rose's lawyer, the one who'd told me about my odd inheritance, just to let him know I'd arrived. But I decided to leave that for the morning.

Struggling with the bags and the candle, I made more noise than necessary clattering up the stairs to the second floor where Rose had lived. There was a master suite, but that was Rose's domain, and I wasn't comfortable taking it over, not just yet. So I opted for the greenroom, the one I always slept in whenever I stayed over.

I dropped one of my bags at the doorway going into the room and I let the other fall to the floor several steps later.

The room, even in candlelight, was cheery. The walls had been painted long ago with climbing Lady Banks roses and pale blue wisteria. The antique oak Lincoln bed, the art nouveau lamps, the two-hundred-year-old Persian rugs all gave the room an air of such comfort that I once again had the sensation of homecoming.

I nudged my suitcases with my feet in the general direction of the closet. Then I got a look at myself in the mirror of the vanity next to the closet. My hair was up and wound in such a way as to hide most of the premature gray. The Irish sweater, comfortable in Atlanta's version of autumn, was too hot in Enigma's humidity. And why had I worn the jeans with the torn knees? Wasn't I getting just a little too old for that look, my mother would have asked?

I shook off that particular ghost and then headed back downstairs, taper in hand.

I knew it was too much to hope that there might be something to eat in the kitchen, but that's where I went nevertheless, because hope springs eternal in the hungry stomach.

The kitchen was in a back corner of the house, and it was small, but Rose had decked it out with the best: a Wolf dual-fuel range that must have cost a fortune, a Sub-Zero refrigerator, almost as expensive. The kitchen table had once belonged to Flannery O'Connor. There was a cast-iron skillet somewhere that she had stolen from the Broadway set of *The Fantasticks*. And in the cupboard, there was china given to her by Gwen Verdon when Rose had been in the chorus of *Chicago*. Where the money had come from or how she'd grown so close to such famous people were mysteries gone to the grave with my aunt.

Unfortunately, most of the food items left in the fridge and pantry had also gone to graves of their own. Blue chicken, fuzzy bread, and blossoming cheese were all to be thrown out in the morning. A lonely can of pinto beans and a nearly empty bag of jasmine rice would have to do for my evening meal.

But before I could find pans for the pathetic repast, a smell of burning juniper suddenly assaulted the kitchen air, the unique, bittersweet combination of fresh pine and earthy balsamic. Juniper was a protector, Rose always told me—it's why she planted so much around the house and garden. She said that when Mary and Joseph were trying to keep baby Jesus from Herod, a juniper tree hid them.

I stood there in the dark room trying to understand where the smell was coming from when a flickering red light began to spatter the back windowpanes. I took a few steps toward the window before I saw the flames.

The gazebo in the backyard garden was on fire.

2

I DROPPED THE BAG of rice and ran out the kitchen door. Twenty feet away, the old wooden gazebo, the center of the garden for a hundred years, was burning. I thought first to get water from the kitchen, then remembered the garden hose. The spigot was near the kitchen back door. It was a little hard to find in the growing darkness, but when I located it, I turned the water on full blast and dragged the hose across the lawn to the fire.

The hose was only marginally more useful than spitting on the fire would have been, but I thought it would be a good stopgap measure, especially drenching the ground and plants around the gazebo, mostly burning juniper.

If I had been a different person, I might have dragged a cell phone out of some pocket and called 911, but I didn't own a cell phone. So when the fire was subdued a bit, I dashed back into the house, to the desk in the parlor, where there was an actual telephone, and dialed the emergency number.

The fire truck was there in seven minutes, one of the benefits of a small town. The fire was out in short order, and the team of three firemen was very nice to me in the Southern Gentleman way.

"Okay then, ma'am, I'm Captain Jordon, and I believe we got her if she don't jump."

Assuming that meant the fire was mostly out, I thanked him with a nod.

Black hair, chiseled jaw, he stood over six feet tall, and the fireman's hat only added to his stature. I didn't recognize him, which almost certainly meant that he wasn't from Enigma.

"It's no telling what might have happened if you hadn't been here," he went on. "Which, excuse me for asking, but why *are* you here? The lady that owns this place has been dead for a couple of weeks."

Right. I stuck out my hand. "I'm Madeline Brimley, Rose's niece. She left the . . . the bookshop to me."

"Oh." He took my hand very delicately. "That'll explain it. I guess. What started the fire, do you know?"

"I *just* got here," I told him, staring at the smoking ruins of the gazebo. "Like fifteen minutes ago or something. I took my bags into the house and went to the kitchen to see if there was something to eat and there it was: fire."

"I see." He let go of my hand. "Well. Your deck, or whatever that was, got doused with gasoline. I mean like a whole lot. And if what you say is accurate, it looks to me like somebody set this fire right when you got here, from the burn rate. And all. Did you happen to see anybody?"

"I didn't look," I said. "You mean that somebody poured gas on that thing and then waited until I got here to light it on fire?"

He nodded, staring into my eyes. "That's one possibility."

He stood silent for a little too long and I finally realized what he was thinking.

"Wait." I shook my head. "Do you think *I* did this? I'm the one who called the fire department!"

"Well." He looked away at last. "Either which way, I got to report this to the police. It's arson."

I kept going. "You think I drove down from Atlanta, put my suitcases in a room upstairs, and then set my own inheritance on *fire*?"

His affability wore off just a little. "Ma'am, I don't know you. I don't know who owns this house. I don't know anything about this situation."

"I grew up here," I said, squinting. "You'd know that if you were from Enigma."

"Albany," he answered curtly.

Albany, Georgia, was only an hour away, but it was a city of 70,000 or so as opposed to Enigma's 1,251.

"I see." I nodded once. "Well, thank you for putting out the fire. You tell the police whatever you want. I'm going inside now to unpack. And I'm also going to try to forget about somebody watching me from the gazebo and then setting it on fire. Thanks for the nightmares."

With that I spun around and stormed back into the house. I went right to my sad little can of pinto beans, opened it, and watched the firemen pack up. Captain Jordon made notes in some kind of log, stared at the house for a moment, and then got into his fire truck and they all drove away.

The silence after they were gone was very, very loud.

Then the beans began to boil, a bubbling whisper. I turned off the burner and thought about sweeping the rice up off the floor. Instead I found one of Gwen Verdon's china bowls and a relatively clean spoon and stared at the smoke rising from the gazebo. It mixed with the first moonlight enough to make the backyard garden look like something from a Bela Lugosi movie.

I looked around the kitchen and talked louder than I should have. "Not the welcome I was expecting, Aunt Rose."

Sometimes lots of noise can chase the ghosts away. And sometimes it can't.

I could almost hear Rose say "Atlanta"—and I knew she was shaking her head. Shaking her head because I hadn't stayed in New York.

So, beans gone, rice swept up, pot and bowl in the sink, I gave up. The moon was high, and the silver slant of light through the open windows nearly hid the smoldering ruins in the backyard. But the smell of it, mixed with juniper, was beginning to give me a headache.

Up the stairs, too tired to unpack, I collapsed onto the bed in the greenroom, clothes and all.

The greenroom. Appropriate, or at least Rose might have thought so. The greenroom, of course, was where actors waited just before they went onstage. Rose always asked me, in phone calls and letters, why I was waiting in Atlanta. Why I hadn't already gone back to New York. And now it wasn't even worth going back to Atlanta.

I stared at the painted wisteria, frozen forever in just that state of bloom, never quite fully blossomed.

"Thanks for the metaphors," I sang out loud to the memory of Rose.

The memory made no answer.

So I kicked off my high tops and rolled over on the bed. I lay there for a moment, afraid that I was too tired to sleep, trying to keep out the image of some monster setting fires in the back. And what about the fireman? What about *that* guy? He was going to tell the cops that I started the fire. I was going to have to deal with small-town cops.

I rolled over so that I wouldn't have to face the damning wisteria, and there, peering up at me from the scarred hardwood floor, was the largest cat I'd ever seen, black and round.

"Are you really here?" I asked him, "or are you another memory—of all the cats who used to live here?"

He answered with a very real and hearty grunt.

"Okay," I told him. "Come on up."

I patted the bed and he launched himself onto the pillow beside me, purring louder than a Volkswagen. I lay back and he settled in.

"In the morning," I said to the cat, "you'll have to tell me who's been taking care of you since Rose . . ."

I just couldn't finish that sentence.

The smell of wet smoldering wood was getting worse, but I couldn't quite get myself off the bed to close the windows. And the metaphors just kept on coming. I couldn't *quite* get up the gumption to do something that would be good for me. Something that I *knew* would make me feel better.

When I was ten or eleven, I would often spend the night with Aunt Rose. In this very room. Why couldn't I just let the memories of those nights—free from my parents, free from my room in my parents' house—wash over me? They were great nights.

I turned on my back and stared up at the ceiling, the glass light fixture, the cracks in the paint, and the spiderwebs. I guess I was afraid I'd dream about fire.

"'For in that sleep of death what dreams may come?'" I asked the cat in my best Hamlet.

The cat did not immediately respond.

I'd played Hamlet twice. Once in an all-woman cast, once in a production so bad that we often began Act II in front of an empty house. Often.

I suddenly bolted up. "Enough!"

I said it loud enough that the cat looked up and the crickets momentarily stopped their music. I hadn't even noticed that they were singing until they stopped. I missed the sound. Isn't that always the way? You don't miss your water until your well runs dry. I loved that song. Wait. What song was that line from? Wait.

"You know what's happening, right?" I said to the cat. "I'm spiraling. Mind roulette, insomniac's free association, sleepless stream of consciousness."

It had to stop; I was exhausted.

Maybe I should get up and go downstairs and read, I thought. Find some long, boring book and I'd be out in five minutes.

Then the phone downstairs began to ring.

I glanced at my watch. The telephone on Rose's desk downstairs was ringing after most people in Enigma had gone to bed. And it didn't stop.

I thought I could let it ring forever, but after a couple of minutes it began to drive me crazy.

"Are you going to answer that?" I asked the cat.

He didn't even open his eyes.

I slid my legs over the side of the bed. By the time I was down the stairs and into the parlor I would have done almost anything to make the ringing stop.

I grabbed the receiver and barked before it even got to my mouth.

"What?"

There was a momentary silence, and I was about to hang up. Wrong number, prank call, some drunk.

But then: "Clear out!"

The man's voice was gravelly and red hot.

"Who is this?" I demanded.

"Clear out of that damn house, girl!"

"Who *is* this?" I repeated.

"Leave now, *right* now," he whispered fiercely. "Next time I'll burn down that whole house. Burn it down with you inside! You hear me?"

And then: a long, dark dial tone.

3

I OPENED THE BOOKSHOP at ten o'clock the next morning. On the dot. What was I supposed to do, let some drunk chase me away with a phone call? It only made me mad. I woke up riled. My aunt wanted me to have her place—for some unknown reason—so I wanted me to have it too. If I left town, it would be like abandoning Rose.

I hadn't slept well. Any noise—creaking house, hooting owl, snoring cat—had me up and looking out the window down at the backyard to see if someone was there, torch in hand, about to lay siege to the house.

I probably should have gone to get groceries, but when I found coffee and a French press, I also discovered an unopened package of oat bars and what appeared to be a new bag of cat food. The "best by" date on the oat bars was smudged, so I just pretended they were delicious and not at all life-threateningly expired. And anyway, when I washed them down with three cups of coffee, they were fine. The cat food bag was sealed, so I opened it and poured too much into the cat's bowl by the back door, even though the cat was nowhere to be seen.

So, sleep-deprived, cranked on coffee, cat-less, and mad

at everything in general, I opened the bookshop. Now under new management.

I don't know what I expected. Rose had been dead for several weeks and the shop had been closed for weeks before that, when she was in the hospital. Maybe if I'd come down to visit her while she was still alive, she would have told me in person why she left the shop to me. We'd talked on the phone the week she died, but I had no idea how sick she was because she kept telling me that she was fine. She was just in the hospital for some tests, that's all.

And of course there hadn't been any local news about a new owner or any sort of "Grand Reopening!" announcement about the shop. So nothing could have prepared me for my first customer.

At 10:07 the front door flew open and in strode Philomena Waldrop. She was Rose's closest friend and the best imaginable sight. Before I could speak, she had me in her arms, tight as could be, and she was laughing.

"Lord, sugar, here you are." She stood back, still holding onto my shoulders. "And look at you, just as pretty as you want to be. Oh!"

She crushed me to her once more.

"Phil," I managed to say. "Thank God you're here."

No idea why I was so relieved to see her, but suddenly everything was all right.

Rose and Philomena were as close as sisters, and Philomena was just as much my aunt, despite any lack of a blood connection.

Phil was indomitable. That's probably why she and Rose were friends. Dr. Philomena Waldrop was now the head of the psychology department of Barnsley College, the small

liberal arts school in Enigma, and a deeply respected member
of the community.

Dr. Waldrop stood nearly six feet tall. She was in her work
clothes: navy blue dress, wide black belt, sky blue scarf. It was
her customary Monday morning lecture outfit. She had long
ago chosen outfits for each day of the week, one less thing to
think about in the morning. She had worn a blue dress just
like that one every Monday since I'd been in high school.

"I'm surprised to see you," I finally managed to say. "How
did you know I was here?"

She looked away. "Oh. Well. I drive by here every morning on my way to the college. I don't know why. It's out of the
way. But when I saw that beat-up old car you drive, I knew
you were here! And here you are!"

With that, she hugged me again. I realized then that she
was wearing Joy. It was Rose's perfume.

"Well," she went on. "Tell me all about everything."

I nodded. "I guess I'm okay. It's just . . . you know, I'm sad
about the reason I'm here, obviously. But. Do you want some
coffee? I found a French press."

I headed for the kitchen. She hesitated.

"Rose never left the cash box unattended," she admonished.

I surveyed the empty rooms. "There's nobody here."
"Nevertheless."

She wouldn't budge until I made sure the cash box was
locked up in the large desk drawer, and then she followed me
into the kitchen.

"You seem to be a little more than just *sad*," she observed.
"You seem a little frightened, I can see that."

"I didn't sleep well," I told her, veering into the kitchen,
and going to the stove. "And for another thing, look, I have

to light the stovetop with a match. The electricity's off. That's why I'm not using the electric kettle over there."

Phil looked around. "Why is the electricity off? It shouldn't be. I mean I don't think it was shut off. Rose had everything in this house on autopay, including good old Colquitt Electric Membership Corporation. Did you check the circuit breaker thing?"

I lit the burner under the antique kettle from the big box of kitchen matches beside the stove. "The *what*?"

She went through the kitchen to the mud porch just inside the back door. I followed. There was a panel beside the door. She opened it.

"There." She pointed. "The master switch or whatever it's called. It's off, see?"

And with a flip of that switch the lights in the kitchen came on.

"Huh." I shook my head.

The kettle on the stovetop started whistling.

"That was fast," Phil said, turning toward the noise.

"Still hot from my—I, like, just made the first batch. There's no cream, but I found packets of Splenda if you want."

"No, I like my coffee straight . . . no chaser." She followed me back into the kitchen and went immediately to the cupboard and got out a particular cup.

"That's how I like it," she said, eyes lowered, leaning in toward me.

I suddenly realized what she was doing. It delighted me and I was eager to play along.

"*Straight, No Chaser* by Thelonious Monk, Doctor Waldrop." I took the kettle off the burner.

"You remembered!" She was clearly delighted.

Philomena and Rose had, together, the largest collection

of old jazz records on the planet. Or, at least, in South Georgia. They spent hours listening to them in the "mystery section" of the shop, which would have been the dining room if the house were a house and not a shop.

"Of course I remember," I said. "You and Rose packed my head with *so* much useless knowledge about jazz, the players, the composers, the tunes."

She laughed. "Knowledge is never useless, sweetheart. You can't ever tell when you're going to need to know who played bass on Miles Davis's first recording."

It was a test, and I knew it.

"Depends on what you mean by 'first recording' but if you mean his first as a band leader, the 1946 sessions featuring Charlie Parker, *that* bassist was none other than Mister Nelson Boyd."

She squealed like a teenager. "Right!"

And it merited *another* crushing hug.

When it was done, I got to the French press, emptied the old grounds into the trash, and put fresh grounds in. Hot water, press up, I took the handle and picked up my cup.

"Front porch?" I suggested. "You've got your mug, I see."

She nodded and followed me back through the house and we found the giant cat sitting by the screen door.

"Oh, good," Phil murmured. "Cannonball's still here."

"He's one of Rose's cats, then."

She nodded. "Last one. I wonder who's been taking care of him."

"Named after Cannonball Adderley, I assume." I smiled.

Phil nodded, pleased, and the three of us went out onto the front porch. The cat wandered off. I set the press on the porch floor between two rockers whose seats were intact and sat down gingerly in one. She took the other less carefully and we stared out into the morning.

"So," I began, casually setting up my punch line. "I had quite the welcome home last night. Electricity off, no food in the house, all the windows open, strange noises, odd memories—oh, and someone set the gazebo on fire."

Her head jutted forward very suddenly. *"What?"*

"Uh-huh," I assured her. "I set my bags down, smelled the smoke, and had to run out and turn the garden hose on it."

She stood. "I want to see it."

"Can we . . . can we just sit here for another second?" I asked. "There's more."

She blinked and her head turned in the direction of the backyard. "Oh. Well, I suppose. What *more?*"

"Lots more, actually."

She sat back down, and I pushed the plunger down in the French press. I really hadn't given it quite enough time, but I wanted to pour Philomena a cup as a kind of odd hospitality. Never tell your troubles over an empty cup.

"The fire department came," I went on. "They put out the fire, of course, but then this guy, this Captain Jordon, he looks at me and gives me the stink eye because he thinks *I* set the fire."

"You? Why would he . . . wait a minute. Mike Jordon? Well. You know he's from Albany, so he wouldn't recognize who you were."

"You know the guy?"

She nodded. "Goes to my church."

"Well, I tried to tell him who I was," I said. "And that this place was mine, but I think he might have reported me to the police."

"The police? Good Lord." She shook her head. "Small-town drama. It'll all be sorted out in no time. Our local constabulary consists primarily of two buffoons and a sweet idiot. You won't have any trouble with them. Dumb as they are, they're good boys. Got the idiot in my Intro to Psych class, as a matter of fact. Look, can we go out back? I want to see the gazebo. You know, of course, that Rose and I planted all that juniper back there."

I poured myself a little more coffee. "There's more."

"More? More than being accused of arson by that nice boy fireman?"

"He's not nice and he's not a boy," I told her. "And yes, I haven't told you the worst thing."

She composed herself, sipped her coffee, and nodded.

"Tell me, then," she said.

"So, when Captain Nice Boy left, I tried to go to bed," I continued. "But I couldn't sleep, like I said."

"First night in a new place," she commiserated.

"I guess. Only all of a sudden, the phone rang. And kept ringing. And wouldn't stop. So I got out of bed and came down to the desk and answered it. It was some man, some hoarse, monster-movie man, and he told me to get out of the house or the next time he'd burn the whole place down with me in it."

Philomena was struck dumb and motionless. She'd taken the fire in stride. Same for the fireman's suspicion of me. But this reaction was visceral; she was clearly shaken.

"Who would *say* such a thing?" she whispered harshly.

"I was more scared by the fire and the fire captain," I told her. "That was very real. The weird phone call? It seemed more . . . sorry, but it seemed more theatrical."

"What did you say to him?" she asked breathlessly.

"I didn't have the chance to say anything. He hung up."

"I . . . I'd be terrified," she managed to say. "I mean, you have *got* to talk to the police about that."

"Oh no, I don't," I told her.

"But, sugar. That person threatened to kill you! Would you at least call Rusty Thompson and tell *him*?"

"Why would I tell him?" I shook my head. "Talk is talk. Like I said, I was more concerned about the fire in the backyard."

I think she believed me.

The thing was, I hadn't unpacked anything. I hadn't even begun to think about taking the rest of my things out of Igor. Fire in the backyard, after-midnight phone threats—maybe I could sell the shop; get some kind of teaching gig at FSU. Or maybe I could just get back in my car and drive until I ran out of gas and get a waitress job wherever I'd stopped. I was the only actor I knew who had never waited tables. Maybe it was about time I started.

Then I felt Phil's hand on mine.

"It'll be all right," she said, like she'd read all my thoughts.

And in the sound of her voice was every other time she'd said those same words to me. I let my breath go, and with it went the largest part of my anxiety. That was the Philomena magic.

"Okay," I said. "You say you want to go see the gazebo, or what's left of it?"

She stood again and held out her mug. "Fortification, please."

I topped her off and we headed through the house and into the backyard garden.

The garden was always a source of pride for Rose. And for Philomena, who had done most of the heavy work. Rose was good at selecting and finding unusual plants. Phil was good with a shovel.

The more formal part of the garden was surrounded by a picket fence, but the inside of the fence was hidden by neatly trimmed azaleas, double bloomers, so they were still showing a few mauve and lavender blossoms. At the very back of the yard there were ten peach trees, but they'd long since given up their fruit. The rest of the yard was packed. Every inch. Cosmos, verbena, yarrow, zinnias, black-eyed Susans, purple coneflowers, Shasta daisies, cardinal flowers, coreopsis, gaillardias, and mile-high sunflowers—something was blooming nearly all the time. Even in October the color held on. And the garden design was as quirky as it was profuse. Odd concrete statues of Greek gods and cemetery angels seemed to be overseeing the flowers and the shrubs, supervising. Neatly arranged pebble pathways wound around moss-covered granite stones. Odd ground covers surrounded baffling topiary creatures. Of course there were rosebushes everywhere.

And at the center of the floribunda sat the throne room of the garden, the gazebo. Big enough for twenty people, it had been built in the nineteenth century by the original owners of the house, railway magnates of some sort, relatives of Rose. The thing was seven sided, for luck, and had been painted red for prosperity. Waist-high railings acted as backing for the wraparound benches inside. There were sconces for candles and several places for oil lamps. The roof was delicately curved outward seven times, one for each side, and decked with slate roof tiles. The ceiling inside was painted with clouds and blue sky.

Or had been.

Now the place looked more like a charred skeleton, and the ceiling was midnight in a coal mine.

"Oh." Philomena stopped short a few steps into the yard, staring at the derelict.

"I know," I agreed sadly, a few steps ahead of her. "And take a look at what's left of the juniper you guys planted all around it."

She looked down at the ground. The trailing juniper was charred and gnarled, unrecognizable.

Phil sniffed. "Can we go back inside?"

I took her arm and back inside we went.

"I just didn't think it would look so . . . so . . ." She couldn't finish the sentence.

"Yeah. If the fire brigade hadn't gotten here so quickly, I don't think there'd be anything left at all."

We sat down at the kitchen table. She stared down at the table; I ran my hand over the well-worn surface.

"You guys used to tell me that this table belonged to Flannery O'Connor," I said, mostly to change her mood.

"It did," she answered absently, tears still in her eyes. "We have to get someone to repair that gazebo. I mean it."

"All right." I nodded. "If I stay, I'll call someone today."

She looked up at me. Her expression was so strange that, for a second, I didn't recognize her at all.

"If you stay? Where would you go if you didn't stay here? Back to Atlanta, I guess." I thought it was odd that she said her last sentence more as encouragement than anything else.

"No, not Atlanta."

Before I could decide if I wanted to elaborate, the telephone rang.

Philomena froze. I turned my head in the direction of the noise and stood up.

"Don't answer it!" she whispered, as if the person on the other end of the phone might hear her. "What if it's that man from last night?"

"It's not likely to be the guy who called last night," I said, heading for the desk in the other room. "That kind of call doesn't happen on a sunny morning at ten thirty."

"Well, who *could* it be?"

"With any luck," I told her, "it could be a customer."

"Everyone knows Rose is gone," Phil said, following me. "And nobody knows you're here."

"Well." I turned to face her. "*Somebody* knows I'm here."

Her eyes got bigger.

"Old Juniper Bookshop," I said with more satisfaction than I'd expected. "How can I help you?"

"Yes." The man was young and definitely a local, he'd made two syllables out of the word. "Umm, would this be Madeline Brimley?"

"It would," I said.

"Ma'am, this is Officer Sanders, Enigma Police Department."

I hesitated.

"Ma'am?" he ventured.

"Yes, sorry, Officer," I said. "I assume this is about the fire in my backyard last night."

"Oh, yes ma'am, it is. See, Captain Jordon, he—"

"Captain Jordon seems to be a suspicious sort of person," I interrupted. "And he jumped to conclusions last night. He's a conclusion jumper."

Phil sidled up to me. "Who is it?" she whispered.

I put my hand over the receiver. "Sanders. Know him?"

"Billy Sanders?" She grinned. "Oh my. I just remembered that you know him."

The name sounded familiar. I went back to the phone.

"Billy," I said, "I'm Rose Brimley's niece. She left this bookshop to me. Maybe you knew Rose. Maybe you bought a textbook here. See, I think I'd like to keep the place intact for a while. I'm not interested in burning it down."

"You don't remember me," he said softly.

He sounded hurt. I covered up the phone again and whispered to Phil.

"How do I know this guy?" I asked.

"He's Hope and Donny's boy," she began.

But I could hear Billy's voice.

"You used to babysit me," he was saying.

I went back to the phone. "You're Hope and Donny's boy, right?"

Phil rolled her eyes.

"Right! You do remember. I mean, you only babysat me twice. I was nine. I didn't really need a babysitter, and you weren't but six years older than me . . ."

"Of course I remember you, Billy," I assured him. "I just never expected that you'd grow up to be a policeman."

"Well," he said, "I hung Sheetrock for a while before the police academy, but that was a *whole* lot of *boring*, so, you know."

"You know I didn't set my gazebo on fire," I said flatly.

He was silent for a second or two.

"But somebody did," he said. "And according to Captain Jordon, they did it right when you got there, so maybe I should come out and have a look. Discuss it further. Also, condolences on the passing of your aunt. I knew her well. She was a firecracker."

My smile grew. "She was."

"Tell him about the phone call!" Phil whispered insistently.

I shook my head, but Officer Sanders had heard her voice.

"You got customers already?" he asked.

"It's Doctor Waldrop," I said quickly. "She just dropped by to welcome me home."

"I *love* her," he said reverently. "She's a great teacher. Tell her Billy says hey."

"Uh-huh."

Before I could go on, he said, "All right then. I'll be over there in a hour or so."

"Oh." I wasn't crazy about that. "Today?"

"I ought to be there by noon," he said. "And when I do get there, maybe you can tell me what phone call Doctor Waldrop was talking about."

He hung up before I could think of what to say.

4

BY TWO O'CLOCK that afternoon Officer Sanders had still not made an appearance. But nearly a dozen other people had. Some were, I realized, regular customers.

An older woman in a black dress and a dark green pillbox hat wanted me to know that she would buy any mystery book in which a cat solved the crime. She introduced herself as Idell Glassie and told me that Rose had always kept her well supplied. She was eager for my assurance that she would have the same treatment under the new management. I gave her my guarantee that she'd continue to be a satisfied customer.

But most of the customers were students from the college. Apparently when Phil had gone to teach her first class, she'd told everyone that the Old Juniper Bookshop was open. And then she'd given all her students a new reading list for every one of her classes.

Running the place was strange and it was familiar. Familiar because I'd spent a lot of my younger years helping people navigate Rose's haphazard organizational system. Strange because I was the owner now, the one selling the books, the person who got the money and gave the receipts and made small talk. Wandering through the rooms in the shop, trying to help people find books, felt like a kind of déjà vu.

Each room was allegedly dedicated to a general genre—the dining room was supposed to be the mystery section, but there were also two cases of poetry, and an entire wall dedicated to records. Most of those records were the jazz platters that Rose and Phil listened to, but some of them were records of authors reading their work. I had listened to Dylan Thomas read "And Death Shall Have No Dominion," for example, about a hundred times, whether I'd wanted to or not. The parlor, where the desk was, contained most of the contemporary books, fiction and nonfiction. The study was devoted to history, biography, and older nonfiction. There were alcoves for philosophy, corners for cookbooks, a small science fiction section, and, of course, an entire wall of plays and books about the theatre. A smaller room—maybe it had been a kind of second parlor—was entirely dedicated to college textbooks, the bread and butter of the bookshop. Everywhere there were chairs and sofas for lounging, mostly antiques that had been in the house for more than a hundred years.

And then there was a tiny room filled with rare books and first editions that weren't for sale. You could only look at them in the shop. I had no idea what that room had been when the house was strictly a home, but Rose always called it "the private library." It was small, but bookshelves were on all four walls, floor to ceiling, and packed. It baffled me and I had often asked Rose why she had it in the shop since there was no money to be made from it. Why hadn't she put all those expensive volumes somewhere upstairs? Another mystery that Rose had taken to her grave.

The morning ran its course, both reassuring and hilarious.

Hilarious because the student customers, these kids, were all still apprentice human beings, but they thought they were grown. Reassuring because college students, despite hair-styles and clothes and the clichés of a younger language, were almost exactly the same as they'd been when I was in college.

Several of the boys flirted. A girl offered me a free ticket to the College Follies—she was featured in a performance of "Helpless" from *Hamilton*. Another girl bought *The Bell Jar*, *The Feminine Mystique*, and, most impressively to me, *Feminist Theory: From Margin to Center*, by bell hooks, which I always thought was a fantastic book. I was about to compli-ment the kid on her choices when she told me, in a very droll voice, that Women in Society was the most boring course she'd ever taken, but it was required for her sociology degree. So I just smiled and took her money.

And one girl lingered. She'd come into the shop around eleven o'clock and wandered, obviously not looking for any-thing in particular. She could have been a shoplifter. I kept my eye on her.

At last my former babysitting charge strode though the front door. Once I saw his face, I remembered him better. When he was little, he was a shy kid, and we'd watched Turner Classic Movies together. He especially liked Hammer horror films, the comforting kind where there's always fog in a grave-yard and a secret bookcase doorway to the mad doctor's labo-ratory. And in the end, when the dawn comes again, everything is all right.

"There he is," I said, trying to keep my voice steady.

"Hey, look at you," he said right back, grinning. "And look at all your business!"

"Philomena—Doctor Waldrop sent this particular busi-ness my way this morning," I told him.

"Nice." He kept staring. "And it's nice to see you. Man, I didn't think I'd ever see you again. When you left town, you were solid *gone*. From then on all we ever heard was that you were a famous theatrical personality in Atlanta."

"What? Where did you hear a thing like that?"

He looked around the place. "Your aunt. She was very proud. For the last several years she would eat at Mae Etta's diner and read articles about you, and reviews if they were good, to anyone who'd listen. After I joined the force, I had lunch there every day. So, actually, I couldn't avoid you."

I always thought that Rose hadn't approved of my so-called career in Atlanta.

So I managed to say, "That surprises me."

The customers in the shop all did their best to ignore the policeman in the room, but one of the boys who had flirted with me made his way very carefully to the back door and slipped out, eyes averted.

"I didn't really expect that you'd have so many customers today," Officer Sanders said. "Makes it a little more difficult to talk about what happened here last night. But can you take a moment in the backyard with me or is this a bad time?"

I lowered my voice. "To tell the truth, I didn't expect this much business either. I'm not sure what to do."

Out of nowhere, the girl I thought might be a shoplifter appeared behind me.

"I could watch things for a minute," she said softly.

I turned in my seat. There she was in her blue cotton dress and army boots. Her blond hair was braided down her back, and her wire-rimmed glasses gave her a stern look that the sweetness of her voice belied. She smiled shyly and then looked down.

"That's very kind of you to suggest it," I said hesitantly. "But I don't know."

"You don't know me." She stuck out her hand. "I'm Tandy Fletcher."

"Glad to meet you, Tandy Fletcher," I said, taking her hand. "I'm Madeline Brimley."

"Oh," she fired back, "I know who you are."

And then she looked down again. "I used to help Rose. Sometimes."

"That'll be fine, it'll be all right," said Officer Sanders. "Thank you, Tandy."

"Hey, Billy," she said, her voice barely audible.

"She's in the Intro to Psych class," he told me. "With Doctor Waldrop. Same one I'm taking, as a matter of fact."

"Ah." I stood.

"We won't be but a minute or two," he told Tandy.

She nodded and then stared at the chair behind the desk.

I pulled it out a little. "It's okay. If you're going to run the joint, I guess you could have a seat."

I headed for the back door. Officer Sanders followed.

Outside the sun was shining, and it was relatively warm. Sparrows were singing from the peach trees. The garden was lovely. Except for the wreck at the heart of it.

"Man." Officer Sanders stared. "They really burned that thing up."

"Yes, they did," I agreed.

He walked over to what was left of the gazebo, touched it, looked at his hand, then rubbed the soot off onto his pants. He sniffed around, squatted, and looked at the ground, stood and kicked a little of the burnt juniper with the tip of his boot.

"You can still smell the gasoline a little," he said, more to himself than to me.

"Hey, there's something!" I volunteered. "Search the place. You won't find any kind of gas can, or anything like that, with my fingerprints on it. Go on. Look."

He smiled. "I don't believe that'll be necessary."

"No, seriously," I began.

"Miss Brimley," he told me, "I don't for a second believe that you did this. Captain Jordon, he's just doing his job to report it, but he don't know you, or your aunt, or anything, really. If I had to guess, I'd say some kids came over here last night, not knowing you'd be here. They were here to smoke some weed or get drunk. They saw you or heard you, and they had a little accident. Took off. That's all."

I stared. "That's all?"

He nodded. "You should probably figure out what kind of insurance your aunt had and see does it cover this kind of thing. Rusty Thompson would know, he's Rose's lawyer." He lowered his voice. "You know, I used to come here in high school with Cindy Perkins. After dark, if you see what I mean."

"I know that this always used to be a great make-out spot, if that's what you mean," I said slowly.

He grinned. "Yes, ma'am, that *is* what I mean."

"I never had any personal experience—"

"It's just that I'd hate to deprive future generations of the same opportunity," he interrupted. "I'd like to see this thing rebuilt."

I was surprised that I smiled back. "Me too."

"Right, then," he said in obvious conclusion, "I'll let you get back to work. Bodes well for your return that you got a crowd on your first real day here."

I was hoping that I didn't look as relieved as I felt.

"It does, it really does," I said. "Well. Tell your momma and daddy I said hey."

He just smiled. I only learned later that they'd both been gone for several years.

Back inside, Tandy was selling books. There was a line. Apparently, people were more willing to buy from someone they knew. Or at least that was my guess.

"Okay, then, Tandy," Officer Sanders said as he passed the desk.

"Bye, Billy," she said sweetly, not looking at him.

He was at the door, with his hand on the handle, just about to step outside and be gone for good, when he stopped and turned around.

"By the way," he said, once again searching my eyes for something or other, "what was that phone call Doctor Waldrop was talking about?"

"Oh." I nodded. "Right. It was nothing. Crank call. You know. Kids or something."

He stared for a whole lot longer than I wanted him to.

"Uh-*huh*," he finally said. "Well, if it happens again, you let me know, hear? Can't have that kind of foolishness."

He reached into a pocket and produced a card with his phone number on it. I took it, nodding.

"No," I agreed, looking down at the card. "No, we cannot have that kind of foolishness."

He stared for another second or two, and then he was gone.

I turned to Tandy. She was still busy with the rest of the line of customers, but when the policeman left, she looked over at me.

"You want your seat back?" She started to stand.

"No." I smiled. "You're doing great. I should hire you."

Her face lit up a little too much at that, and I realized instantly that I shouldn't have said it. So instead of continuing to engage with her, I abandoned the room in favor of the kitchen, thinking I'd have more coffee.

But once I was in the kitchen my stomach reminded me that I really hadn't eaten enough in the past . . . well, really in the past couple of days. Coffee would do nothing to assuage my hunger. I needed to go grocery shopping.

So I ignored the French press and went back into the parlor.

"No, but seriously," I said to Tandy, walking in, "would you mind holding down the fort for a minute? I have *got* to get some groceries in this house. The pantry's bare."

Once again, Tandy's face burned bright. "Oh. Yes. I'd love to. Thanks."

The other students in the room didn't seem to care one way or the other. I checked my back pocket for the old wallet, fished the car keys out of the front pocket, and launched myself out into the world.

It took me five minutes to rearrange things in the car to make room for a bag of groceries—and that hadn't been easy—so my exit wasn't as speedy or as dramatic as I'd wanted it to be. But in no time at all I was on my way.

I headed for the Stop & Shop on Highway 82. It was only a convenience store, but I could at least pick up milk and eggs and ice cream and beer. The essentials. I figured to go to Tifton later for a real grocery run, maybe a Whole Foods or something.

I pulled into the Stop & Shop. There was only one other car in the parking lot. Good. The last thing I needed was to run into some old high school buddy who wanted to reminisce or a friend of Rose's who'd spend twenty minutes telling me how much they understood my pain and how sorry they were that she was dead.

Out of the car, into the store, straight to the refrigerated section. Milk, eggs, bacon, ready-made biscuits, and some kind of sausage with a winking pig on the packaging. Just the ticket. And, naturally, a six-pack of Bud, because, when in Rome.

Clutching my prizes, wishing I'd thought to get a hand cart, I stumbled to the cash register. Just as I let everything tumble to the counter, I heard a voice behind me.

"Health food nut."

I turned.

There, in a T-shirt and gray jeans, stood Captain Jordon of the fire brigade. He looked just a little too much like a life-sized action figure.

I nodded. "I just thought that these sausages might have enough grease in them to help me start another fire. Maybe the front porch this time."

"Billy Sanders called me the second he left your place," the fireman said. "You appear to be off the hook. But I don't know how much I trust his opinion. I think he might be sweet on you."

"Gross." I lowered my eyelids. "I used to *babysit* him."

"Okay." He was holding a six-pack of Coors.

"Bye, then," I said to him, and then I turned back to the cashier.

The cashier was a kid with a nose ring and dyed black hair. She looked about twelve.

"Will that be all, ma'am?" she asked me.

"*Big* box of matches," I told her loudly.

"Ma'am?"

"Never mind," I said. "This'll do it."

I kept my back to Captain Jordon for the rest of my time in the store, and he kept his mouth shut. As I was walking out, I heard him speak very gently to the cashier.

"Hey, Jaime," he said. "How's your mama?"

"Hey, Mike," she answered sweetly. "She's out of intensive care. She—"

The door closed behind me; I didn't hear the rest of the conversation.

By the time I got back to the house, even though I hadn't been gone more than twenty minutes, the place had all but cleared out.

There was one guy lounging on the sofa in the mystery room; Tandy was still sitting at the desk carefully arranging small bills.

"Everybody still pays in cash?" I asked, coming through the room.

"Oh, no." Tandy stood up. "Rose, you know, used to have a—"

"Cash only policy." I nodded. "I remember. I'd be surprised if that were still in effect."

"It's not. We have a credit card thing now, you know." She glanced at my plastic bag. "You need help with that?"

I shook my head. It was only one bag. Tandy followed me into the kitchen. The guy in the mystery room got up from the sofa and was out the door. I set my bag down on the kitchen table.

"Thank you for helping out while I was gone," I said to Tandy. "I had to get something to eat in this house."

She nodded. "I love this place. I come in here all the time. Or, I mean I did before . . . I loved your Aunt Rose."

I took a closer look at her face. It might have been made

out of perfect porcelain, except for the blush of sadness around the eyes.

"I did too," I told her. "Still do, I guess."

"Uh-huh," she said absently. "You know, I could help out every day. Like I did today."

"I don't know." I started unpacking my bounty. "Do you really think the shop makes the kind of money that would merit an employee? What did we make today so far, twenty bucks?"

"Umm, no ma'am," she began. "I took in over a thousand dollars, near fifteen hundred."

I nearly dropped my eggs.

"What?" I glared a little too intensely.

"Well," she began quickly, "see, the textbook that Doctor Waldrop assigned cost over a hundred dollars, and I sold eight. Then there were a number of other books on the reading list, and they were all at least twenty each. Then there was that girl from that Women in Society class. And, umm, I bought a book of Mary Oliver poems. I love her."

"Jesus." I managed to get the eggs into the fridge without much damage. "I walk out of the house for twenty minutes, and when I come back, I'm a thousand-aire."

She smiled. "Minus the overhead. And, look, if you want you some *good* eggs, don't eat those sorry things you just now put in your icebox. I can get you some from home that's just come out of the hen. They'd be so much better."

"Farm girl."

"Yes, ma'am," she told me proudly. "It's small, but we get by. Just shy of a hundred and eighty acres. Peanuts and chickens mostly."

"I see."

There was a calm moment of silence before Tandy spoke

again, and I could hear the sadness in her voice. Or was it sadness? Maybe it was something more, I couldn't tell.

"So, what do you think? About my coming in to help you. See, I don't want any pay, actually, so it don't really matter about you being a thousand-aire or completely broke."

I felt my head tilt entirely of its own will. "Why would you want to do that?"

She looked away. Her shoulders lifted. "I like it here. I always liked it here."

I stared. "There's more to it than that."

After a breath and a pause, she nodded. "It's nothing. I had a little fight with my roommate. My college roommate? Rae. We were best friends growing up together, so I figure we'll get over it. See, Momma wanted me to stay living at home, but I wanted to be—I don't know. I wanted to feel grown."

I smiled. She saw.

"I see that look on your face and I know it don't make me all the way grown to live in a college dorm." She sighed. "I mean, I guess we're lucky to have a dormitory at all at little bitty old Barnsley College. But I thought it would be like a transition for me. Out of my family and into the world, a *slightly* bigger, you know, world."

"Like a halfway house."

That made her smile. "Right."

"And you want to be in a bigger world?"

"Bigger than Enigma?" She laughed, but it wasn't a happy sound. "It don't hardly get a whole lot *smaller*, does it?"

"It does not," I agreed. "So what's the problem with your roommate?"

"No big deal." She smiled sweetly. "I expect it'll all be forgotten tomorrow."

"Okay. So otherwise, how's the first-year college experience?"

"I like classes. I want to—there's a lot more to know than what you get out of a beer can. I aim to be gone from this town in a few years."

I sat down at the kitchen table, and, with a small gesture, invited her to do the same.

"What's your major?" I asked her.

"Psychology," she said, but it was almost an apology. "I want to . . . I think I want to help people. I'm going to someplace bigger for graduate school. Get my doctorate. Maybe even go to New York like Rose did."

I watched her face. A thousand dreams played across those poreless cheeks, and in those deep green eyes, in a single second. I knew because I'd had that face, that same face, when I was her age. About a million times, sitting in that same kitchen, talking with Rose.

And I had a sudden overwhelming desire to tell her all the things that would go wrong with dreams that grand. Rose went to New York to be a star and spent thirty years in the chorus. And I'd lasted exactly seven weeks in New York. New York eats Enigma for breakfast. And it's not even a full breakfast, it's the continental.

But after a second or two I turned down the role of Dream Crusher and just smiled.

"Well, you can come here anytime you want to, and if you feel like working, I guess I can't stop you." I leaned back.

The light outside began to fade. It was a little too early for sunset yet, so I assumed that the sky was clouding up.

"Tell you what," I said, hands on the tabletop. "Why don't you help me close these windows down here. I think it might rain."

I stood, so she did too.

"These windows were all open when I got here yester-day," I said, headed for the parlor. "I guess Rose left them open when she went into the hospital."

Tandy was at my side; she shook her head. "No, they were all closed yesterday morning."

I stopped. I turned her way. "They were? How do you know that?"

"Oh, um, I come by here every day," she said before she thought better of it. "This sounds stupid, but I drive by, now, hoping I might see Rose. Still. You know, sitting on the porch or some such. I mean, I know she's gone. But."

It became clear to me that Rose had meant that much to Tandy. I didn't say anything else about that because I didn't know what to say. So I just went for the first window.

But as I put my hands on the sill, I turned to Tandy.

"So, wait a minute. Who opened all these windows yesterday—between the time you drove by and the time I got here?"

"Oh." Tandy looked around. "Right. Reckon who did that?"

5

WHEN I CAME downstairs the next morning, I saw Tandy sitting in one of the rockers on the front porch. I hadn't slept well again, and I was trying to decide if I was irritated by her or not when she stood and knocked on the door.

I'd finally taken a shower and changed my clothes. I was in sweats and slippers, not quite ready to receive company.

Still, I couldn't ignore her. So I opened the door.

"Hey," she said, breezing in holding a large brown paper grocery bag. "I brought you some eggs, some real eggs, and some bacon from over at Porter's Smokehouse—it's so good—and some biscuits I just made you this morning over in Mama's kitchen. Buttermilk biscuits!"

Without another word she headed for my kitchen. I watched. I couldn't quite get my mouth to form words. Before I could move, there were noises in the kitchen. And Tandy was humming.

I followed the sounds, and there she was at the stove, cast-iron skillet in hand. She was in another cotton dress, pale green, with a blue jean jacket and the same work boots.

"Where'd you find that skillet?" I asked.

"Scrambled or fried?" she answered.

"Coffee," I said.

She nodded. "Daddy's the same way. Can't think without that first cup of coffee in his hand. You like the French press? That's what Rose liked."

All I could do was nod.

She went to work. She pulled whole coffee beans out of her grocery bag, turned on the oven, started an eye on the stovetop, and found a coffee grinder in what appeared to me to be a single motion. She was like a dancer, or like poetry.

She caught me staring and stopped her forward motion.

"I used to do this for Rose all the time." The sadness in her voice filled up the entire room.

In no time we were both sitting at the kitchen table. And I'll have to take a moment to say a word about her biscuits. If you could scoop a handful of cloud, mix it with just-churned butter, put wildflower honey on it, teach it to sing, and have an angel kiss it, it wouldn't have been as good as those biscuits. I ate three. Tandy watched, chin in hand, eyes bright.

"Tandy." I shook my head. "Forget psychology. You should open a restaurant."

"The average salary for any kind of psychologist is around a hundred thousand dollars a year," she said. "Whereas your average salary for a restaurant worker anywhere in America is about ten an hour."

"Ah," I said, "you've done your research; hard to argue with."

"Yes, I did," she told me.

There was a noise at the front door, and then Philomena called out.

"Anybody home?" she cooed.

"In the kitchen," I said without moving.

Seconds later she appeared in the kitchen doorway. She was in her Tuesday outfit: sand-colored dress, black scarf, low-heeled black shoes.

"Tandy!" she sang.

"Morning, Doctor Waldrop," Tandy answered.

"Tandy Fletcher," Phil told me, "is my absolute *favorite* student. And she's made you breakfast, I see. She used to do that for Rose all the time."

Tandy stood up and started clearing the dishes. Philomena sat down at the table.

"I understand you had a good day yesterday, business-wise," she said slyly.

"Yes," I acknowledged. "Thanks to you."

"Well." She tossed her head.

Tandy brought Philomena a cup of coffee and refilled mine from the last of the French press, careful not to let any of the dregs drift into my cup.

"I think Tandy, here, just might be my elfin helper from now on," I told Phil, sipping. "Especially if she keeps making those biscuits."

Philomena looked at Tandy; Tandy shrugged.

"Just wanted to stop by, check in," Philomena said, her coffee cup poised midair.

"Officer Billy visited yesterday," I told her. "And I ran into that fireman at the Stop and Shop. He's a real peach."

She nodded, acknowledging the heavy sarcasm in my voice. "Cute though."

"He looks like a Ken doll." I stood. "I gotta go put on some real clothes. Just in case we have more customers today."

"Oh, you'll have more," Phil assured me, downing her

coffee. "Word's gotten out that the shop is open. You'll probably have double today what you did yesterday. Probably see some old friends come by! Won't that be nice?"

I had no idea why I was more irritated than delighted by that prospect, but no matter what, I didn't want to be in sweatpants when other people—especially "old friends"—showed up. In a town the size of Enigma, that kind of thing leads to nicknames. Maddy Sweatpants. Sister Sweats. Miss Can't Be Bothered To Dress Properly When People Come Over.

But before I took my first steps toward the stairs, the phone rang.

"I wish my own phone had rung this much," I mumbled, "when I was in New York. I'd probably still be in the theatre game."

And I launched myself into the parlor.

Once there, sitting on the desktop, I picked up the phone.

"Old Juniper Bookshop," I began. "How may I—"

"I done told you once," the gravelly voice warned me. "If you don't clear out of that house, it'll come down around you in a furnace of flame!"

"Who the *hell* is this? If you think—"

But he hung up.

"Madeline?" Philomena called from the kitchen.

A second later she was in the doorway to the parlor.

I hung up the phone and stood. "My secret admirer."

Phil froze, her eyes wide. "Was it that man who threatened you? Did he do it again?"

"He did."

She came to me. "Honeybee, you have *got* to tell the police about this. Tell Billy."

"Wasn't nearly as scary as before," I said. "A call like that on a golden autumn day seems more like a bad joke than a serious threat."

Tandy came into the room. "What is it?"

"Nothing," I said. "I'm going upstairs to change clothes."

"I'm staying here," Philomena insisted. "I'm not leaving this house until you call the police."

"Don't be ridiculous," I told her. "You have classes to teach, and I have work to do. Also I have Tandy Fletcher with me, so I will fear no evil."

"What *is* it?" Tandy repeated.

"Some man is making threatening phone calls to Madeline," Phil said before I could stop her. "He's saying he'll burn down the house."

Tandy put her hand up to her chest. "And he already burned down the old gazebo out back," she whispered. "We all heard about that."

"Okay, but, you know, it's just a crank phone call!" I said, a little louder than I needed to.

"No, it's not," Philomena protested. "Why would anyone do that? You have to take this more seriously. You have to call the police!"

"I don't *have* to call the police!" I countered, full volume.

"Why not?" Tandy asked, still whispering.

I counted the reasons off on my fingers. "I don't care for policemen in general. I used to *babysit* Billy Sanders so forgive me if my faith in his police skills is somewhat lacking. And there's nothing to the threat. Seriously, this house has been here for over a hundred years. Who in the hell would want to burn it down? What reason would there be? I'm going upstairs to put on better clothes. Tandy, mind the store. Phil, go to work. It'll all be fine. Honestly."

And with that I stormed upstairs.

But once upstairs in the greenroom, I realized how fast my heart was beating. What if it wasn't a prank? What if, for some reason, someone actually wanted to burn down the house?

I changed as quickly as I could. I found an outfit that seemed right: blue and white horizontal striped top, a little like the French sailor's uniform, a billowy knee-length black skirt, and harmless black flats. A dab of lip gloss, a shake of the head to frizz out the hair, a spot of toothpaste on the tongue to clear away the coffee breath, and a very Fosse-like stare into the bathroom mirror, "It's showtime, folks." Then I was down the stairs, trying to avoid thinking about—anything, really.

Thankfully, Dr. Waldrop was gone. Tandy was at the desk. The sun was in through the open window. Autumn was in the air.

"You opened the window?" I asked Tandy absently.

"The fresh air's nice, don't you think? You look good."

"Doctor Waldrop is a worrier," I began.

"She said this was the second call from that man."

"Yeah," I admitted, going to the nearest bookcase and pretending to arrange something or other. "I like to take care of things myself. I mean, you've lived here all your life. Have you *ever* heard anyone talk about burning down this old house?"

She was silent for a heartbeat. Then: "Not everybody in this town liked Rose as much as I did."

"Get out of here," I admonished. "She was a beloved odd-ball character. Who didn't love her?"

Tandy's face changed and she wouldn't look at me. "Rose had her secrets."

I stared, but Tandy didn't look up. "What secrets are you talking about?"

"You lived here all your life 'til you were near my age," she chided. "You ought to know what I'm talking about. Like where did her money come from? How did she keep a bookstore going in this day and age? And, you know—why? I mean, Rose was an odd person. And it was a lot of people who thought there was more to her than she let on."

"Okay, she wasn't a member of the garden club or any particular church congregation if that's what you mean. But . . ."

"No, she had *secrets*, is what I'm saying," Tandy snapped, a little feistier than I would have thought she could be.

I nodded. "Okay, I guess there could be something to that. Let's talk about it."

But before we could go any further in our exploration of fear-of-the-*other* in a small southern town, the first customers wandered in.

"Here they come," Tandy said, her mood completely changed back to the sweet farm girl. "Maybe you'll see some old friends today! I overheard Doctor Waldrop say you might."

I shook my head. "That's less likely than you might think. I kept to myself when I lived here, and I didn't have a lot of friends. And the friends I did have got out of this town as soon as they could. So aside from Doctor Waldrop, I can't think of anyone who'd remember me, honestly. I mean, I've been gone almost seventeen years."

She smiled. "You never can tell. Billy Sanders remembered you, for one."

I did not respond to that.

And as it turned out, Phil had been partly correct in her

assessment: word had gotten out about the shop. The customers doubled from the day before, but most of them were still from the college.

I'd confess to being surprised at the number of nonacademic visitors, actual people wanting actual books. I didn't know any of them, so maybe they were new in town or something. Or new since I'd left town, anyway. That was more likely. But no matter what, there it was, right in front of me, that rarest of American phenomena: the busy independent bookstore. Maybe it was the twenty-first century somewhere in the world, but in Enigma, it looked a lot like the 1990s to me, when Rose had first opened the shop.

It was, in short, a very busy day.

At one point a young man in overalls and work boots, face a little smudged, waited until there was no one standing near us to ask me if I would get something from the poetry section for him—the way Rose had always done. I nodded discreetly. He wanted the collected poems of Lorca and stood by the desk while I went to get it for him, all the while looking around the shop to make certain no one was watching.

When he was gone, Tandy sidled up to me and whispered, "That's Coulter Jennings. He's shy."

That's all she would say, but there was obviously more to that story.

At around one o'clock I manned the desk and Tandy made lunch for us both.

She dipped bread in whisked eggs to make them sort of like French toast, then fried maybe twenty pieces of bacon—the whole house smelled like a barbecue joint—and made bacon, lettuce, and tomato sandwiches so good that there ought to have been a better name for them. And they didn't even have mayonnaise on them. No idea what she did. Sandwich of the gods.

Around five o'clock the place calmed down. Tandy and I sat, slouched down, on the green French antique sofa in the parlor, exhausted.

"I haven't worked that hard since I was in children's theatre," I murmured.

"I believe this was the busiest day I ever saw here," Tandy agreed. "You were in children's theatre?"

"I toured a Grimm's fairy tale show," I said. "Twenty songs, all with dance numbers, and a *brutal* question and answer after."

She managed to turn her head my way. "Why was it brutal?"

"The stage manager would come out with us and say to the crowd of schoolkids, 'Anyone have a question about the show?' and every hand would go up. So she'd point to someone, and the kid would say, like, 'We just got a puppy! His name is Albert.' And it would go on like that for half an hour. Swear to God, not one single word about the actual show."

"This was in Atlanta?"

I nodded. "And environs."

She sighed. "Rose used to tell me about all the famous people she met in New York. Tell the truth, I'd never heard of any of them."

I nodded. "She used to do the same thing with me."

"Umm," she said after a moment. "I don't know what to call you."

"What do you mean?" I asked lazily.

"I mean I used to call Rose by her name."

"Oh. Right. So call me Madeline, okay?"

"Okay." She sat silently for nearly a full minute. "Madeline?"

"Mmm?" I answered, eyes closed.

"What would you think if I was to stay here tonight?"

"What?" Eyes opened. "Stay here in the house? Why?"

"I like it here," she said.

"Yeah, me too," I agreed, "but you have a farmhouse *and* a dorm room you could go to, right?"

"I do." She sat up. "But, don't you want you some company here all alone?"

"Well, no," I told her, sitting up and looking into her eyes. "I mean, where would you sleep? Upstairs?"

"Oh no, ma'am," she said quickly. "I'd sleep down here. The sofa next to the library room, the room with the rare books? It's real comfortable, that sofa. I ... I slept there before."

"You did? Rose let you stay here?"

She nodded. "She said you used to do the same thing when you were about my age—you know, sleep over here."

That's when I finally realized what should have been obvious to me all along. Tandy, aside from being a lovely human being and a superior cook, was also the ghost of my younger self. She was me; I was Rose. I sat up; it was a very odd sensation. And in light of that particular personal revelation, how could I refuse her request?

"Well," I said slowly, "if Rose let you stay here, I guess kind of I have to let you do it too."

She looked down, smiling. "I guess you do."

"One condition: you make dinner."

She nodded. "Just in case you said yes and let me stay here, I brought some things in that grocery bag this morning so I could do that. Make dinner. How do you feel about fried chicken?"

"If it's half as good as your biscuits, I have deeply religious feelings about it."

She stood. "It'll be ready at six."

And she was gone.

Okay, it wasn't just that she was my younger self, and it wasn't just that I was appreciative of all her really hard work; and it wasn't even *just* that I wanted to see how good that fried chicken dinner was going to be. I had to admit to myself that I did want the company, and I was going to feel safer with someone else in the house.

Because maybe I did take the phone calls a little more seriously than I wanted to admit to Philomena.

Whatever it was, by seven o'clock that evening, there was nothing left on my dinner plate but collard green broth, a few chicken bones, and a scrape of gravy.

The kitchen was filled with a comforting deep-fried smell and my spirit was filled with a love of all humankind. And just as I was about to begin a very complicated soliloquy praising Tandy's culinary talents to the sky, she stood up from the table.

"Banana pudding," she announced and went to the fridge.

Out came my favorite childhood dessert: vanilla pudding, ripe banana slices, Nilla Wafers, and bronzed meringue.

"Oh my God," I whispered.

"I know it's your favorite," Tandy said, unable to hide her delight. "Rose told me. Every time I made it for her."

I looked up at her. "I hope you'll take this in the spirit with which it's given, Tandy Fletcher, but I kind of feel like I've died and gone to heaven."

She nodded sagely. "Banana pudding *will* make a person feel like that."

And she set my bowl before me.

Happy that she understood, I dug in. And when it was gone, it was *all* gone. I'd used my finger, without an iota of embarrassment, to clean the bowl spotless.

I sat back, hands clasped in prayer. "Tandy. *Tandy.* Best meal this decade."

She beamed. "Glad you liked it."

"And I'm glad you're staying here tonight," I confessed.

"Does it feel odd, coming back here after so many years gone?" she asked.

"It does," I admitted. "I spent almost all of my free time in this place when I was a kid. And then, when I left for college, at the stupid age of seventeen, I just never came back. I mean, Rose and I kept up. First with letters and then in these recent years on, you know, Facebook video talks."

"Not Zoom?" she asked, but she was making fun of it.

"The Facebook thing was easier for her. But now that I'm back, it seems . . . yeah, it is weird. It's like I never left, and like I was never here at the same time."

"She said you went to New York right after college?"

I shifted uncomfortably in my seat. "For a while. Then I got a lot of gigs in Atlanta. Good ones. And I just stayed there."

"Why?"

I sat forward. "Long story. For another time. And it's my turn to do the dishes."

"Nuh-uh." She stood at once and took the empty bowls from the table. "Still my turn."

"Okay," I said, "then I'll go straighten up the desk and the shelves and generally tidy up the shop. You don't see it while they're here, but after they're gone you realize how messy book customers are."

"I *know*," she agreed, taking the bowls to the sink.

So, I went to clean up the store; Tandy stayed to clean up the kitchen.

Standing there in the middle of the largest room, I took in the store, really, for the first time since I'd been back. Breathed it in and listened to it. The way the October wind whistled through some of the windows, the creaking of the walls as the day cooled. Every door hinge played a different melody. All the floorboards sang their different parts: the one by the nearest fireplace was a soprano with an attitude. The baritone section by the door all got along swimmingly. The group of altos in the dining room were always a little off-key, God bless them. And there was one tenor on the staircase that clearly could have gone pro if it had wanted to. But some voices were content to stay in small towns and sing in the community choir. It was mainly the wild voices, the ones who never fit into the group, who ran away from town—and were usually never heard from again.

By eight thirty I realized I'd been tidying up with a full-fledged dose of OCD, evening up every shelf, dusting off every surface, adjusting every chair and sofa. I was only just realizing how completely obsessive I'd been when I heard Tandy call from the kitchen.

"Why am I cleaning this kitchen floor with a sponge on my hands and knees?"

I went in, and sure enough: sudsy bucket, giant sponge, down on her knees.

"Stop it," I admonished her. "Stop it right now. And, also, I'm kind of doing the same thing in the other rooms. I don't think the place has been this clean and tidy in ten years."

She laughed and tossed the sponge into the bucket, then stood.

"What's the matter with us?" she asked lightly.

I looked around. "We miss Rose. And we're trying not to think about that."

She nodded slowly. "Reckon."

After that admission, I felt every bit of energy leave my body, and all I wanted was a bed and a long night's sleep. Tandy looked about the same.

"Let's call it a night, what do you say?" I suggested.

"Right," she agreed.

"Do you know where to get your blankets or whatever for the sofa in the thing, the room?"

She picked up the bucket. "Done it a million times."

"Okay, then." I sighed. "You probably won't get this reference, Tandy Fletcher, but I think this is the beginning of a beautiful friendship."

"*Casablanca*." She smiled. "Rose's favorite movie."

"So it was." And that was that.

I turned and went upstairs, praying I was headed for a good night's sleep.

Up in the greenroom I opened the window closest to the bed. The air was a little chilly and very delicious; the tree frogs and crickets were wildly alive. The moon was generous with its silver, ladled it over everything: the garden, the woods behind, the distant fields—even the skeleton of the gazebo was hoary—was that the word? *Hoary?* No idea why that particular descriptive took my brain, but it did. Hoary. There. I'd thought it three times. Three times is the charm.

Man was I tired.

Into my comfy cotton pjs, toothbrush in my mouth, I

abandoned all adjectives in favor of melody. I began humming "As Time Goes By."

I stumbled into bed, clicked off the lamp, closed my eyes, and vanished into dreamland. How long I stayed there I had no idea.

Panic woke me.

I didn't know why at first. Then there was the smell. Then there was the sound, the faint crackling sound. Something was burning. I sat up in bed and shot a glance to the window. There was nothing burning out there.

I threw off the covers and lumbered out of the room, down the stairs.

Tandy was on the floor, splayed and still. The door of the shop was on fire.

I ran to Tandy, but the flames jumped. White smoke seared my eyes. I began to cough. Had to get the flames out.

I ran into the kitchen and found the bucket Tandy had used, filled it with water, and ran back to the door.

The door frame and the floor around Tandy were all burning; the flames were jumping, angry, red and black, or was that already soot?

I tossed the water onto the fire. That only made more smoke.

I grabbed Tandy by the arm and dragged her away from the heat.

I grabbed a sofa pillow from the parlor and started beating the flames on the floor, then on the frame. That helped. Then the door. The smoke was worse, but the flames were smaller. Back into the kitchen for another bucket of water. And again. And again.

The smoke was much worse then. Made it harder to see. But the fire was mostly out.

I was coughing so violently that I thought I might have cracked a rib, the pain in my side was wickedly intense. I tried to think what to do next.

I ran to the nearest bathroom next to the staircase and wet all the towels there. Back to the doorway and used them to beat at the wood again and again and again. I heard myself making growling fear noises, little yelps, and guttural grunts.

I don't know how long I batted at the smoldering door, but finally there was only smoke and black wood. I went to the parlor windows and threw them open. Then I grabbed the phone and called for the fire department, only seconds removed from hysteria.

I could hear the siren over the phone before I hung up.

Breathing like a sprinter, I stumbled and tumbled across the room and tried to get Tandy up and out of the house. I grabbed her hand.

"You—are you okay?" I gasped. "Jesus that was scary."

I stared down at her. She was very still.

"Tandy?"

I shook her shoulder, and she rolled over onto her back. That's when I saw the blood. It drenched her pretty green cotton dress.

"What the hell?" I muttered.

I reached for one of the nearby towels I'd discarded on the floor and pressed it to her stomach.

"Tandy?" I shook her whole body. "Tandy!"

But she didn't answer, and she wasn't breathing.

Tandy was dead.

little sooty and he was sweating. There were flecks of foam on his rubber jacket.

"What?" I mumbled.

He took the water from the other fireman and forced it into my hand. "Drink this now."

My stare returned to the bottle.

Behind Jordon, a shadow charged in through the blackened doorway and screamed.

"Get away from her!" Philomena's voice was shrill, hysterical.

She brushed past Jordon and threw her arms around me. There was a crinkling sound and I realized that I was wrapped in one of those silver blankets too. I had a sudden flashing thought that I might also be dead.

And then I started to cry. I could hold it in when the cold, rude men were all around me, but Phil's tenderness broke down all my resistance.

She steered me into the closest chair, a big, overstuffed beige thing. Then she took the water bottle, unscrewed the cap, and put the plastic to my lips.

"Drink this, sweetheart."

I did. I drank the whole bottle.

"Was that you outside just now," I asked her, "reading the riot act to somebody?"

"They weren't going to let me in." She turned to glare at Jordon. "I heard the sirens and then I saw the smoke coming from this direction and I—I tell you I just panicked! You know. I remembered those phone calls! I jumped in the car and got here just right as they were getting everything tamped down, I think. But they wouldn't let me in. And then one of the men said you were dead! That's when I came in."

6

BY THE TIME the smoke was finally clearing, and the smell of wet wood filled the house, I was almost able to speak. Captain Jordon was all business.

"I called the police," he said, stone-faced.

I nodded.

"The girl is dead," he went on.

I nodded.

"Stabbed," he told me harshly.

I coughed. "Her name is Tandy."

There were maybe five other firemen in the room or on the porch, and someone was out in the yard fussing at them, but I couldn't hear what was being said. I couldn't concentrate on anything. I barely understood what was going on.

Someone had thrown one of those silver emergency blankets on the floor and it took every ounce of brainpower I had for me to realize that it was probably covering Tandy.

One of the firemen said something to me and offered me a water bottle. I stared at it.

"You need to drink some water," Captain Jordon said.

I turned my stare in his direction. His face was red and a

She stood and stormed over to Jordon, nearly nose to nose.

"What in the hell is the matter with you?" she demanded to know. "What was Madeline doing just standing there? Why isn't she on a stretcher?"

"Ma'am, she wouldn't move away from this body on the floor here—" Jordon began.

"Did you *just* notice how I had no problem moving her over to that chair? And I'm a woman twice your age and half your weight. I mean, what is the *matter* with you?"

Then I heard Billy Sanders intervene.

"Captain Jordon," he began in a very official-sounding voice, "I believe I would also like to know why Madeline is not on a stretcher."

"Officer Sanders," Jordon said, straining his patience, "two of my men tried to get her onto a stretcher and she started screaming. She kicked one man in the privates and popped another one in his chin with her elbow. I believe his jaw might be dislocated!"

I blinked. I didn't remember doing anything like that.

"It's a dead body in her house," Billy roared, "and that house is on fire! Or ain't you never heard of *shock*?"

"Who's dead?" Phil murmured. "They said it was Madeline."

"Well, Madeline said the name *Tandy*, so—" Jordon began.

Phil shrieked. Billy made a lower sound.

"It's Tandy," I said, and I started to cry again.

Billy cleared his throat three times before he said, "Tandy Fletcher."

"What was she doing here at this time of night?" Jordon wanted to know.

"She was staying with me," I managed to say.

"Why?" Jordon asked flatly.

"Well if you must know," Phil snapped, "Madeline has received several threatening phone calls and I expect she wanted a little company!"

There was a brief silence.

"Phone calls?" Jordon asked.

"There was more than the one Doctor Waldrop told me about?" Billy added.

I looked up and nodded. "The first phone call told me to get out of town right after the gazebo fire. He said he'd burn the whole house down with me in it next time. I guess that's what this was."

Both men started talking at once and at the top of their lungs, so I ignored them. I turned to Phil.

"And I didn't ask her to stay here," I said. "She asked me. She was having some kind of trouble with her roommate at the college. But I *was* glad for the company."

By that time Billy had taken several quick strides and was standing next to me.

"Let's get a hold of this," he said. "You got two threatening phone calls and the only person you told was Doctor Waldrop?"

Jordon intervened. "Did anyone else hear these alleged phone calls?"

Phil stood up. "I was in the room for the second one," she told Jordon indignantly. "Right here in this room."

Not entirely true, but I was grateful for her support.

"Also Tandy knew about the calls," I offered.

"I *mean*," Billy railed, "why didn't you tell me about the calls?"

I looked around at the wreckage, tried to block out the

smell when I sniffed, and nodded. "I thought it was just some crank calls. I should have told you, though. I see that now."

Billy let out a breath, and when I looked up at him, I could tell he was working hard to keep his temper in check.

"I might be able to get some kind of phone records," he said, measuring every word. "Maybe find out who called."

"There haven't been that many calls since I got here," I said. "There won't be many to go through, I mean."

Billy shook his head. "Well, it's not too many people that know you're back in town yet." Then he glanced at Jordon. "I contacted the coroner from up at Tifton. He's coming but there's no idea when he'll be here."

"Does she need to wait for him?" Phil asked Billy. "Can't they take her to the hospital now?"

I stood up. "I'm not going to the hospital. I'm not leaving Tandy."

"You're in shock," Jordon began, clearly aggravated, "you're suffering from smoke inhalation, and you've got a pretty good burn on your left hand."

I looked down. My left hand was red as a tomato and suddenly it felt like ice.

"Yeah," I said, "I don't know how that happened. I'll put some butter on it."

"You'll put a cold pack on it," Jordon said, moving my way, "and you'll let our EMT check your vitals without kicking him, or I'll ask Officer Sanders to arrest you for assault."

Billy's head snapped back. "I guess you could *ask*, but this woman has suffered a traumatic event and all I'm going to do is sit with her until I get my head right about what happened here tonight."

With that he stormed over to the desk, grabbed the chair, dragged it my way, and pointed to the chair I'd been sitting in. He did it with such authority that I sat down immediately without thinking.

"Now—" he began.

"Captain Jordon," I interrupted. "I'm very sorry I was mean to your firemen. I actually have no memory of doing that. But a person I cared about just died and I probably wasn't in the mood to be manhandled by burly stump-jumpers in rubber suits. So thanks for dealing with the embers of the fire that I put out myself before you got here, but now, if you wouldn't mind, please get lost. I'm being interviewed by the police."

I adjusted my chair so that I was face-to-face with Billy.

And then the most unexpected thing happened. Captain Mike Jordon of the local fire brigade began to laugh.

"Swear to God, you're a firecracker, Miss Brimley." He shook his head.

It made me mad because I thought he was making fun of me or maybe belittling my circumstance. But when I started to offer him some of the remarkably disgusting curses I'd learned over my years of hearing backstage profanity—and believe me, actors can out-curse sailors *any* day—I saw the expression on his face. There wasn't a hint of mocking superiority or any typical kind of masculine condescension. There was only a weird version of admiration.

Before I could gather myself to make any response to that, he'd turned and walked away.

Billy smiled sweetly at me. "I thought he'd *never* leave."

That made me laugh a little, and I was more grateful for that than I would have been for a shot of tequila. Although I wouldn't have turned down the tequila.

"Tell me about the phone calls," Billy said, completely focused on me.

"Well, like I said, the first one came right after the gazebo fire. The second one came when I guess it was obvious that I'd opened the bookshop and didn't look like I was leaving town." I glanced at Phil, who'd taken a seat on the arm of my chair. "Philomena heard my side of that one, and Tandy was here too."

But just saying Tandy's name out loud made me choke up a little again.

"Man's voice," Billy prodded.

"Right." I sipped a breath. "Sounded, you know, not like a kid, not like an old man. Hoarse, but I think that was on purpose, to sound scary. Local accent. I mean, sounded local. Other than that . . ."

"Can you remember exact words?" He asked.

I closed my eyes. "Wait."

It was a weird kind of trick I had as an actor—lots of other actors I knew had it too. With a little concentration and a lifelong practice of sense memories, I could often remember, word for word, something that had been said to me, if it was recent enough.

I began, trancelike, eyes still closed. "The first time he said, 'Clear out' and then, 'Clear out of that damn house, girl' and then, 'Leave now, *right* now. Next time I'll burn down that whole house. Burn it down with you inside! You hear me?'"

I opened my eyes.

Billy's eyes were wide. "That's impressive."

I nodded and closed my eyes again. "Second time he said, 'I done told you once. If you don't clear out of that house, it'll come down around you in a furnace of flame.'"

"'Furnace of flame.'" Philomena shook her head.

Billy looked around. "Well, it looks like that's what he tried to do tonight, don't it."

The firemen were packing up and, with all the windows open, the smoke was completely gone. There was a funny smell in the air, but it was hard to tell what it was.

"All right, we're done," Captain Jordon called out.

His crew began to leave.

"There's no structural damage, not even to the door frame," he said in my direction. "But it'll need to be replaced quick as you can get to it. It'll smell funny in here for a while, maybe a week. You might consider staying somewhere else for a while. And I believe there might be some kind of city ordinance about opening a store after a fire, but I don't know how it would apply to a place like this, since you live here too."

"Okay," I said, trying to think of what else to say to him.

"Good night then," he told me.

He took a second to look down at the body, and then he left.

"He might be right about not staying here tonight," Billy began.

"I want to stay here," I said, even though I didn't know why, exactly.

"I'll stay with her," Phil volunteered instantly. "Or she can stay with me."

"Right." Billy stood up. "If you want to go on upstairs, that's okay. I'll be here. I got to wait for the coroner. And now with this new mess about these phone calls, I believe I'll get a couple of other boys over here to collect some, you know, evidence."

"I don't like to leave Tandy just lying there," I said.

Billy sighed. "I know what you mean. But we got to keep her just like that until we get a little more information, you understand."

"I guess I do," I told him.

"God," Billy said, staring at the phone on the nearby desk. "I got to call her family."

He sounded a little sick.

"She made the greatest biscuits in the world," I mumbled.

I heard the sound of my voice. It was the sound of someone who probably should have gone to the hospital after all.

Phil put her arm around me. "Come on, sweetheart. Let's get you upstairs."

"Can't I stay until the coroner gets here?" I asked Billy, completely realizing how little sense I was making.

"Wait, I just realized," Billy said, obviously gathering himself. "Is it . . . did she die from the fire? The smoke? I ain't looked at the body yet."

I swallowed. "Oh. I thought you knew."

"Knew what?"

"I think she was stabbed." I blew out a breath. "That's what Jordon said. There was blood all over her. I saw that."

"Stabbed?" Billy's voice was ghostly.

"My God," Phil whispered, hand to mouth.

And the tears came on again. "She was the sweetest person I ever met. Who would want to do such a thing to her?"

Philomena and Billy both went silent, glaring at me.

"You understand what happened here, don't you?" Billy finally said.

"Of course I do," I said, irritated. "The guy who threatened to burn my house down killed Tandy Fletcher!"

Philomena put her hand on my shoulder. "Not . . . exactly, darling."

"That man came here to burn your house down," Billy said, cold as ice, "and when he seen a girl come at him, he killed her. But, Maddy . . . he didn't know it was Tandy."

I squeezed my eyes shut for a second. "What?"

"Sugar, he . . ." but Phil couldn't finish her sentence and looked to Billy for help.

"Maddy," Billy said. "That man came here to kill *you*."

7

I WOKE UP LATE the next morning. Everything about the previous day was a fun house mirror. Distorted images and trombone voices. I sat up in bed. The autumn sunlight shouting through the window was rude and reassuring at the same time.

I heard noises downstairs, and my first thought was that Tandy was making breakfast. My bare feet hit the cold floor before I remembered that Tandy was dead.

It only took me another second to realize that I was probably hearing Philomena. I looked down at myself. Somehow, I'd gotten into sweats. And the icy wooden floor told me that October had finally turned a little chilly. I looked around for shoes, saw my high-tops, pulled them on untied, and lumbered toward the staircase.

"Phil?" I called out.

"Oh!" she answered, chirping. "You're up! Good."

I managed my way down the stairs, avoided looking at the front door, and made it into the kitchen. Philomena was standing at the stove, wrapped in one of Rose's huge aprons. It had Paris things on it, Eiffel Tower, Arc de Triomphe, baguette.

Whatever she was cooking filled the air; it erased or at least covered the burnt wood smell.

"Sage and apple sausage," she announced. "And a mushroom omelet. I was making it for myself. I didn't know when you'd be up. But it's yours now."

I took a seat at the kitchen table. "I couldn't."

But she heard the lack of conviction in my protest and brought me a plate almost immediately.

"Thanks for staying here," I said with my mouth full.

"I was worried about you," she said, beginning another omelet.

"Where did you sleep?"

"In Rose's room," she answered.

I couldn't figure out why that struck me as odd. Just because I didn't want to sleep in there shouldn't have meant that Philomena couldn't do it. But there was something in her voice that made it seem strange.

So I tried to laugh it off. "You weren't afraid of Rose's ghost?"

"Oh." She stopped her food preparations for a second. "I see her ghost all the time."

I held my breath for a second, but the sausage smelled so good that I chose to eat instead of think. Eventually Phil sat down at the table with me, and we ate in comfortable silence until our plates were empty and our coffee cups had been refilled.

"Now," she said, sliding her plate away from her. "Let's talk about what you're going to do."

"What I'm going to do?"

"Well, I've turned away a dozen customers this morning already," she said, looking down at the tabletop. "I just told them there'd been another fire, and you wouldn't be open for a while. But you *know* that word about Tandy will be all over town before sunset. And the news about a maniac trying to kill you. I'm sorry, but even given how gruesome it is, it's the most spreadable town gossip in decades."

"Yeah." I sipped from my cup. "I guess it would be."

Cannonball chose that moment to wander into the kitchen. His mouth and nose were smeared with soot.

"There you are," Phil said to him. "What have you been into?"

He sat down in response and began to try cleaning his face, but all he succeeded in doing was smearing the soot around.

Phil got up, found a paper towel, dapped it in sink water, and went to the cat. He looked up at her. She tried cleaning his face, but it was clear that the paper towel was a cat toy and not a cleaning implement at all. He batted it, nipped at it, and batted it again until Phil gave up and dropped it onto the floor. Cannonball fell upon it then with a sudden enthusiasm and wrestled it into submission. It was a pleasant three-minute diversion from the awful exercise of answering Philomena's original question.

She repeated it. "So what are you going to do?"

"I have to tell you," I said with a sigh, "I don't think my heart is in this enterprise anymore. I mean, I know I only just met Tandy, but *man* I latched on to her. When we were sitting at this table yesterday, she was *me*. And . . . I was Rose. I can't see how I could stay here now. You know, not to mention that somebody wants to kill me. There's that."

Again Phil wouldn't look at me. "I see."

I could tell that she was disappointed. But it also seemed to me that she understood. How could she not?

"So." I finished my coffee. "What do I do?"

She took in a hard, deep breath. "Well. I suppose you call Rusty Thompson, don't you? Arrange to sell the place."

"Sell it?"

"Don't tell me you don't need the money," Phil said softly.

"Oh, I need the money. Especially if I sell the place where I currently live." I folded my arms. "And I don't really want to go back to Atlanta."

"New York?"

"Never again. Makes me tired just thinking about it. And after staying in a Victorian mansion for a couple of days, the thought of living in an eight-by-ten studio apartment in Brooklyn is just too depressing. No. Not New York."

"What about Savannah?" she suggested. "I love Savannah."

I looked up at her. "You're full of suggestions, Doctor Waldrop."

She met my eyes. "I'm trying to figure out what would make you happy. Excuse me, but Rose had the idea that you haven't been happy as an actor for years."

"Nobody's *happy* as an actor," I said. "You're unhappy until you get a gig, and then you're just relieved. Happiness isn't really a part of that world."

"Rose was happy," she said, a little sadly.

"Yeah, but Rose was happy with everything. She found a snail on the back door here once and she celebrated like it was a rich uncle with good news and money."

Philomena sighed. "Yes. That was Rose."

"But back to the problem at hand," I said.

"You could teach," Phil interrupted, a little energized by the idea. "You could start a theatre program at Barnsley!"

"Academia?" I made a face that I hoped would convey my extreme revulsion. "I'd rather be tossed into a pit of flesh-eating vipers."

"Oh, sweetheart, academia *is* a pit of flesh-eating vipers," she said. "But teaching is a different story. First, it would satisfy your performance desires because every class is a brand-new show. And you would fall in love with the students. I always do."

"You fell in love with Tandy." I don't know why I said that, it just popped out.

"I did." That's all.

I stood. "Well, I don't think I'm made for Enigma in general at this point. And I'm probably not the professorial kind. So, I think I'll give old Rusty a call and see if can I unload this dump."

And with that I was off to the desk in the other room.

I heard her say, mostly to herself, "It's not a *dump*." And she began clearing the dishes.

I went to the desk. The desk where Tandy had been sitting only the day before. I sat down and stared at the phone before I realized I had no idea what Rusty's number was. So I hustled up the stairs to my notebook and back down to the phone, only to find Cannonball in my chair.

"Okay," I told him, "you call Rusty, then. But what are you going to say to him?"

He stared at me, thought about it, and hopped off the chair.

"That's what I thought," I said.

I sat, dialed, and waited. It rang nine times before someone answered.

"Thompson and Associates," said a very tired woman.

"Hi, I'm calling Rusty—"

"And this is regarding . . . ?" she murmured and then waited.

"This is Madeline Brimley; I need to speak to Rusty about my aunt Rose's house in Enigma."

"Rose?" Her voice had changed completely; it was full of life and light. "I *loved* her. So you're the niece. She talked about you all the time."

"She did?"

"Just hang on a second, sugar," she said. "We're up to our elbows in this stupid real estate fraud case, and we've all been up the whole night. Rusty's still asleep in his chair, poor thing. But he'll want to talk to you."

Before I could tell her that I'd call back, she'd put me on hold.

After another interminable wait, Rusty's chipper voice assaulted me.

"Miss Brimley! What can I do you for?"

"Hey, Mister Thompson," I began, "I hear you're not getting enough sleep."

"Well, who needs sleep when you love your work? What's up?"

"Umm. Well, I've run into a little bit of a stumbling block here at my aunt Rose's house."

His voice shifted seamlessly to concern mode. "I'm sorry to hear that. What is it?"

"Okay." I took a deep breath. "I don't think it's going to work out for me here and I'm going to have to sell the house."

Silence.

"Rusty?"

"You just got there, like, yesterday, right?" he asked slowly.

"Day before," I corrected, "but, see, someone was killed here last night, and some man has threatened to burn the place down with me in it if I don't clear out. So . . ."

Another silence.

"Someone was killed there?" His voice was finally the voice of a real person, not a professional attitude.

My voice, on the other hand, sounded a little like a bad door hinge. "A college kid. Someone who, apparently, helped my aunt run the bookstore. And I've received these phone calls—"

"College kid?" He gasped. "It wasn't little Tandy Fletcher?"

"It . . . it was. How could you possibly know that?"

"Rose used to talk about her," he whispered slowly, "and I know the family. What the hell happened? She was the sweetest little girl."

"The killer thought she was me," I said, hoping I didn't sound as unhinged as I felt. "That's what the police said. See, I got these phone calls—"

"Who would kill a kid like Tandy?"

"Nobody," I snapped, twice my previous volume. "The guy thought he was killing *me*, Rusty. He burned down the gazebo in the garden and then he called and then he called again and then he set fire to the house and stabbed Tandy Fletcher a whole bunch of times, thinking it was me, and that's why I need to sell the house and get out. Do you understand?"

My sudden tirade induced yet another moment of silence.

"Oh," he said at last.

"So can you help me with that, *Rusty*?" I prodded, still at the top of my voice. "Or do I need to find somebody else?"

He heaved a sigh the size of Texas. "I apologize, Madeline. I'm focused now. You been through a bad thing, a very bad thing, and I'm sorry for your . . . trouble. You've gotten the police involved, you said?"

"Yes." I was still a little wound up.

"All right. All right." He groaned, sounded like he was sitting way back in his chair. "See, I handle all the Fletchers' farm loans, bank loans, you understand, and I got to know the whole family real well. I might be a little bit in shock."

I exhaled. "Yeah. Imagine how I feel."

"I can't," he admitted. "You got somebody who can stay with you at the moment?"

"Doctor Waldrop from over at the college," I said. "She and my aunt—"

"I know Philomena," he said instantly. "So that's good."

"So about selling the place," I began, slowly calming.

"Yeah," he said quickly. "I'm afraid you can't do that. Not right now."

My turn to be silent for a second.

"What?" I finally said.

He made a low, long sound leading into his response: "Your aunt, she was kind of a riddle, you know? I mean, she had her secrets."

I got an instant chill. That's just what Tandy had told me.

"What secrets are you talking about, Rusty?" I ventured.

"Well, for one thing, there's a codicil to the will your aunt made," he said slowly, "that I suppose you haven't seen."

"A *codicil*?"

"Right," he went on. "Your aunt wanted the bookstore to continue to do business after she was gone. I guess it was a legacy kind of thing. And she seemed to be concerned that you might just sell the place, you know, for the money, without even coming down here. So. The amendment says that the house, the store, the money—all of it—does not completely pass to you until you've lived in the place for six months. Legally, you don't own it yet. So you can't sell it yet."

"I can't . . . so who *does* own the place?"

"Well, technically, I do," he said, "or my firm does, as the executor of the estate. But since the estate was left to you, I can't legally sell it either. I'm sorry to say, you're stuck with it until next spring. And I mean you've got to stay there to get the complete inheritance."

"I have to *live* in it for six months?"

"That's what the codicil says, yes ma'am."

"What if I don't?" I asked, trying not to panic. "What if I just leave? You own it then? You could sell it?"

"That would be a mess," he told me. "For one thing, I signed a letter of agreement that says I can't sell the house to anyone for the same six months. And then I'm supposed to offer it to Jay Garner."

"Jay . . . who's that?"

"He was some actor Rose met in New York right when she first got there," he said. "She said he was the governor in that stupid musical *The Best Little Whorehouse in Texas*, from, like, the seventies."

"It won a Tony." I had no idea why I wanted him to know that.

"She was an understudy for the female lead," he went on.

"Right. So what about this Jay Garner?"

"That's part of the mess. He passed away in 2011, and she never changed that part of the will. Tell the truth, I didn't even remember it until she passed, and I got in touch with you."

"Oh for God's sake!" I exploded. "This is ridiculous! I can't stay in a house where somebody wants to kill me!"

"Okay," he said quickly, "but, see, you can't sell the house. And if you don't stay in it, you can't inherit it either. So get the police to post a guard. Get Doctor Waldrop to move in for a while. Get a dog. And maybe a gun?"

"A *gun*?"

"I'm sorry, Madeline," he went on, even more distractedly. "The way Rose set this deal up, we're just stuck."

"*We're* stuck?" I shook my head. "If we're in this together, why don't *you* come live here with me?"

He actually chuckled. "I think my wife might have something to say about that. So, look: give me a day or three to get out from under this real estate fraud case, and then let me see if I can't figure out something that doesn't keep you trapped in some bad B-movie, hear?"

And, weirdly, his shift to a lighter tone popped me out of my panic somehow.

"I *am* trapped in a bad B-movie," I told him.

"Just gimme a couple of days," he said, and he even managed to sound reassuring.

"Okay." I sighed. "And sorry to be, you know, a hysterical stereotype. Momentarily."

"I think you sound brave and righteous," he said, almost fatherly.

"Thanks, Rusty," I said. "But just, you know, a couple of days, right?"

I heard someone in his office hollering, and several people started talking at once. Rusty groaned.

"Lord. Gotta go."

And he hung up.

So there I was, stuck in a creaky old house with the ghost of my dead aunt and a maniac trying to kill me. Welcome to Enigma.

8

I GOT UP FROM the desk before Philomena called out from the kitchen.

"That didn't sound like it went well," she allowed.

"It didn't," I said, coming back into the kitchen. "I can't sell the place until I've lived here for six months."

I collapsed into the kitchen chair where I'd been sitting for breakfast.

Phil stopped what she was doing and turned around to face me. "What?"

"Aunt Rose put a thing in the will," I mumbled. "Is there any coffee left?"

"She did *what*?" Phil pressed.

"A *codicil*," I told her, "says I have to live in the house for six months before I completely inherit. If I don't, I lose everything."

Philomena's shoulders sagged, her face went pale, and she tried to say something, but the words wouldn't come out.

"I know," I said, agreeing with her astonishment.

"What are you going to do?"

"I have no idea, but I'm not just going to sit here and

hope for the best," I announced. "I'm going to pester Billy. I'm going to garner other allies. I mean *besides* you. Find out who the hell would want me out of town bad enough to kill me. Bad enough to burn down the house. So, I guess, *that's* what I'm going to do. There."

"Oh." She drifted toward the French press, picked it up without looking at it, and brought it to me.

"Any thoughts?" I asked her. "I mean, about who could help me?"

She sat, poured us both some more coffee, set down the press, and appeared to consider my question with a very fierce intensity.

Then her head snapped up. "You know who we should call? Gloria Coleman!"

And with that she was up and headed for the phone.

"Who's that?"

Her sudden enthusiasm was a little alarming; I followed her into the next room.

"Gloria Coleman," she repeated. "You'll love her. She's our first and only *female* Episcopal priest! Can you imagine?"

She dialed the phone.

"Her story is like something in a book," Phil went on. "She was born at the edge of the Okefenokee Swamp. Her parents were squatters on government land, but they'd made friends with the local park rangers, so they were allowed to live there. I mean surreptitiously."

"That does sound interesting," I said uncertainly, "but—"

She held up her hand and said into the phone, "Gloria? Yes, it's Philomena Waldrop. Listen. I've got a kind of emergency. Is there any chance you might come over to Rose's bookshop?"

She nodded as she listened to the reply.

"That's right, it's her niece," she said after a moment. "And she's in real trouble. Can you come now?"

The response made Phil smile and she hung up.

"She'll be right over," she told me.

"Right." I nodded. "Why?"

"*Why* what, dear?" Phil asked absently.

"Why are you so happy that an Episcopal priest is coming over?"

"Oh, I see. Well, she's new in town, like you. She's had a smidge of trouble with the hoi polloi, like you. And she's a priest, which is really just a different kind of actor, like you, don't you think?"

"But how is it that you think this priest might help my current situation, exactly?" I insisted.

"I told you," she answered. "She's received threats like you have."

"What do you mean?"

"I'm a lay reader at the church," she said. "The only woman lay reader, I might add. So because of that, Gloria confides in me. She's gotten some frankly horrible threats from the community."

"She's been here how long?" I asked.

"About six months, I think," she said. "So I think we should put our heads together, we three. Don't you?"

I just stood there. "I don't know."

She shrugged. "You'll see."

Ten minutes later we were sitting on the front porch. Phil had made another French press. The morning was still chilly, but it wouldn't last long. The sun was warm, and the sky was an autumnal blue, like some kind of aquamarine stone, hard and clear.

We'd only just gotten settled in when the remarkable

figure of Gloria Coleman appeared, motoring our way with a bulldozer's determination. She couldn't have stood more than five foot two. Her reddish hair was cut short enough to qualify as a crew cut. Her black suit couldn't quite disguise the fact that she was twenty pounds overweight. But she was moving with the speed and elegance of a dancer. It was a confusing combination of attributes.

When she saw that we were sitting on the porch waiting for her, she waved and hollered, "Doctor Waldrop!"

"Father Coleman!" Phil answered, laughing.

Seconds later, the priest was standing in front of me.

"Gloria Coleman," she announced, hand thrust my way.

I took her hand, endured a crushing grip, and made a halfhearted gesture toward a rocking chair.

She shook her head. "Let's talk inside."

And without another word she launched herself into the house.

Gloria took up residence on the antique French sofa. Philomena sat in the nearest overstuffed armchair. I dragged the chair from behind the desk. For some reason I had the feeling that I didn't want to get particularly cozy. Once we were all seated, an uncomfortable silence prevailed long enough for me to start asking ridiculous questions.

"Doctor Waldrop said you were born in a swamp," I ventured. "Is that true?"

"It is!" she answered. "Land of the alligator and the ibis. We weren't supposed to be there, you understand. My family. We were on government land, or, really, Oconee land if you want to get technical about it. Still, my parents were very likable people, and they had the gift of gab, you know. So they just talked their way into the scheme of things there, and that was that. *Man*, it was a great place to grow up. Wild, beautiful, hot. I hated to leave it."

I was already beginning to see why the local population might have been a little standoffish with the Reverend Coleman.

But what I said was, "Why *did* you leave?"

"Ah." She nodded. "The folks died. I stayed for a while, but I got lonesome, so I walked out of the swamp, all the way to Savannah. No money. No schooling, or no traditional schooling anyway. I slept on the streets for a while. Savannah's a fine place for that. Then I got work as a janitor in an Episcopal church. It was a *great* job."

And with that I was beginning to see why Phil liked this woman. Her enthusiasm for just about everything in life, no matter how mean, was infectious.

"That's what made you want to be a priest," I assumed.

"The guy there, Father Davis?" She grinned and shook her head. "I never met anybody half as . . . I don't know, kind or happy or just great. So, yeah, he was the guy. And he didn't bat an eye when I said I wanted to be a priest. Two years after I started working there, he arranged it so that the church paid for my seminary education. And then a couple of years later, voilà: short, happy, lady priest!"

"And they sent you here?" I asked.

"God, no," she told me. "I've been at this for ten years now, first back in Savannah with Father Davis, then up in Atlanta for a bit. They sent me here when old Father Glenn retired."

"*Retired*." Phil rolled her eyes.

"All right, Doctor Waldrop," Gloria chided. "He was just being a good Episcopalian priest."

Phil looked at me. "He drank too much, he was thrice divorced, and oh my Lord he was *impossibly* loquacious."

Gloria nodded. "Those are all practically requirements for ordination in the Episcopal Church."

"So he *retired*," Phil said, "to his girlfriend's seaside cottage in St. Simons."

"So, see, I've only been in Enigma for a few months," Gloria concluded.

"But we digress," I said, hoping to get to my point. "Why am I talking to an Episcopal priest about my current situation?"

"Madeline has received death threats," Phil told Gloria, "and someone tried to burn this house down. And—and a girl was killed here last night."

Gloria nodded. "I already heard. So that's why Philomena called me. I've been getting threatening phone calls too. Practically since the day I got here."

"Same person," Phil pronounced. "Same guy is threatening you both. That's what I think."

I stared at them both for a minute before I started slowly shaking my head.

"No, I don't think so." I sat back. "There's a big difference between—"

"This is a very small town!" Phil snapped. "The odds of there being more than one idiot of that particular ilk are very small indeed, in my opinion."

"But my guy is more than an idiot, Phil," I said softly. "He's a murderer."

"Mm-hmm," Phil mumbled curtly. "Tell Madeline the nature of your phone calls, Father Coleman."

"Second day I was here," she responded, "the man called and told me to pack up, leave town. A couple of days later, when I didn't, he called back and said he was looking at me through the sight of his deer rifle, could see me in the window, sitting in my office. Told me how easy it would be to put a bullet through my 'fuzzy' head."

"See?" Phil glared at me.

"What did you say?" I asked.

"I told him if he didn't like my haircut, he should shoot my stylist, not me." Gloria grinned again. "But he had already hung up."

"Yeah, my guy didn't leave much room for witty repartee either," I admitted. "But that still doesn't prove—"

"Don't be ridiculous," Phil objected. "It's the same man!"

"I'm sorry, Phil," I said, "I just disagree with you. But I'm very glad you've introduced me to Gloria because after only a few moments with her, I *do* agree with you about one thing. If the three of us put our heads together, we'll probably be able to figure all this out."

"You mean who's calling me," Gloria asked, "or who's killing you?"

"Both." I slowly examined their faces. "Look at us. We're the fabled Weird Sisters. I have a very odd feeling that we can probably do *anything*."

Philomena nodded and giggled a little too manically. "We *are* the witches from the Scottish play! 'Double, double, toil and trouble!'"

"'Peace!'" Gloria snapped instantly. "'The charm's wound up.'"

I think you could probably have heard us laughing from at least a half mile away.

9

WE WEREN'T LAUGHING later that night. I'd spent most of the
day trying to clean up as best I could. The door frame and
the floor at the entrance were charred and probably unsafe.
I didn't want to bother Philomena again, she'd gone to hold
her classes, but I really needed to find someone who could fix
it all up in a hurry. Repair the damage, and maybe rebuild the
gazebo too.

I'd seen plenty of movies and television shows about someone being killed in someone's house, of course, but they never
show what it's like after everyone leaves and it's up to the poor
slob who lives there to try to put things back to normal. Or
to show that *normal* wasn't really a thing you could get back
to after something like that happened. In your house. I was
having a long streak of out-of-body experiences.

I guess that's why the phone made me jump.

It was just after sunset. There was still a little hazy light
on the horizon. Everything was amber. Or sepia-toned like
some old movie.

Heart thrashing, I answered the phone on the third ring.

"Madeline!" Philomena gasped before I could say anything. "Get over here to the church right now!"

I didn't say anything instantly, so she snapped at me.

"Madeline! Do you hear me?"

"I do," I told her. "What are you talking about?"

"The church!" she yelled.

"What church, Phil?" I asked her. "I'm trying to clean up—"

"Gloria's church is under attack! She needs help. I called Billy, but he didn't answer. We've got to help her! They're trying to set it on fire!"

And she hung up.

I looked around the room. There was still a smell of wet charcoal and heavy anxiety in the air. I was still in my sweats, and my hair was a chaos of brambles.

Not to mention that I wasn't certain I remembered where the Episcopal church was.

Still, we'd made a pact. Sort of. And if Philomena was that agitated, something was going on.

So without another thought I headed upstairs for my tennis shoes and my car keys. Halfway up the stairs I realized how eager I was to get out of the house, to do something more than clean soot and obsess about what was happening to me. It was good to think outside myself.

After that minor revelation, I flew up the stairs and back down in under a minute, swerving through the burnt doorway without even bothering to lock the door.

As it turned out, the problem of remembering the exact location of the Episcopal church wasn't much of an issue. I saw it. Just across the street and what amounted to a block down.

I shoved the keys into the pocket of my sweatpants and took off. I hadn't gotten more than ten feet when I heard the commotion. Men were yelling. And it sounded like they were building something. In spite of the sudden clench in my stomach, I ran toward the church.

The scene that presented itself was a little out of a Frankenstein movie, villagers with pitchforks. Five or maybe six men were menacing the parking lot to the side of the church. They were yelling things at the church that I couldn't understand. They were obviously drunk. And they had torn down part of what looked like an All Saints' Day display in the churchyard—big plywood panels with kids' paintings on them. They were dismantling the panels and piling them up in the parking lot. They were trying to set the pile on fire, but there was a good cold wind, and they couldn't quite manage it.

I pulled my hair back and slowed down.

"Hey, boys!" I called out in my best small-town-girl demeanor. "What are y'all doing?"

One of the men turned to me and snarled, "You'd best get on away from here, little girl."

Despite the fact that I found it hilarious to be called "little girl," I did my best to stay in character: small-town curious citizen just out for an evening jog.

"Y'all making a display?" I said, ambling toward them.

The man who'd yelled at me, overalls and a flannel shirt, work boots and three-day whiskers—a real stereotype—dropped the two-by-four he was carrying and took a few steps my way.

"This ain't none of your business," he growled. "Go on, now."

I saw the look in his eye. I'd seen it in bars and sometimes in boyfriends. It was a glassy, zombie look, the kind that said he wouldn't remember anything about this when the morning came. In other words, the dangerous kind. He was drunk enough to do something wrong.

"Hold on," I told him, backing away.

"I don't believe I know you," he snarled, lumbering closer.

I didn't know what to say. If he knew me, would it be less threatening? A couple of the other men glanced our way. I was feeling weird and amped up enough to take on one drunk, but three was beyond my limit. I kept backing away.

"How about you come over here and join us, sweetheart!" one of the other men jeered. "We're gonna have us a little old bonfire."

And for no reason I could understand, the threat of fire clicked on a certain rage in the center of my soul, just like flipping a switch. My face got hot, every muscle I had tensed, and my hands turned into fists.

"I don't think so, *Jethro*," I growled at the guy closest to me.

The entire scene had the makings of a really serious life moment, but I wasn't about to back down. I was tired and sad and hungry, and the only thing on my mind was all the ways I could do damage to the guy coming at me.

And just at that moment, Gloria and Philomena appeared in the front doorway of the church.

"Madeline!" Gloria called out, chipper and happy. "How nice of you to drop by."

Like nothing else was going on.

But Philomena's eyes were huge. "Madeline! Get away from that man!"

I shook my head. I looked back at the men. They were gathering. I felt a sickening combination of fear and anger in my bones. I was shivering and ready to jump. At that moment, I might have done anything. Even seeing a dead body in my new home wasn't as surreal as that moment.

To make matters even stranger, Gloria motored down the

church stairs, clerical collar, black suit, sensible shoes, holding up a six-pack of Budweiser in her hand.

"You boys seem to be having a little trouble getting your fire started," she called out amiably. "Let's have a beer and see if we can't work this out."

She handed the six-pack to the nearest goon and reached into her suitcoat pocket, producing a box of kitchen matches.

"Kind of a windy night," she said. "Maybe if y'all gather round that way, kind of make a semicircle, block the breeze, we might get her lit."

The men were clearly confused, looking at each other for answers. But the prospect of another beer seemed clear to them. After the slightest of pauses, they each took one, and then, slowly, silently, moved to block the chilly breeze.

Not a one of them could think of anything to say, and I was a little dumbstruck myself. The sight of a female minister kneeling beside a pile of plywood and striking a match was difficult to comprehend. But Gloria managed to find a splintered part of one of the panels and, on the third match, set it on fire.

She stood back, proud. "There you go. That what you had in mind?"

She looked around at the assembled. The men were silent and frozen, very confused about the odd turn of events, utterly unable to quite understand what was happening.

Gloria leveled a very benevolent gaze on one of the men and said, "Too bad, though, Floyd. This one, the one that's burning, is the one your Debbie painted. I think it was Saint John the Baptist. See? It's got her name on the bottom there."

And, momentarily forgetting himself, Floyd tilted his head so that he could see the blue and white image on the panel.

But before Floyd could grapple with the facts, one of the men, a stubby red-faced piglet, snapped everyone out of the temporary peace Gloria had tried to create.

"You ain't got no *right* to be here in our town!" he shouted at Gloria.

He was spitting his words and hot as a gunshot.

But Gloria stayed calm. "Uh-huh," she began.

"Speck Dixon!" Philomena appeared behind her, apparently emboldened by Gloria's performance, or maybe by her own fear. "You are *not* a member of this congregation. I would suggest that you leave the fitness of our pastoral care to those of us who *are*."

I knew she meant it to be more scathing than it was, but it made me love her more.

"This ain't no *real* church," the stubby man went on. Had Philomena called him *Speck*? Had I heard that right?

Floyd finally found his voice. "That *is* Debbie's name down there at the bottom."

"It is," Gloria assured him. "Maybe we should put the fire out?"

Floyd looked over at Speck.

"And you should know that I've called the police!" Philomena announced.

That didn't seem to matter to the crowd, or maybe they just couldn't grasp the concept that what they were doing might be a police matter. They were really drunk. But Floyd swigged his beer, crumpled the can, tossed it into the parking lot, and began stamping out the fire.

"Every one of those panels was painted by some little kid just like Debbie," Gloria observed more quietly than before. "Makes me wonder what you guys think you're doing, exactly."

I picked up that thread, still shaking. "Some child is going to walk by here tomorrow and look up at Daddy and ask him what happened to her picture of a saint. I'll be sitting on those steps over there and I'll tell her exactly what happened. In detail. Because I have nothing better to do since somebody tried to burn down my house and I can't open my store."

Gloria looked over at me, beaming. "And I'll be right there with her."

Philomena looked around. "I have to teach in the morning. But maybe I can come by after lunch."

Speck was only more irritated, more red-faced, and louder, turning his ire on his cohorts. "It don't matter what you say!"

Philomena stepped forward, chin out, and shouted the little stubby man down. "I've known you since you were a nasty little boy, Speck Dixon, and I've a good mind to call up your mother right now and tell her what you're doing."

One of the other men laughed at that, and two or three more looked away.

"I don't care who you call!" Speck screamed. "I'll take down this whole damn church!"

But the scene had lost some of its momentum thanks to Gloria's odd fire-starter performance. The man who'd stomped out the fire, Floyd, sniffed and looked around like he'd lost something.

"I'm gone," he said, and just wandered off.

Speck lumbered over the smoking plywood, careless of his dragging pants' cuffs, and got a little too close to Gloria.

"You don't belong here," he rumbled. "This church don't belong here; you get that into your head. We're all Baptist down here. You understand me?"

Gloria locked eyes with the guy. "No, I don't think I'll ever understand a person like you, Mister Dixon. And as for

St. Thomas Aquinas church, it was one of the first in this county. Goes back to 1906, same year as the college was founded. Probably by the same people. The Baptist church, on the other hand, didn't come along until 1943, after the Depression. Do I have my dates right, Doctor Waldrop?"

Phil took another few steps closer to Gloria. "Why, yes you do, Reverend Coleman."

"And we have a congregation of almost sixty," Gloria went on. "So not *everyone* around here is a Baptist. Am I right about my figures, Doctor Waldrop?"

"Fifty-three, to be exact," Phil answered.

Gloria lowered her voice and spoke very slowly, without any hint of aggression. "And if you ever come onto church property and tear anything up again, I will personally give you a demonstration of the rifle marksmanship skills I learned as a child in the Okefenokee Swamp. Do you understand *me*, Mister Dixon?"

Speck put his face so close to Gloria's that they were almost touching. "It's more than a few sticks of plywood that can burn down around here."

Gloria turned to Philomena. "That kind of sounded like a threat, didn't it?"

"When Billy Sanders gets here," Phil said, staring at Speck, "it's the first thing I'm going to tell him about."

"Boys!" Speck called out.

But the other men had already begun to disperse. The sun had completely set so it was impossible to see their faces, and they were silent, but all of their momentum was gone.

Speck Dixon shook his head in disgust, grunted, and turned away.

The scene was ending.

"Thanks for coming over, Madeline," Gloria told me

softly. "Come on in the church for a minute, hear? Philomena?"

Philomena let go a heavy breath and headed up the steps.

I nodded, but I stood my ground until it was clear that
all the men were really leaving. Most of them just walked
away. Speck got into an old Ford pickup and roared down the
street, fast and loud as he could manage.

Stars began to blink on, and I went into the church, through
the red doors, past the vestibule. But I froze in the doorway to
the nave.

I stared and couldn't think of any other way to put it than,
"This place is, like, hysterically *Anglican*."

Arched wooden beams, dark carved pews, dramatic
stained glass. The cross at the altar was ornate, and the flowers were fresh. The low light gave the whole place a kind of
smoky ambiance. Or maybe it was the candles. I even thought
there might be a hint of frankincense in the air.

Gloria looked around. "It is, isn't it."

She had plunked down in the last pew on the right. Phil
was sitting beside her, fidgeting nervously.

"I mean it's like a cliché of an Episcopal church," I went
on. "I don't know what I was expecting, but this surpasses it.
I must have walked by this place a million times when I was
a kid. I never even noticed it. Certainly never came inside."

"Your parents weren't religious?" Gloria asked me.

"Not remotely," I answered, stepping into the wonderful
world of liberal Christianity. "And Rose was downright anti-
religion."

"Don't say that," Philomena snapped, still twiddling. "The
theatre was her church."

I nodded. "Good point."

"But, listen, we have to get the police here right now." Philomena leaned toward me. "Now that we know."

I blinked. "Now that we know what?"

"Now that we know it was Speck Dixon who killed Tandy!" She stood up, her voice rising. "We've got to tell that to Billy Sanders right now!"

"Philomena, take a breath." I shook my head and sat down in the pew across the aisle from Gloria.

"What makes you think that stubby little man had anything to do with Tandy?" Gloria asked.

"And what exactly do we go to Billy Sanders *with*, Phil?" I added.

"With what just happened!" Phil was still a little wound up from the scene, apparently.

"That guy, Speck, he does seem like a moron," I admitted. "And, okay, maybe a firebug, but that's a long way from . . . help me here, Father Coleman. You don't think that guy's the person who killed Tandy."

"I don't." But her face was contorted. "But you have to admit that was a weird scene just now."

I grinned. "I actually thought you handled it brilliantly. Helping them start the fire was—I mean, it really confused those guys. It confused me."

"Speck *is* the only guy who's threatened me in person," Gloria went on. "But I couldn't say for sure that it was him on the phone."

"Same here," I agreed. "Didn't really sound like the same voice to me. Or, I mean, I couldn't tell. And, anyway, this Speck character was right there in the parking lot, out in the open, not making an anonymous phone call. Not the same behavior pattern, right?"

"Behavior pattern?" Phil repeated. "What are you talking about? Is that some kind of actor thing?"

I laughed, mostly to release a little of my tension. "Maybe. Look, why did you call me to come to this shindig anyway, Phil?"

"I called everybody," she said. "I called Billy first, but when he didn't answer I called five or six other people. You just got here first."

"Yeah," I said, "turns out I live just down the street. I didn't quite realize that. Swear to God, Gloria, I spent most of my young life in the bookshop and I didn't even remember this place was here." I looked around a little more carefully. "This beautiful place."

"Stop it!" Phil snapped. "What's the matter with you two? These men just threatened us. Speck Dixon is no joke. He's a good old son of a good old boy going way back over a hundred years. *He's the guy!*"

I hadn't realized that Philomena was so rattled. Or, scared, really. She'd been frightened by the gaggle of goons. I wasn't sure why my fear had turned so quickly into a fool-hardy kind of anger. Maybe it was because I was still so enraged from what had happened at the bookshop. Or sleep deprived. Or maybe I was an odd kind of numb. I really couldn't tell.

Gloria saw Phil's lingering fear too and took her hand.

"It's okay, Philomena," she said softly. "A guy like Speck Dixon is always more talk than action. I've been dealing with men like that most of my life. My guess is that you have too. I mean, academia is not exactly the most female-friendly environment in the world, is it?"

That made me laugh.

But it was clear that Philomena was trying really hard not

to cry. "It's not. It's horrible sometimes. And Madeline, honey, thank you for coming when I called. I guess nobody else did. I should have said thank you right when you got here. It's just . . . it's been a very difficult couple of days."

"Yes, it has," I told her softly.

I remembered Philomena as being a little tougher than that. But maybe it was just my kid's perspective of her. When you're a kid you figure most adults can handle anything; most adults know what they're doing. I'd left Enigma when I was seventeen. It's only after you're thirty that you realize what's really true about being an adult. Or at least that's the way it was for me. Still, Phil seemed more upset by the events of this particular evening than I would have imagined. Especially considering how relatively calm Gloria and I were.

Which prompted me to say, "Gloria, why are you and I so calm? Phil's right. Those guys were pretty scary."

She nodded. "I'll break it down for you. Do you know the number one fear of most people in the world? Survey says: speaking in front of a group of people. You've spent most of your adult life doing that. So have I. So what's a little small-town foolishness compared to that, apparently?"

"But Phil teaches college," I protested, "and she has to talk in front of students every day."

Gloria waved me off. "Not the same thing."

"It's kind of the same thing," Phil objected weakly.

"Students are intimidated by teachers," Gloria went on. "They're being graded by the teacher. It's just the opposite for us. Actors are being graded by the audience. Plus, only half of any audience wants to be in the theatre anyway. The other half was dragged there by their wives."

It was an old joke, but it still made me smile.

"Philomena thinks that you and I have commonality,"

I told Gloria, "because a priest is like an actor. That's why you weren't scared?"

Gloria shook her head. "No, and anyway she got it wrong. *Lawyers* are actors, priests are something else."

"Okay," I said, still smiling, "so then why weren't you scared?"

"Me?" She shook her head. "I lived in a swamp half my life. Alligators big as Buicks, a dozen varieties of poisonous snakes, bugs that can eat your hand off while you're asleep. Shoot. Speck Dixon can't hold a candle."

"Teachers are a *little* like actors," Phil mumbled on, only a little absently.

"No—" Gloria began.

But before that ridiculous debate could get any further, Billy Sanders charged into the nave.

"What happened here?" he asked, all out of breath.

10

PHILOMENA GLARED AT Billy. "You're a little late to the party. The culprits have absconded."

Billy looked to Gloria. "What was all that mess out in your parking lot? It looks like it was a little fire out there."

Gloria nodded. "I set that."

"Speck Dixon and four or five other men were here, Billy," Philomena said angrily. "They threatened us. They were going to burn the children's paintings of saints, but Gloria stopped them.

"By setting fire to them first," Gloria said.

Billy was silent.

"I was here fixing the flowers on the altar," Phil went on, "when I heard the commotion."

"I was in my office," Gloria said, "but I heard them too."

Billy turned my way. "What about you? What are you doing here?"

"Doctor Waldrop called me," I told him. "I was cleaning up my house. You know, from the fire. And the murder."

I didn't want to be deliberately confrontational with Billy. He was okay. I was just feeling a little aggressive in general, I guess.

"Why did you call her?" Billy asked Philomena.

Phil sighed, irritated. "I called everybody. She showed up first."

"I live just down the street," I said.

"Yeah," Billy snapped. "I know where you live. What were these men doing here exactly?"

"The Reverend Coleman has been receiving the same kind of threats that Madeline's gotten," Philomena answered. "She just hasn't reported them to you. This, tonight, was the culmination of those threats, I believe. And by the way, when I called you, I got your voicemail. That does not instill confidence in the constabulary. *Voicemail*."

Billy's jaw clenched and his lips thinned.

"I was at the coroner's in Tifton," he said, measuring his words, "getting Tandy's autopsy report."

That put an end to our antagonism toward Billy.

"I'm sorry, Billy," Philomena said softly.

He looked down hard, but he spoke very softly. "I was just talking to Tandy in your class two days ago. I believe she might have been the sweetest person on the planet."

"Any surprises from the autopsy?" Gloria asked, clearly steering Billy back to his official capacity.

"No." He drew in a long breath. "She died of a stab wound. Just one. Had smoke in her lungs, so she didn't die right away."

"It was Speck," Philomena said.

Billy's jaw clenched again. It was taking all his self-control to keep himself calm, we could all see it.

"What makes you say that?" he asked.

"His performance here!" Philomena told him.

"Okay." He took a couple of breaths. "Madeline, was Speck

Dixon the one that threatened you the phone? Or Reverend Coleman, same question."

"Hard to say," I admitted.

"The guy who called me," Gloria said, "kind of disguised his voice, kind of growly."

"Same here," I said. "Whispery. And, for my money anyway, I don't think it was that guy, Speck."

"Why not?" Billy asked.

"There's a difference between a drunken toad who doesn't want a woman priest in town," I said, "and a person who would murder somebody as sweet as Tandy Fletcher."

Gloria nodded. "I'd have to agree with that."

"No!" Philomena insisted, counting off her list of facts on her fingers. "One, he starts fires. Two, he hates Episcopalians. Three, he . . . he's a bad person. Four—"

Billy stopped her. "I'll go talk to him. He certainly can't come onto church property and harass the minister. Who else was with him? You said four or five others?"

"Floyd Tucker was one," Gloria said. "His little girl comes to Sunday school here. For some reason. He doesn't. He's not a member of our congregation."

"Debbie most likely comes here with the Garner twins," Billy said. "I believe Jed and Millie Garner go to this church."

"Oh." Gloria nodded. "They do. I see the twins and Debbie together all the time. Good call, Officer."

"Uh-huh," he said, "who else?"

"I don't know anybody in town anymore," I said.

"I just got to Enigma myself," Gloria told him. "I only know Floyd because I've seen him with Debbie."

"It was getting dark, and I didn't have my glasses on," Philomena added. "So I didn't recognize anybody else."

Billy took a second. "Well, like I said, I'll go talk to Speck. But Doctor Waldrop, he's a moron, not a murderer."

"You're just saying that because he's well-to-do!" she snapped. "Because of his family!"

Something in Billy just gave up then. His face went blank.

"I'm sorry you'd think that about me," he answered softly.

He nodded once, turned around, and was gone.

"I don't think he quite deserved that, Philomena," Gloria chided gently.

"Speck," she grumbled, like his name was a curse word.

I stood. "Well, it's not that this hasn't been fun, but I think I'll go home now."

"You're not staying in that house alone," Philomena said instantly. "I'm coming with you."

"Thanks for coming here, Madeline," Gloria said to me. "Considering everything that's happened to you since you got here, it was kind of above and beyond."

"I only came because I thought there was going to be a bonfire," I said, angling toward the vestibule. "Who doesn't like a good October bonfire?"

"It's not a joke," Phil said, following me.

"You know," Gloria said, escorting us toward the door, "Saint Thomas Aquinas, for whom this church is named, is the patron saint of students, booksellers, academics, and theologians. Among other things."

I turned. "You're making that up."

"Swear to God," she answered, hand on her heart. "That covers the three of us, plus Tandy Fletcher."

"Well," Philomena scoffed, "Saint Thomas needs to work a little harder. Because he didn't help poor Tandy very much. And Madeline's clearly not safe. And I love Billy, but I don't have much faith in his ability as a detective."

"No, I don't either," I agreed.

"What I was saying about Saint Thomas," Gloria said as we walked out of the church and down the stone steps, "is that maybe he brought us together. To help each other."

"We did come together tonight," I said. "It was sort of great, the three of us standing up to the mob."

"I don't know if those drunks amounted to a mob," Gloria said, "but, yeah, like that."

"Or." I stopped dead in my tracks.

The other two almost ran into me.

"What if we were brought together," I went on, "to find out who killed Tandy?"

The stars were out in full, and the moon was climbing high in the sky. There was an October chill in the air. An owl called out from behind the church. A crow answered. Lights had come on in the few houses down at the other end of the street. Someone was baking cornbread. The wind picked up, swirled and crackled a cloud of leaves.

"You're right, sugar," said Philomena firmly. "That's what we're going to do. We're going to track down the man who murdered that child."

"Amen to that," Gloria confirmed.

And for the first time since I'd come back to Enigma, I felt right about something.

11

THE NEXT MORNING was another one of those golden autumn days, apple-crunching air, hard-slanted sunlight, cold-water breezes. Philomena had indeed stayed the night with me, and I'd slept like the dead until nearly eleven in the morning.

When I trundled down the stairs, still in my sweats, and hit the step with the baritone groan, I stopped for a second. I considered that I might ought to listen to the house a little bit more. Like maybe it had been trying to tell me something.

But that thought was immediately dispelled by the smell of coffee coming from the kitchen. There were no cloud biscuits there, but the coffee was steaming, and Philomena seemed to have calmed down.

"I turned more customers away," she announced when I came into the kitchen. "They didn't seem to care if the doorway was charred, and if they knew about Tandy, they didn't mention it. Thank God. Oh, by the way, look what I found."

She was sitting at the table, coffee mug in hand, leaning over her laptop. She pointed to the counter at a new-looking electric kettle, plugged in and turned on. It was sitting next to the French press.

"Where'd you get that?" I asked, shuffling in.

"It's a Mueller Ultra Kettle," she said absently, staring at her computer screen. "Rose got it from Amazon a couple of months ago."

"Cool," I said. "Also, thanks for staying here last night."

She looked up from her computer. "It was a very strange night, to me."

"It was to me too." I poured my java into a mug that had owls on it, the only one on the counter. "You seem to be recovered from it. And I haven't slept like that in several years."

I collapsed into the chair across from her.

"I've just been arranging for someone to come over here and do a little handyman work," she said, looking back down at the screen. "He's coming right over."

"Handyman?" I sipped.

"David Madison," she gushed all of a sudden. "Sugar, you will *love* him. He's the master gardener at the college, but he can do absolutely anything. I already wanted to get him over here to fix the gazebo, but now he can work on the doorway too. He's a genius at woodwork. He builds garden trellises you could use at Versailles. I really can't wait for you to meet him."

I leaned back in my chair. "Sounds like somebody's got a crush."

She smiled. "Don't be ridiculous. He's *your* age." She waited a beat before she sang out, "And he's single."

"Hold on," I told her. "Is this someone who's going to repair my house, or ask me out?"

She shrugged, closing her laptop. "Why couldn't it be both?"

"You're trying to fix me up." I took in more coffee. "I don't want that."

"Just wait until you hear his story," she said, waving a hand over her head enthusiastically. "He ran away from home at the age of twelve. Ended up in Kentucky to study poetry and organic gardening with—you would never guess—Wendell Berry!"

"I do love Wendell Berry," I agreed, mostly just playing along.

"Then he earned a living playing the fiddle with itinerant string bands all around this part of the country. Then he got this job at the college about ten years ago. Honey, he knows more about gardening than Rose and I put together. And he's so *handsome*!"

"I'm not really in the market, Phil," I said, swigging the rest of my coffee. "Maybe let's put the matchmaking on hold until after we've stopped someone from killing me?"

"All right," she said, deliberately sounding as skeptical as she could.

"Have you cooled down about this so-called Speck Davis?"

"Dixon," she corrected. "And no I have not. I genuinely believe he's the culprit."

"Based on what?" I complained. "You don't have any actual proof of anything—"

"Then we'll find proof," she interrupted. "You and Gloria and I, we'll *find* proof."

She was so committed to the moment that I didn't have the heart to contradict her.

"Okay, Doctor Waldrop," I said gently. "We'll find proof; we'll find something."

I took my coffee with me back to my bedroom. Changed clothes, brushed my hair, dabbed a little Dove deodorant on the armpits, and went back downstairs.

"When is this guy coming over?" I called out to Phil when I hit the bottom of the stairs.

"Five minutes ago," said a very deep voice from the front porch.

And suddenly there he was in the doorway. Laughing, black hair, kempt stubble, gray jeans, T-shirt, work boots, and single.

"David Madison," he said.

"As foretold," I responded, trying not to stutter.

"This doorway's nothing," he went on. "Once I get the trim and molding, shouldn't take more than a couple of hours. And some paint. The floor here's burnt, but not bad. You won't have to replace any of the boards. You could sand it and stain it, I think. Won't look the same, but you could finesse that. But the gazebo is another story."

"Where's Philomena?" I asked.

"She went on over to the university. She's got a one o'clock class to prepare for."

"Right, right." I nodded. "I'm Madeline Brimley. You probably already figured that out."

"I did." He smiled. "I knew Rose. She was a remarkable person."

"She was to me," I told him. "So what about the gazebo?"

"Yeah," he said, heading toward me. "Pretty much have to start over with that. Take away all the burnt wood and everything, just build a new one."

"Okay—" I began.

He was, in fact, heading for the kitchen and, I realized, the back door. "Let's have a look."

I followed. Phil had cleared the kitchen table, but there were a few dishes in the sink, and a little coffee left in the press.

"You need some coffee?" I called after him.

"No, thanks," he said without looking back. "I don't really drink coffee."

I'd only put on a sweater and jeans, but it was enough. The day was warming up nicely, and the sun was strong in the garden. Strong enough to make me squint.

David had stopped at the pile of ashes where the gazebo had been.

"I haven't called anybody about the insurance yet," I began, drawing up closer to him. "I don't know if I can afford to rebuild this thing."

He nodded. "Well. The thing is, the Old Juniper gazebo is kind of a historical landmark. You really have to replace it. So I'm going to do it, and you'll pay me whenever you can, how about that?"

I glanced at the house. "It's a bookshop. If I can't get insurance money to cover this, you'll be a great-grandpa before I can pay you back."

"Okay, that's a deal," he told me. "I'll finish the gazebo, and then get right to work on the having children and grandchildren part of the plan. You put a dollar or two away a day, and I'll check back in with you when little Cecily has a baby."

"Cecily?"

He leveled a very serious look at me. "That's going to be my granddaughter's name. You're not making fun of it, are you?"

"God no," I said. "I was just worried that the other kids might make fun of her in middle school."

He turned back to the wreckage of the gazebo on the ground. "Oh, I'm sure they will. But she's going to be the concert master of the New York Philharmonic, so what does she care?"

"So she'll take up the violin," I said, "like her great-grandfather."

His smile got bigger. "Philomena told you about that."

"She did," I confirmed. "She also said you worked with Wendell Berry."

"I *studied* with him," he corrected.

"Gardening or poetry?"

"Little of both." He finally turned my way. "I also birthed a baby once, planted seaweed professionally, and raised a bear cub in the wild until it got big enough to make me nervous and I turned him out."

"None of that's true," I insisted.

He looked around, like he was taking in everything he could see, taking it into the deepest part of himself.

"I don't know if there's any other life besides this one," he told me quietly. "So I believe in the sampler plate. The tasting menu. The smorgasbord. I want to do a little bit of everything that I want to do. So, I believe I'll be a jack-of-all-trades, master of none as they say. Which brings us back to your gazebo."

"I think it's going to be *your* gazebo," I told him, "but okay. What about it?"

"Do you want it to be a copy of what was here, or do you want it to be a new design?"

"The original design came with the house, I think." I looked back at the house. "I mean, I'd certainly want it to match the house, right?"

"I think so," he agreed.

"Plus, as the historic make-out spot that it's been for decades, we have a responsibility to, you know, young lovers all over this great land of ours."

He studied the space where the gazebo had been. "So

each of the benches on all seven sides would have to seat two people comfortably."

"At least," I agreed. "And I'm impressed that you knew that the original had seven sides."

He looked down. "I might have observed it from the inside a time or two myself."

"So you understand the value of a personal commitment to the work," I said.

"I understand that better than anybody you know."

And even though I wasn't quite sure what we were talking about, I knew it was somehow suggestive.

So I deliberately changed the tone. "Seriously, though, let me see what the insurance situation is before you do anything, okay?"

"Okay," he said and headed back toward the house. "But I'll get started on the doorway and all today. I need to get a chip from the wall to match the paint. I think the door trim was just a gloss white. Is that okay?"

"Sure." I shrugged.

I fell in beside him as we aimed for the back door. I wasn't a short person, but I had to look up to catch his eye.

"You know who else was called a jack-of-all-trades, don't you," I said. "And when it was said about him, it was meant as a criticism."

"Who's that?"

"Shakespeare," I said. "It's the only remaining printed notice of his work. Some guy named Greene gave him a bad review, called him a Johannes Factotum and accused him of plagiarism. Johannes Factotum is basically a jack-of-all-trades."

We stepped inside the house.

"Wow," he said. "I guess that Greene guy is sorry now."

"Oh, yeah," I said. "Very embarrassed. Look. I figure you've probably heard about everything that happened here. I love Philomena, but she's not exactly the—what should I say?—soul of discretion."

"She's a gossip," he said, striding though the kitchen.

"Right."

"She told me." He didn't look at me. "I didn't really know Tandy Fletcher, but I liked her. I met her a couple of times. One of her brothers, Frank, helps me out; he's on the college grounds crew. Frank didn't much care for the fact that Tandy was going to college, or that she spent so much time with Rose here at the bookshop. But in general, they're a farm family, the Fletchers. And I mean that in the best sense. Good uncomplicated people. Who you think they are is who they really are."

"That seemed to apply to Tandy," I said.

He heard the sadness in my voice.

"I'm sorry you're in the middle of something," he said.

It was an odd phrase, but it seemed to be a lot more accurate to me than the more typical "I'm sorry for your loss" or "I'm sorry for your trouble." I *was* in the middle of something.

So I was prompted to ask, "Any idea just what I'm in the middle of?"

He stopped walking. We were almost to the front door.

"As long as I've been in this little town," he began, "I've tried to steer clear of politics, religion, and a certain brand of local sociology. The problem is, those things haven't bothered to steer clear of me, so I've been forced to become aware of certain phenomena which I'd rather not know anything about."

"For example," I prompted.

"For example," he obliged, "a woman who was a New

York actor and then came back home to turn a big old house into a bookstore, she's not quite right. And a woman who's an Episcopal priest? Forget it. And a woman from the big city of Atlanta who comes wading into all that mess, who does she think she is? And she's a threat. I don't know why. I don't know what she threatens. And it isn't just a question of conservative values versus liberal theatre types. There's something more to it than that."

"Like what?" I stared at the side of his face.

"I don't really know," he said, "but I wonder if the psychology of it might go something like this. Rose grew up here, you grew up here, and you both got out. Why would you both come back? There's something suspicious about that. Especially since I've talked to so many people here whose only wish in life is to get out of this town and into a larger world. Larger than Enigma, Georgia, population one thousand seven hundred and twenty-three."

I nodded slowly. "That was Tandy."

"That's her brother Frank."

"That was me when I was Tandy's age," I said.

"So why did you come back?"

"Me?" I opened my arms. "Didn't feel like I had any other options. The bookstore felt like my salvation when I first heard about it, really."

"Yeah, how's that working out for you?"

I had to laugh. "Not very well at the moment."

Further conversation with David Madison—or was it some odd brand of flirting—was brought to a halt when two kids appeared in the doorway. One of them was Coulter Jennings, the kid who liked poetry but didn't want anyone to know.

"We heard you weren't open," he said.

"But," the other one began, and then she studied the burnt door fame. "We wanted to see."

David waved them off instantly.

"You can't come in here," he warned them, "until the place is back up to code. That's what the police said. I'm sorry. Won't be but a few days. But you have to leave now."

They backed away, staring.

"Okay, then," one said.

And they were gone.

"Umm," I said. "If you keep scaring my customers away, I'll never be able to pay you for the gazebo."

He shook his head. "Those weren't customers; those were gawkers. Don't you think?"

"One of them, maybe." I stared out the door at the sunshine. "But the thing is, I actually do want to open up as soon as possible. I don't want it to look like the fire or even the murder is going to keep this place closed. You've got to stand up to stuff like that, right?"

"You are definitely Rose's niece." He laughed. "She was just as feisty."

"My point is," I said, only a little irritated, "that I want to be open. Even to gawkers. So don't chase anybody else away again, okay?"

He took a second. "You're right. Sorry. I hadn't considered that. This place being open and busy, that's the best way to tell everybody that you can't be scared off. I get that."

I was a little taken aback by his agreement. And a little attracted by it.

"Okay," I mumbled. "Umm. Thanks."

And just like that, I didn't know what to say to him. I didn't know how to tell him I was glad that he was there, appreciative of his help, and maybe a little lonely for male conversation. Whatever *that* was. Jesus. A couple of fires and a murder only made me more aggressive, but a guy who's nice to me made me tongue-tied and confused. What the hell was going on in my head?

Luckily, Gloria Coleman appeared in the doorway at that exact moment, crisp new black suit, snow-white clerical collar, eyes bright.

"David!" she called out.

"Gloria," he answered.

"Glad you're here." She barreled into the room. "Come and talk with Madeline and me."

"I was just about to go get the stuff I need to fix this doorway," he protested.

"Won't take but a minute or two," Gloria said, already halfway to the kitchen.

I looked at David. "You don't drink coffee, so—do you drink tea?"

"Rose . . . always had that Earl Grey," he said hesitantly.

I nodded. "It's still here."

By the time we got into the kitchen Gloria had already poured a cup of coffee from the dregs of the French press and seated herself at the table.

"I've been thinking," she said without any preamble.

David joined her at the table. "Nothing good can come from that."

I went to the cabinet where the tea was, got out the good old Earl Grey, put water in the electric kettle, and waited for Gloria to continue.

"Last night there were some men at the church," she told David. "Their plan was to scare me by burning up the children's All Saints' Day display out front. That didn't quite come to fruition, but Philomena thinks that their ad hoc leader, Speck Dixon, is the same person who's been threatening Madeline and me. And that makes her think that he's the same person who killed Tandy Fletcher."

David's head jutted forward. "What?"

"I know," Gloria said.

"I don't think so." David shook his head. "Speck is more of a doofus than a threat. I don't think he's got it in him to kill anybody."

"He was pretty scary last night," I chimed in.

Gloria glanced my way. "You weren't scared." She turned to David. "You should have seen her."

"I'm sure," he said. "So what makes Philomena think that Speck is the one—"

"Fire starter," Gloria interrupted. "He was the one trying to start a fire out of the children's display."

"I drove right by the church," David said, thinking. "I didn't notice anything about it."

"One of the panels might be a little singed," Gloria said, grinning. "But we managed to save the rest—Philomena, Madeline, and me."

He sat back.

"That's a formidable trio. And I get the fire starter connection," David went on. "But it's not really much to go on, is it?"

"No," Gloria said.

The water in the electric kettle started to rumble. I got out two cups, dropped a tea bag in each one, and waited for the kettle.

"The thing is," I said, "I promised Phil this morning that

we'd try to find something that *would* be proof. In my mind it would be proof that Speck didn't do it, but what if Phil's intuition is right?"

David nodded. "Wouldn't be the first time. She's got a weird knack sometimes."

"She does," I said.

The water came to a boil, and the kettle turned itself off. I poured, then delivered the steeping tea to the table.

"I just realized I drank the last of the coffee," Gloria said, looking at our teacups. "Sorry. You want me to make some more?"

"I'm having tea with David," I told her, eyebrows up. "But if you want more coffee, I can make it."

She pushed her mug away from her. "I've probably had too much already."

"So just what are you going to do to get the kind of proof Philomena wants?" David asked, dunking his tea bag up and down.

"Good question," I said. "I mean, for me, I'd start by trying to figure out why anyone would want to burn down this bookshop, I guess. Any ideas about that?"

"Maybe there are people in town who might object to some of the books in this place, as I was kind of saying a minute ago," David ventured. "But also Rose seemed to have a lot of money for the owner of a bookshop, and some people were—"

"Curious about that?" Gloria said.

"Irritated about that," David went on.

"Could be something to that, I guess," Gloria nodded, "but I think it might be something more immediate, more contemporary, like the small-town objection to an outsider horning in on a business like this. I have a little personal experience in that particular department."

"Huh," I said. "Tandy said something like that."

"People had gotten used to Rose," David said, "but a new woman in town, an outsider, taking things over, that might rile somebody, I guess. Doesn't seem like quite enough for, you know, arson and murder, though, does it?"

"I'm not exactly an outsider," I objected. "I was born here."

"But you've been gone nearly twenty years," Gloria said.

"And once again," he said. "You got out of here. Why would you come back? What's your angle? You've got to be up to something."

David lifted his tea bag, squeezed it a little between finger and thumb, set the bag on the table, and tossed back half the cup at one gulp.

"Well, I'm with you and Philomena," Gloria said to me. "We've got to investigate. We've got to ask questions. We've got to find stuff out."

"Because who else is going to do it?" I sipped from my cup, bag and all.

"Well, there's the police," David ventured.

Gloria and I glared him down.

"Billy Sanders?" I asked.

David set his teacup down and blew out a breath. "Yeah, you're right. You guys have to investigate this yourselves."

"You don't want to help?" I asked, mostly just teasing.

"I think my talents are better employed here at this house," he said. "Fixing the door, starting on the gazebo, that sort of thing."

With that, he stood. "All right, then. I'm off to the Home Depot in Tifton."

I stood immediately. "I'll walk you out."

Gloria looked down and smiled. I followed David through the house and out into the front yard.

The day had suddenly become overcast. Heavy, fast-moving dark clouds were crowded together in the sky. When we arrived at his pickup, I had to ooh and aah just a little. It was a gray Jeep Gladiator.

"This is one of the coolest trucks of all time," I said in hushed tones.

He laughed. "How in the world would you know anything about that?"

"I had a small part, a very small part, on an episode of *NCIS*," I said, a little embarrassed for some reason. "There was a Jeep Gladiator in the segment I was in. I fell in love."

"Well," he said, hand on the door, "it is a great truck."

Way in the distance there was a deep rolling thunder. The sky grew darker.

"Is it going to rain?" I asked, looking up at the clouds. "Where did that come from?"

"That's October for you," David said. "Just when you think the sun is out and everything is bright and shiny, here comes a rainstorm dark as night."

"Yeah." The deeper implication of his pronouncement was not lost on me.

And that was that. He got in his Jeep Gladiator and drove away. I stood in the yard watching his truck until it was too far away to see, and it began to rain.

12

I SPENT THE REST of the rainy morning finishing my cleaning work at the front of the house. Gloria was camped out on one of the old sofas nearby, working on a sermon on her iPad mini, silent as the grave, so I assumed her work was going well. As for me, scraping the sooty layers off the door frame proved ridiculous. There was always another layer under the one I was scrubbing. The floor was a little less cussed, but it was a mess too. Still, it was good to be preoccupied by something besides death threats and murder. Focusing on something relatively small, focusing hard, kept me sane.

At around one o'clock I realized I was hungry. I also realized that Gloria had stayed in the house more to keep me company than to work on her sermon when I saw her slumped down in an overstuffed chair and asleep, dead to the world.

I tiptoed toward the kitchen, but my stealth was in vain. Philomena suddenly appeared in the front door with takeout bags from Mona and Memaw's BBQ.

"Yoo-hoo!" she sang as she barged in.

Gloria sat up so suddenly that her iPad clattered to the floor.

"I brought barbecue!" Phil continued, headed for the kitchen.

"I'm *starved*," Gloria declared, still not completely awake but rising from her chair.

I had to laugh. "Come on, then."

We followed Phil into the other room.

"Oh, I brought us each a Diet Coke too," Phil said, setting her bags on the kitchen table and beginning to unpack.

"How did you know there would be three of us?" I asked.

"I called Gloria when I left and told her to come over," Phil said with a sly look on her face.

"Yes, I just put that together," I said.

"And," she went on, "I thought that you and David might need a chaperone."

"Ha," I answered without a hint of mirth. "The only thing that David and I need is insurance money."

"Right," Phil agreed. "Have you checked on that?"

"I don't know who to call," I admitted.

"Rusty," Phil said, popping the top off a tub of coleslaw.

"Yeah, I thought of that." I fished in the silverware drawer for forks and spoons. "But the last time I called him he was swamped. And I was calling him about selling this place, re-member?"

"Oh that's right," she said.

"Selling?" Gloria snapped.

"Umm, I thought maybe I should just sell the place and get out of Dodge," I told her.

"But you found your courage and changed your mind," Gloria said.

"No," I told her. "I found out that I can't sell it because I won't legally own it until I've lived here for six months."

"Really?" Gloria sat down.

There was a very brief second of silence. Philomena stopped pacing.

"Nancy Drew?" Philomena said straight-faced. "Really. How old are you? Those books were written before your *parents* were born."

"It's a TV show," Gloria objected. "It's on right now. It's got ghosts and stuff."

"And *murder*," I confirmed before I turned to Gloria. "See. I can say it when I want to."

"All right!" Phil topped us. "If you think talking to people about Tandy is what you want to do, then I can't stop you. Do you know where to find Frank?"

I shook my head. "I think I want to talk to Tandy's roommate at the college first."

"Why?" Phil asked.

"Just do." I loaded some more coleslaw on my plate. "The reason Tandy was staying with me was because she had a fight with her roommate. I thought I'd go see what that was about, you know?"

I didn't want to tell her that I mostly just wanted to know more about Tandy. To feel like I was grieving for a full, real person, and not just my shallow understanding of her. It was the kind of thing I might have done as an actor trying to create a full character study.

Phil stared, then gave up. "Well, maybe I should have thought of this before, but Rose told me, when her health began to decline, that she owed a lot of money. Maybe there's something there."

"You mean medical bills? I asked.

"No," Phil said. "No."

But that was all.

So I nodded. "You'll look into that, then."

"Right," Gloria concluded. "We've all got our first assignments. I'll start on mine soon as I finish this very good barbecue."

"Yeah." I stood. "I'll go over to the college this afternoon and see if I can find Tandy's roommate. If I can remember her name."

"Rae Tucker," Phil supplied. "She's in the same Intro to Psych class that Billy is taking. The one that Tandy was in."

"Thanks," I said. "Is there more than one female dorm?"

"Just one," she said. "North Hall."

"Great." I held up my empty plate. "And this *is* very good barbecue."

Phil sighed and sat back. "I thought you'd both like it."

But her face had gone all sad. She folded her arms and stared down.

"What is it?" I asked her softly.

"Oh, I was only thinking about what you said," she told me. "That you had to live in a haunted house before you could inherit it."

"Right."

"Well, the thing is," she went on, barely audibly, "it is haunted. I see Rose here all the time. Still. Every time I come here, in fact."

I put my hand on hers. "Me too."

Philomena looked around the room, and then the whisper of a smile touched her lips.

"Maybe that's really why she didn't want you to sell it," Phil said. "Because she knew she'd still be here."

13

THE CAMPUS OF Barnsley College had always been a mystery to me. It was founded in 1906 by wandering Quakers and set in a landscape dedicated to no less than Frederick Law Olmsted, who had died only a few years before the college was built. Rose had always compared it to the town in *Brigadoon*. When I was much younger, she told me that it vanished every evening and came back just at sunrise. When I asked her where it went at night, she told me that it went to a land of eternal enlightenment. When I asked her where *that* was, she said she wasn't sure, but it was probably wasn't in Georgia.

There were tall magnolias and purple crape myrtle trees, double blooming azaleas under pink dogwoods, a border of muhly grass that looked like a mist all autumn. The rain had gone, the air was crisp. In my head I was singing, "On a Clear Day (You Can See Forever)." I continued with various other songs from musicals that applied to the scene, in addition to my *Brigadoon* recollections, until I deliberately put a stop to them. But that's what the campus had always engendered in me, a goofy kind of theatrical fantasy. In short, it didn't seem real.

And David's new work was everywhere. Or, anyway,

there were large areas that were completely new to me, so it pleased me to assume they were his. He'd created a two-acre meadow: tall grasses and wildflowers and short shrubs where thousands of late-season butterflies and migrating birds were dancing in the air. He'd also installed what appeared to be a kitchen garden close to the dining hall that was still producing the season's last greens and okra and squash. And he'd somehow made it look like another flower garden. That was probably the mums and the pansies. However he'd done it, it was beautiful.

There were students everywhere. Some were obviously on their way to classes, others were at benches and tables, talking, flirting, laughing. Again, it didn't seem real to me, the happy, cavorting students in my otherwise world of universal confusion.

I parked and got out of my car. I wandered onto the closest lawn, and for a second, just a second, I was afraid to touch anything or say anything because I thought it might all just disappear. But then somebody yelled at me, and I turned just in time to grab a red Frisbee that was about to hit me in the head. My catch earned me raucous applause. And when I flipped the Frisbee back whence it had come, the boys gave me another enthusiastic round.

The spell was broken, so I approached three girls around a table made from rough tree limbs and hand-hewn wooden planks.

"Hey," I said. "I'm looking for North Hall."

One of the girls, with long braids and owl glasses, pointed. "The big one right there. It's a dorm."

"Right," I said. "Actually looking for Rae Tucker, do you know her?"

The kid with the glasses laughed. The other two shook their heads.

"She's probably still asleep," the one in the turtleneck sweater said.

"Second floor," Owl Glasses told me. "Room ten."

"Are you Madeline Brimley?" the third girl asked me shyly. She was dressed in a sweatshirt that had the words "Spirit of Adventure in an Age of Indifference" written on it.

"Depends," I said. "Are you a process server?"

Turtleneck laughed, the other two were baffled.

"Sorry, yes," I said immediately. "I am Madeline Brimley."

"Oh, okay," Sweatshirt said. "I loved Rose. I'm glad you're keeping the store open. It's, like, the greatest place in the world."

Which shot me in the heart because it reminded me of Tandy's naïveté. I loved the shop, but it probably wasn't even the greatest place in the county, let alone the world.

But what I said was, "Thanks."

I took one more second to study their faces and I didn't see a trace of awareness that Tandy was dead. Maybe they didn't know her. Maybe they hadn't heard the news. Either way, I was glad. I didn't feel like sharing my grief with anyone. I wanted to keep it all to myself.

So I just waved and headed toward North Hall.

The entrance was gothic stone, with a crest over the door that involved an eagle and a sword, like something out of Arthurian mythology. The halls were all dark wood, and the staircase went up to a landing that sported a diamond-patterned stained-glass window that nearly filled the whole wall. Up from the landing to the second floor I noticed that the steps were worn, and I suddenly had an image of all the thousands of students who'd gone up and down them for over a hundred years.

Room ten was at the end of the hall on the right. All the doors were closed. When I was standing in front of number ten, I was suddenly hesitant to knock. I had no idea what I was going to ask Rae, or to say to her about Tandy, or what her reaction to Tandy's death might be, or how I would handle it if she fell apart.

But fools rush in, so I knocked.

There was no answer, so I knocked harder.

Still nothing, so I tried the handle. It turned and the door creaked open.

The room was dark, the blinds were closed, and I did my best not to take it in, not to think about the notion that it had been Tandy's room.

The person in the bed against the wall began to groan.

"What?" she snarled.

"Rae?"

"What?" she repeated.

I tried out an official-sounding voice.

"My name is Madeline Brimley and I need to ask you a few questions."

She said a few unintelligible words, and several more that wouldn't do in polite company, and then she sat up.

I could see in the half-light that she was fully dressed, wrinkled shirt, tangled ribbon in her hair, mascara slightly runny. She looked around the room, apparently trying to determine whose room it was. Satisfied that it was her own, she drew her legs out from under the sheets. Her denim miniskirt was hiked up to an embarrassing level and she was still wearing shoes, some kind of high-heeled ankle boots. Then she sneezed three times.

"Do you have coffee?" she mumbled.

"I don't," I said apologetically. "I'll buy you some, though."

"What time is it?" She tried and failed to stand.

"I guess it's about two thirty," I said.

"In the *morning*?"

"Afternoon," I assured her.

"Oh." She coughed. "I missed my psych class again."

"Come on," I said. "Let's get you some coffee."

She finally managed to stand, however unsteadily. "I got *so* drunk last night."

"I can tell," I said.

"My roommate got killed," she said unsteadily.

So the news was out.

"I know." I sighed.

"Are you a cop?" she asked, looking warily my way.

"No," I said. "I'm an actor."

That seemed to confuse her sufficiently so I turned around and walked out of the room.

"Wait a minute," she called out, following me. "Did you say you're an *actor*?"

I stopped at the top of the stairs.

"I was with Tandy when she died," I said, hoping to hit her with a little sobering reality.

She stumbled to my side. "You're that new one. The new person at that bookstore."

"Uh-huh." I gave her a cold stare, another tactic designed to snap her out of her hangover.

"That's where she got killed, that store," she said, her eyes clearing just a little.

"Right."

"And you were with her when it happened?"

"I was."

She took a very deep breath. Then: "Oh."

Five minutes later we were in the dining hall. It was less industrial than I'd imagined. There was a pizza station and a salad bar. There was also, of course, a Starbucks coffee station. It wasn't manned, but there was a choice of five coffees and some kind of automated espresso machine.

Rae filled up a mug with Ethiopian brew. I tried out the espresso. We found a table far away from the bright windows and not too close to any other people. I studied Rae's face as she downed her coffee. The runny mascara looked to be from crying, so maybe Tandy's death had hit that hard.

"I got *really* drunk last night," Rae whispered.

"So you said," I told her.

"I did?" She gulped more coffee.

"Tandy told me," I said, "that you two were roommates because you'd known each other all your lives, which she thought would make it easier for her to leave home. Something like that."

Rae nodded, staring off into space, clearly shaken.

"I can't believe Tandy's dead." She sounded like a zombie, and she closed her eyes. "We grew up together. Same age, same class in school. I'd spend the night with her on their farm out there. And then Tandy's come in town and stay with me and my grandma. It was . . . great."

"You lived with your grandmother?" I asked.

"Uh-huh." More coffee. "I don't know who my daddy was, and my mama died in childbirth, you know, with me, so."

"That sounds hard."

She looked up. "I guess. I didn't know anything else, so it didn't seem . . . it was just the way it was. Except that I always loved going to Tandy's farm and being there with that big old family and all. When I was out there with them, with the

Fletchers, I felt like I was in that family, like I was Tandy's sister, you know?"

"Which is why you guys decided to be college room-mates."

"Uh-huh." She smiled, but it was a sad expression. "We were an odd pair. She was a Goody Two-shoes and I'm just, you know, normal."

"How do you mean?"

"She would *never* stay out late, she'd never take a drink of hard liquor, she'd never go to frat parties." Rae shook her head. "I mean, it's like she wasn't even *in* college!"

"Maybe she just wanted to learn something," I said, but the second that it came out of my mouth I realized just how much I sounded like somebody's mother, and I regretted it.

"I guess." Rae rolled her eyes.

"She mentioned something about you two having a dis-agreement?" I asked quickly.

"It was nothing." Rae eyed me suspiciously. "We had a fight about a boy is all."

"Really?" I hadn't meant to sound as surprised as I did. "Tandy had a boyfriend?"

"Not exactly; Bo was my boyfriend," she said slowly. "He just flirted with her a little. I think it was mostly to make me jealous. She didn't quite understand that, I don't think."

I sighed. "Yeah, that sounds like something a college boy would do. What's Romeo's name?"

"Huh?" Rae blinked.

"What's the full name of the boyfriend?"

"Oh. Bo Whitaker." She slumped back in her chair.

"What's he like?" I asked. "Tell me about him."

"He's a junior, so he's two years older," she said. "Plus, he's a chemistry major."

"So he's smart," I interrupted.

"Cooks meth," she said right away. "He's majoring in chemistry to get better at cooking crystal meth. Grows a little weed. Sells a little oxy when he can get it. And he already knows a lot about chemistry."

"I see."

I wasn't naïve. I'd always figured there was plenty of weed around when I'd been growing up in Enigma, it's just that I never really thought about it much. Rose's liquor cabinet had such good scotch in it that I never considered anything else. And the Enigma in my memory was a kind of innocent Eden. I was actually shocked to hear about the serpent in the garden.

So I said another stupid *mother* thing. "You know that about him, and you still like him?"

She looked at me like I was a hundred years old. I pressed on.

"Did Tandy know what he does?" I asked.

"I don't know," Rae answered, irritated. "Probably not. But she was always talking about how he wasn't good for me. But, see, he's good-looking and he's got money."

She finished her coffee and stared down into the empty cup.

"I'm sorry about Tandy," I told her softly. "More than you know."

She leaned forward, but still no eye contact. "I went to see Bo at his house last night. He lives in a little place down US 82 with this other boy. I went to tell him about Tandy being dead and all. I was messed up drunk, thinking about Tandy, sad and mad and crazy. But when I got there, *he* was tore up too."

"Drunk? Drugs?"

"No, I mean he was crying like a baby about Tandy!"

"He'd heard about her?" I asked.

As far as I knew there hadn't been any official news about her death.

"Yeah, he heard."

I studied her downturned face. I thought about Bo. And I began to wonder why he was that upset about Tandy's death if he'd just been flirting with her to make Rae jealous.

"Bo was really that distressed about Tandy?" I asked. "You made him sound like a tough guy."

She finally looked up at me. "He's got his sensitive side."

"Apparently," I said. "Crying about some girl he was just using to mess with you."

"Everybody loved Tandy," Rae said. "Everybody that knows about her being dead is all upset about it. And it won't be but a day or two more before *everybody* knows. It's a small town. I heard you used to live here. You don't remember that everybody knows everybody, and when something happens, we all find out about it, and we all feel it?"

"No." I shook my head. "I don't remember that. I never felt that."

"Well." She looked back down. "Then you didn't ever really live here, did you?"

"Maybe not." I finished my espresso. "You want more coffee?"

"It's not helping my hangover," she said. "And now I feel bad again. I don't think I want to talk anymore."

"Oh." I exhaled. "Sorry."

She shrugged and started trying to stand up.

"Hang on," I pressed. "Can you tell me where Bo lives exactly?

Her eyes narrowed. "What for?"

"I'd like to go talk with him."

"Why?" She squeezed her eyes shut for a second, trying to concentrate.

I tried to sound casual about it. "Maybe he knows something that could help find out who killed Tandy. Maybe?"

"Sure," she said slowly. "I guess."

She told me his address then, and even described the surrounding area so I could find it easily. And then she got up from the table and walked a little unsteadily out of the dining hall without once looking back at me.

I sat there for a minute trying to absorb what she'd told me. Tandy's description of Rae had been fairly accurate, brief as it had been. And Rae's portrait of Tandy mostly matched my experience of Tandy. Bo was the surprise.

Tandy may have had a boyfriend. Or something like it. A small-town drug-addled two-timing boyfriend. And suddenly it seemed quite possible that this *Bo* character was somebody to look out for. Maybe he'd come at Tandy in some kind of drug stupor. Maybe he'd killed her. Maybe there wasn't anybody out to kill me after all. It didn't explain the fires, but I suddenly felt a little liberated. Maybe I wasn't a victim after all.

Maybe I was Tandy's avenging angel.

14

WHEN IGOR AND I pulled up in front of the bookshop, Gloria was there. She'd been sitting in one of the rockers, but when I came into view, she bounced up and was anxiously waiting for me on the front steps.

I hadn't even closed my car door when she started talking.

"You'll never believe what I found out!" she shouted. "I think I've solved it!"

I locked the car and hurried her way. "You know who killed Tandy?"

"Oh." She took a second. "I shouldn't have said 'solved it.' I see that now. Because you thought—"

"What have you solved?" I asked, up the stairs and un-locking the shop.

She followed me in.

"I've just found out some very interesting news that per-tains to what's happening in general," she said.

I turned. "What are you talking about?"

"Speck Dixon is in real estate!" She held out her hands as if she'd just revealed the secret of the ages.

I thought my response was appropriate. "Umm . . ."

"Well, you know I was going to see if I could find out more about him, so I called him!"

"How did you get his number?" I asked.

"Facebook!" she told me, all smiles. "He's in real estate, like I said, and his company name and phone number are listed on his Facebook page!"

"Okay," I said, ambling into the house. "So you talked to him."

"He was actually glad I'd called." She could hardly contain herself. "He told me he'd come right over!"

"To the church?"

"Yes! He came to the church!" She lowered her voice. "And when he did, he came with a very strange offer."

I was losing patience with her story and her whole demeanor in general, and I was frankly more interested in telling her my news. So.

"Okay, I want to hear what that was," I told her, "but you'll never guess what I found out about Tandy."

"You found out something too," she surmised. "You met her roommate."

"I did, and it was revealing."

I sat down on the arm of one of the big chairs close to the desk in the den. Gloria collapsed on the green sofa and let out an enthusiastic groan.

"Okay, so what did she tell you, the roommate?" she asked.

"Tandy may have had a boyfriend!" I announced, very proud of my news. "A *druggie*. And he was also the roommate's boyfriend. Rae's boyfriend. At the same time!"

She sat forward, suddenly a lot more interested. "Well. That *is* something."

"It is indeed. Because I now believe that I was not the intended victim of the . . . the . . ."

"Murderer," she filled in.

"Right. I think the boyfriend showed up conked out on meth and got mad enough at Tandy to stab her."

"Okay." She sat back. "Okay. Doesn't explain the fire at the front door, though. Or the gazebo fire."

"Yeah, all right," I said impatiently. "I haven't figured that part out yet, but you see why it's a big deal, right? The *boyfriend* did it. The reverse version of cherchez la femme."

"That most sexist of all detective fiction clichés." She rolled her eyes.

"Yeah," I had to admit. "But still. You know."

"I think we can do better than that."

Her response knocked most of the wind out of my sails. I took a deep breath.

"So, all right, then." I sighed. "What's your news about this Speck Dixon? Which, by the way, makes me ask: who names their child *Speck*?"

"Funny you should ask," she said. "I found that out thanks to my good old-fashioned research about the guy."

"You said you looked him up on Facebook."

"Right," she said, not missing a beat. "His actual given name is Honor Respect Dixon."

I shook my head. "That poor guy. He didn't stand a chance, did he?"

She smiled. "Obviously, *Speck* is the South Georgia diminutive of *Respect*, and there we have it."

"So what's this about his coming to the church with a strange offer?" I asked.

"Right." Her energy bumped up about two levels. "So, he told me, still in the same growling, outraged manner as last night, that if I didn't sell him the land that the church is on, then what happened last night was just a beginning."

"Sell you the land?" I shook my head. "What for?"

"He wouldn't say," she answered. "But he was very clear about how he wouldn't be surprised if things didn't get out of hand; go too far. That's what he said: '*too far*.'"

"So what did you tell him about the land?" I asked.

"The truth," she said, arms out again. "I don't own the land. Not even remotely. The national Episcopal Church owns the land. And that's based on the so-called Dennis Canon."

"What's that?" I asked.

"Doesn't matter," she said, "it just means that the church as an entity owns the land, I have no say-so in the matter."

"And when you told him that . . ." I began.

"Just made him madder. He left snarling like a cartoon character."

"That seems about right."

I let his behavior sink in for a minute before I realized what she was saying, and what it might mean to me.

"Wait a second." I stood up. "I think I just got why you were saying you had something solved. You think that Speck wants to buy my land too. And *he* started these fires here at the shop. He's the one who threatened me on the phone. He wanted to scare me into leaving."

She nodded her head with a frightening amount of energy. "Because he wants *your* land too."

"That's quite a theory." I tried to piece it together.

Gloria stood up too. "The buildings next to you, the ones across from the church, are all empty."

"Yeah," I told her, "I noticed that on my first day in town, driving down Main Street."

"All the businesses at this end of the street are gone. And past your place it's all open fields. I think he's trying to acquire a big chunk of land for something."

"And he thinks that you and I are standing in his way."

"Burn down a rickety old gazebo in your backyard," Gloria said quietly, "torch a couple of kids' plywood saints in the churchyard, scare you and me away. Acquire the land, maybe even on the cheap."

"So that would mean that Philomena was right," I said. My voice was a little weak. "He's the guy. And Billy was right. I *was* the intended victim. Tandy was just the unluckiest houseguest in the world."

"I'm not sure about all *that*," Gloria hedged. "It's kind of a big leap to go from real estate intimidation to actually killing someone."

"It is," I concurred. "But he did seem amped up enough last night. I mean, he seemed like he was the sort of guy to let his anger get the better of him."

"I don't know," she confessed. "But, look, I don't really know what could provoke any person to kill another person. I just don't understand it at all. And to *stab* someone. I mean, that takes a real kind of visceral rage, don't you think?"

"And why would he feel that kind of rage for Tandy?" I stared at the place by the front door where her body had been. "Why would anybody feel that way about Tandy, according to what I know about her at this point?"

"You know who does provoke that kind of ire," she said, still very quietly.

"Around here?" I answered. "Maybe an outsider."

"Especially one who stands in the way of some big money-making real estate scheme."

"*Especially* if liquor was also involved in the decision-making process," I said. "Like it was last night."

"Those guys *were* pretty drunk," she agreed.

"Damn it," I whispered.

"What?" Gloria asked.

I sat back down. "I was just getting settled into the idea that I *wasn't* the one the killer was after. I was kind of convinced that Tandy's boyfriend came here on drugs and killed her."

"Because that's the way it would happen on television," Gloria sniffed. "Your feeble cherchez l'homme theory."

"Yeah." I sighed. "Sorry."

"But now?" Gloria pressed.

"But now," I answered uneasily, "Speck Dixon wants to kill me and burn down my house."

She sat back down too. "At least we're in this together."

"Terror loves company."

"Exactly." She folded her arms, staring into space with a determined look on her face. "Except that we're still just guessing. You don't really know much about Tandy, and I don't really know that much about Speck. And anyway we're not really equipped to form a solid theory about any of this. We're both new in town. We should talk with Philomena a little more. And I hate to say it, but we should probably talk with Billy Sanders a bit too. He's the official investigator here, right?"

I closed my eyes. "I guess you're right. I just have to quit thinking of him as 'Little Billy' and start thinking of him as Officer Sanders."

"So." She sighed. "What's our next move?"

"Talk with Phil? Go to Billy?"

"Take a nap?" she suggested, obviously to break the mood.

"*That's* the best idea." I laughed. "Sleep your troubles away."

"If Speck is the guy," she said, back to business, "and he's stepped up his game from intimidation to murder, we should talk with Billy about some kind of protection."

My brow furrowed. "Is Enigma the kind of place that offers police protection?"

"You're right." She shook her head. "Doesn't seem like it."

But I decided. "We have to at least tell Billy what we've been thinking."

"And what we've found out," she agreed.

"But should I say anything about Rae and Bo at this point?" I hesitated. "Because you're right, I really don't know much about this town anymore."

"What did Rae say to you exactly?" Gloria wanted to know.

"Not a lot, actually." I concentrated. "The thing she was most upset about was the fact that Bo was crying over Tandy's death."

"That seems . . . at least a little callous on her part."

"She'd gone to his house," I said, "to tell him about Tandy."

"But all he could do was cry?" Gloria nodded. "I guess that would be upsetting. But I think it tells us more about this Bo character than it does about Rae."

"Yeah," I agreed. "She mentioned his involvement in drugs. So my first impression of him did not include that level of sensitivity. Maybe he really did like Tandy. Rae said he was only flirting with Tandy to make Rae jealous."

"But what if that's what Rae *wants* to think," Gloria concluded. "You only heard about Bo and his relationship to Tandy from her obviously individuated perspective."

"'Individuated perspective'?" I taunted. "Nice turn of phrase."

"Sorry." She actually blushed. "Every once in a while, my higher education pops out. I try not to let it happen around here. You obviously bring out the worst in me."

"Obviously." I laughed. "You're going to have to tell me about your higher education at some point."

"But you see what I mean, don't you?" she forged ahead. "Rae may have been telling you the truth, but it was only the truth from her point of view. Which isn't the whole story."

"You're absolutely right." I looked out the window. "So how about this. I got Bo's address from Rae. He's got a place out on Highway 82 with some other boy, Rae said. How about if I go talk with him? See if I can find out a little bit more about his situation with Rae and Tandy. You know, from *his* point of view."

"By yourself? I don't think so. He's a drug dealer with a gang."

I smiled. "It's not a gang. They're farm boys, and they're a lot more bored than they are dangerous. They're small-town farm boys with nothing to do and no way to make any pocket money other than a little good old-fashioned local enterprise."

"Yeah, but one of them might have *killed* a very nice young girl," Gloria insisted.

Okay, she had a point. I knew I should probably have talked to Billy about my suspicions. But I knew I didn't want to say anything to Billy about Bo until I knew a little bit more about him, about his story.

So I said to Gloria, a little foolishly in retrospect, "You want to come with me, then?"

She was headed for the door before I'd even finished my sentence.

15

AS IT TURNED out, I was glad that Rae had given me more information than just the address for Bo's house. Even in the bright late-afternoon light there were daunting shadows. She'd said that there wasn't a mailbox or an address marker at the highway. And since the house was back off the road at the end of a dirt and gravel driveway, there would have been no chance of finding the place without knowing, for instance, about the stone bear.

Rae had described it accurately. About seven miles south out of town there was a fairly large granite rock by the right side of the road that looked a little like a sleeping bear. That was the first of several markers that she'd told me about. Once you saw the stone bear, you had to be on the lookout for a large field of cereal rye on the left, a cover crop for the Dillard family's organic acreage. Most of the rest of the farm fields would be bare. Then you had to look for an unmarked county road and the wooded acreage just past it. You had to slow down and look for a nearly hidden dirt path on the right, and that would take you to Bo's house.

We would never have found it without the instructions.

As I turned off 82 and slowly went down the dirt path toward what I really hoped would be Bo's house, I had a strange sense of déjà vu. I knew I'd never been down that particular path before, but it was oddly familiar just the same. I didn't say anything about it to Gloria, not at that moment anyway.

There was a slight bend in the path, and the house came into view. It was a small square place clad in gray old-style as-bestos tiles, had a tin roof with a rusty metal chimney. Pines and scrubby little shrubs surrounded it, wild boxwoods and the like, with a few native bare rose of Sharon limbs here and there.

On the ruined gravel paddock there was a souped-up VW Bug, cut off in front and in back, with a large, chrome dual exhaust sticking straight up out of the engine in back. Next to it was a fairly new Dodge Ram pickup, jacked up, splattered with mud.

As we pulled in closer, we could hear music coming from inside the house. It just wasn't what I was expecting. It sounded like Miles Davis. Was that possible?

Gloria started to get out of the car.

"Don't do that," I told her emphatically. "Just sit here for a minute."

She stared at me, then closed the car door.

"This isn't the kind of house that you just go up to and knock on the front door," I said. "This is the kind of house where you wait to see if someone comes out the door with a shotgun."

A split second later someone appeared in the doorway with a hunting rifle.

I shrugged. "Close enough."

I rolled down my window and stuck my head out.

"I'm a friend of Tandy Fletcher's," I called out. "I came to talk to Bo."

Might as well get right to the point, I thought.

The boy lowered his rifle. A little. He was in his bare feet, wearing messy jeans and a sweatshirt with the arms cut off. His head was shaved but his beard was full.

"I seen that car over at the bookshop," he said to me. Then he scratched his chest, still holding firm to his gun. "It's a Fiat?"

"It's a 500 R," I said.

"1975?"

"'74, but with some '75 parts," I told him. "You've got a good eye."

"Can I come look at it?" he asked a little hesitantly.

"Sure." And that's when I shut the engine off and turned to Gloria. "We can get out now."

She stayed where she was. "He's still holding his gun."

But as she was saying that, he leaned the rifle against the door frame of the house and padded his way toward us.

I got out. "If I didn't have a friend who's into cars, this thing would have been in the junkyard a *long* time ago."

He grinned. "You need you some bodywork."

"Yeah, Igor's been in a few arguments."

"You call your car Igor?" He laughed. "Like in the Frankenstein movies?"

"Uh-huh."

He shook his head. "Girls. What you want to give a car a name for?"

I smiled back. "I don't have a dog."

"Oh." He seemed to accept that as a good enough explanation.

"I'm Madeline," I began, "and this is Gloria."

Gloria climbed out of the car and waved.

Our new friend stared at her clerical collar. "You that new lady preacher."

"I am." She flashed one of the most winning smiles I'd ever seen.

"Is that your VW?" I asked him. "Chopped and channeled like that, some people call that a Baja."

"Some people do," he said absently, examining Igor. "I done the work myself. Could I look at your engine?"

"Of course you can, but be careful of the latch."

He went around to the back of the car and had the hood up before I'd even finished my answer.

"Look at that," he said softly. "You practically rebuilt the whole thing."

"My friend did."

He raised his head up. "Bo! Come out here and look at this old Fiat!"

Bo materialized a little like a dream, taller than expected, black hair, intense eyes, T-shirt, jeans, and also barefoot, despite the chill in the air. He looked a little familiar. My first thought was to tell him that he looked like a young Sam Shepard; my second thought was to realize he probably wouldn't know who that was.

He nodded in my direction. "You're Madeline Brimley, I guess."

"You guess right," I said. "And this is Gloria Coleman."

"Father Coleman," he said, smiling at her. "Do people call you that?"

Gloria smiled back without a hint of guile. "Some do."

"Where on earth did you get parts for this?" the other guy asked, nose down into my car.

"Some came from junkyards," I said. "But my friend is

kind of a genius and he just tooled most of those parts him-self. Isn't he great?"

"He surely is," he whispered respectfully. "He ain't from around here, I know that."

"Actually lives in Canada now," I said. "But he comes to Atlanta every once in a while to visit."

The guy stood up. "Reckon you might give me his con-tact information? This is—I mean! This is amazing work."

"Sure." I turned to Bo. "Invite me in."

The two boys looked at each other for a second.

"The place is kind of a mess," Bo said slowly.

"I don't care about the mess," I told him, and then I low-ered my voice. "And I don't care about anything else you might have in there. In the way of . . . chemical experiments. I came to talk with you about Tandy. We can do it out here in the driveway if you want to."

The other guy sighed very heavily and closed the hood of my car.

"Come on in, then," he said softly.

And he headed for his house, putting his hand on Bo's shoulder for a second as he passed him. Because that guy cared about the way Bo was feeling.

That's why I hadn't been afraid to come out on Highway 82 to a house where wild boys cooked crystal meth, even as sundown was approaching. The wild boys I'd known when I lived in Enigma all had good hearts, every single one of them. Maybe times had changed, but I was banking on some-thing fundamental about these guys, something that was as much in the soil and the air as it was in their upbringing or their schooling or even their current circumstances. I'd al-ways heard Rose talk about the bones of a garden. Even if the weeds seemed to have taken over and the flowers had all gone, you could still tell it was going to be a good garden by the bones of it. You just had to look carefully enough.

I could tell that Bo was trying to say something. He started three or four times to form a sentence. But after a minute he just turned and followed his friend inside.

I glanced over at Gloria. Her eyebrows were raised, and her face was paler than usual, but she sucked in a breath and headed for the house.

The place was a little dark on the inside. Bo's roommate was clearing some stuff off the sturdy coffee table in front of a well-worn red sofa, a square fifties thing that had probably come with the house. Bo clicked on the standing lamp next to it, but the light only made the place gloomier. There was a handmade braided oval rug on the floor, maybe from somebody's great-grandma, and the floor around it hadn't been vacuumed since 1978. No pictures on the walls. No other furniture. No other lighting fixtures.

But there was a great old stereo and Miles Davis was, indeed, playing. It was a record I knew called *Relaxin'* that was recorded a couple years before the famous *Kind of Blue* album. The music was so surreally out of place in that room that I was momentarily speechless.

Gloria was staring at the sofa. Bo went into the next room; it looked like a dining room.

"I guess it'll be okay to sit on that thing," Gloria said. "You've had your tetanus shots, right?"

After I laughed but before I could answer, Bo came back into the room dragging a dinner table chair. He sat in it. So we sat too. Gloria took the uncertain sofa. I sat on the substantial coffee table to be closer to Bo.

"Before I ask you about Tandy," I began, "I have to know about the record you're playing."

He turned toward the stereo. "Miles Davis."

"Yeah, I know," I said.

I started to ask him how in the world he'd know anything about Miles Davis, but then I realized that was exactly the same kind of quasi-offensive question people used to ask me when they found out I was from South Georgia.

So I said, "My aunt Rose used to try to teach me about 'cool school' jazz."

He nodded. "That's Rose's record. I just borrowed it. Tandy likes it because Rose told her to." He took a second to adjust himself to the proper tense. "*Liked* it. I prefer Dizzy Gillespie, but I like Coltrane's work on this one. See? Rose taught Tandy. Tandy taught me."

At that everyone was quiet for a moment, feeling the sense of loss and longing settle over us, palpable as the dust in the room and tender as Miles on the stereo, playing "You're My Everything."

Then, after a deep breath, I began.

"Rae Tucker told me that you were flirting with Tandy to make her, Rae, jealous," I said.

Bo shook his head. "Rae."

"That's not true?" I pressed.

"I was in love with Tandy," he said hopelessly. "Still am. Rae, I don't know what gave her the idea that I liked her, but she . . . I don't know how she got that idea. I love Tandy. I was . . . we were talking about getting married, me and Tandy. Leaving town. Tandy had it in mind to study psychology. Did you know she was on a scholarship there at Barnsley? She was so smart."

Stop the presses. "You were going to get married?" I repeated, sounding almost as stunned as I felt.

"Uh-huh," he continued. "In a year I'll have my chemistry degree and I might have a job as a pharmacologist lined up."

"Rae said you were getting that degree so that you'd be better at cooking crystal meth," I said, still testing Bo's veracity.

"Elbert!" He bellowed the name so suddenly, and at such a volume, that Gloria and I both jumped.

The roommate reappeared with a beer in his hand. "What?"

"Elbert's the guy," Bo said.

I looked over at Elbert.

"What guy?" he said.

"They know about your drug business." Bo stared at me.

He sipped his beer. "I got no idea what you're talking about."

"Elbert is trying to get up enough money to open a garage in Tifton," Bo said, ice cold. "He's good with cars."

"I'm *great* with cars," he corrected.

"He needed my help to create a safer and more useful product," Bo went on, "and I was happy to help because he's my cousin, and I needed the money for me and Tandy."

"Well," Elbert allowed, "he is good at chemistry, and I am his cousin. And plus which, I believe I'm giving him a chance to explore pharmacology on a real-life basis."

And he rewarded himself for such a selfless support of his cousin with another sip of beer.

"But," he continued, "he was, sure enough, saving up the money to run off with Tandy. That's what he told me. Repeatedly."

"You didn't ever hear the phrase 'speed kills'?" I asked Elbert.

He shifted his weight onto one leg. "Methamphetamine is been around for a *long* time, ma'am. They used to give it to soldiers in World War II; keep 'em awake. People take it now to lose weight and get over depression. And people take it for that ADHD."

"It's a party drug that gives you a great rush for a little while," I snapped, "and jangled nerves for the rest of the night."

"So you're familiar with it." He smiled.

And I don't know why, but I smiled back. "Maybe once or twice. Parties in New York. You know, in a previous life."

He hoisted his beer. "Okay, then, here's to that. And also? Rae Tucker don't know which end is up."

With that he hiked up his jeans and launched himself off into some other room again.

"I don't know what all Rae told you," Bo began as Elbert was leaving, "but there is nothing between me and her, and there won't ever be. It was Tandy."

The entire house was filled with the sound of his heartbreak. The slant of setting sun through the front windows made the room golden while I tried to gather my thoughts. But before I had a chance to put them into words, the gold was gone, and the shadows set in.

"I guess Tandy told you," Bo said softly, "about me and her staying at your bookshop after Rose died."

Gloria leaned forward. I swallowed hard.

"What?" I managed to say.

Bo looked down. "Yeah. After Rose died, Tandy just stayed there, kind of taking care of the place. You know, keeping it tidy, feeding the cat. We'd open up the windows to air out the place once a week. Tandy would cook. She's a really good cook. And, I mean, we stayed there together, like, living together, for I don't know how long until we heard about you coming back to Enigma to take over the place."

"You heard about that?" I asked because I was too surprised at that moment by his other news to comment on it.

"Small-town gossip, Miss Brimley."

Gloria cleared her throat. "Did other people know that you and Tandy were living there? Because you were there for over a month, right?"

"Right." He nodded. "But I don't think anybody knew. We were real careful. I never parked my truck there. I only went there after dark. And, seriously, if it had got around that I was spending the night with Tandy, her brother Frank would have killed me by now. I mean, he'd kill me, then he'd take me to the hospital and get me revived *just* so he could kill me again. If there had been *any* gossip about our situation, we wouldn't be having this conversation. Because I'd be very, very dead."

"*That's* the truth," Elbert called out from the other room.

"Frank is a good person," Bo went on, "but he's very protective of his little sister. And he can have a temper on him."

"And he's big," Elbert added from offstage.

Bo nodded. "I wouldn't stand a chance."

It sank in. "You and Tandy were living together at the bookshop."

"Yes," he said, and it was a sad and longing syllable.

"That's why the windows were open when I got there," I went on.

"Probably."

"And that's why Tandy was so comfortable in the house," I continued, more to myself than to anybody in the room. "Why she wanted to stay there with me."

"It was like a second home to her," Bo said.

"Like it was to me when I was her age," I admitted to him.

"Oh. Okay." He closed his eyes. "Can we stop talking about Tandy for a minute?"

The stereo chose that moment to shut off, and the room was eerily silent.

The sun was almost gone. After a minute or so, I had no idea how long it actually was, night birds began to call out, crickets and tree frogs joined in, and night settled over our little world the way a beak closes over a seed.

Thank God Elbert broke the silence. He lumbered back into the room.

"Man. It got *quiet.*"

He went to the stereo, removed the record, put it back in its green cardboard jacket, and snapped on the radio. Gospel music instantly filled the room. Elbert turned it down a little.

"That's more like it," he said. "Anybody else want a beer?"

Gloria's hand shot up. "I wouldn't say no."

Elbert looked around the room for a second before he said, "Well, come on in the kitchen, preacher, and let me see can I get you one."

Gloria hesitated for only a split second before she bobbed up and followed Elbert out of the room.

"I guess I realize now," I told Bo, "that the first thing I should have said to you was, 'I'm sorry for your loss.'"

He didn't look up. "That tired old sentence. What good are words?"

"What good indeed," I concurred. "How about this: I think I loved Tandy too. I think it would be hard not to love her."

"She had a soul like a burning sun," he said.

I didn't know what to say to that bit of perfect poetry.

So I chose to be diminutive. "I mean, her biscuits alone . . ."

And I was quite pleased to see him smile at that.

"Banana pudding," he added.

"What made *that* taste so good?" I agreed.

"Nutmeg," he said instantly. "She told me it was her secret ingredient."

I didn't know about the rest of the world, but I knew that in my little branch of the south, food spoke out when words failed. And if there wasn't any actual food available, *talking* about food would often suffice.

From the other room, Gloria laughed suddenly, and enthusiastically, and Elbert joined in. I was glad to hear them; it broke the mood in the living room.

I stood up from the very uncomfortable coffee table then.

"Thank you, Bo," I said, offering my hand. "This has been quite a melancholy enterprise. But it also filled in a lot of blanks."

"About Tandy," he assumed.

"The police think that I was the intended victim," I said, only a little awkwardly. "Tandy was just . . . in the wrong place at the wrong time. As they say."

"And by *police*," he said, also standing up, "you mean Billy Sanders."

"Right."

He nodded. "Okay. I like Billy and all, but he's not exactly the sharpest nail in the bin, is he?"

"He means well."

"And he was always very sweet to Tandy," Bo agreed. "But as far as solving a situation like this . . ."

He let me fill in the rest of his thought.

"You don't think his theory is right?" I asked.

Bo's lips thinned. His breathing stopped for a second. "Frank Fletcher has got a temper on him. Ask anybody."

"He wouldn't kill his little sister," I said, "no matter what she'd done."

"He wouldn't *mean* to," Bo said slowly. "But I've seen him

when he was blind drunk and crazy mad and just about ready to do anything you can imagine."

I didn't buy it—Bo was just seeing Frank from the "threatened boyfriend" perspective—but I didn't want to argue with him.

"Gloria and I have been having trouble with Speck Dixon," I told him, mostly to see what his reaction would be.

His reaction was to laugh. "Speck Dixon is a punch line. He's always got some big backroom money-making plan that'll all fall apart in a week or two. Nobody takes him seriously. He didn't kill Tandy. He don't even hunt. The only thing I ever saw him kill was a pint of whiskey."

"Huh."

At that, Gloria came rolling into the room, closely followed by Elbert.

"You have got to hear this joke," she said. "Jesus and Moses are playing golf."

"Time for us to go," I said quickly.

Gloria looked around like she was missing something, and then she shrugged.

"Okay."

I headed for the door.

"By the way, Bo," I said. "I'm really happy that you're listening to Miles Davis, but I'm going to want Rose's record back eventually."

"Okay." He smiled. "Can I keep it just a few more days? It makes me think about Tandy, so, you know."

"Of course," I said.

"But like I said," he went on, "I prefer Dizzy Gillespie."

"Anything in particular?" I asked, only testing him a little, the way Rose used to do to me

"'A Night in Tunisia,'" he said instantly.

I waved that away. "You just like Charlie Parker's famous alto break."

"It's not even human," he said.

Elbert looked at Gloria.

"You got any idea what them two are talking about?" he asked her.

"None whatsoever," she answered. "I'm a more Lynyrd Skynyrd, Blackberry Smoke kind of a gal."

"I *love* Blackberry Smoke," Elbert said.

Bo shook his head and said to me, "You see what I have to live with?"

"We'd better get going," I said to Gloria, laughing, "before this gets ugly."

"Wait," Elbert said. "Can you give me the name of your car guy, and some kind of way to get in touch with him? His work is—I ain't never seen work like that."

"His name is George Dockray, and he lives in Canada," I said. "Got a piece of paper? I'll give you his phone number. And tell him Madeline says hey."

Elbert fished in his pocket and produced his cell phone.

"Just put it in here," he told me.

I stared at it. "I don't know how to do that."

He seemed not to understand me. "Don't know how to do what?"

"Look," I said apologetically, "I know it's ridiculous, but I don't have a cell phone and I don't know how to use one."

Gloria blinked. "How does an actor in the twenty-first century *not* have a cell phone?"

"Landline and answering machine," I said quickly. "Let me just tell you the phone number and you put it in your phone, okay?"

It was a much sloppier leave-taking than I was hoping for.

I would have preferred a clean, "Well then, you just bring Rose's record by the shop whenever you want to. Bye."

But it was not to be. Because after the modestly embarrassing cell phone moment, Elbert and Bo accompanied us outside and kept talking. Small talk—microscopically small. When I was younger, I used to call it "leaving like adults." Kids say goodbye and go. Adults say goodbye, talk another ten minutes, say goodbye again, walk to the car, remember something else important, say goodbye a third time, and keep talking through the window as they're pulling out of the driveway.

Which is what happened to Gloria and me. We were out on the highway before Elbert stopped talking.

"So that was educational," I mumbled, picking up speed heading home.

"You want to hear the joke about Moses and Jesus playing golf?" Gloria began.

"No. I want to talk about Bo and Tandy living in the abandoned bookshop together!"

"Yeah," she agreed. "That's a thing."

"I mean, it kind of alters my understanding of Tandy."

"You mean that you thought she was this innocent waif," Gloria said, "when she was actually having sex with her boyfriend in your house."

"Not that so much," I answered, "as the fact that she didn't tell me about it."

"You thought you two were closer than that," Gloria said.

"I thought we were . . ." I gathered myself. "There were ways in which we were the same person. When I was talking to her in the kitchen, I was Rose, and she was me. You know what I mean?"

"Not exactly," she said. "But I get how that could make you feel a certain kind of affinity for the kid."

"Yeah."

The night had gotten as dark as it was going to get, and we drove a little way in silence. There wasn't a moon, or it was stuck behind clouds, and the stars were a poor substitute for it. The only real light anywhere came from Igor's headlights. It was like milk spilling itself onto the blacktop for fifty feet in front of us. The air had gotten chillier, and what we could see of the landscape around us was drenched in October: craggy bare trees, broken down barns, haunted misty fields, the occasional flight of crows. Once in a while we could see that orange kind of light in the windows of distant farmhouses. The color always reminded me of those candy jellied orange slices covered in sugar crystals that I'd gotten in my Halloween bag. The wind picked up and sent leaves flying in the air, just another flight of crows.

"It was a surprise to me," Gloria said at length, "that somebody like Bo would be into the kind of music that he was listening to, what you two were talking about."

"That wasn't Bo," I said softly. "That was Rose."

And with that, the October scene was complete: autumn leaves and bare fields and the ghost of Rose Brimley riding with us in the car on the way home.

16

I WAS SURPRISED TO see Philomena's car parked in front of the shop when we got there. It wasn't late by my standards, but I knew that most people in Enigma were getting ready for bed by the time we rolled up in front of the house.

Then, on the porch, one of the darker shadows moved, and Philomena stepped off the porch coming toward my car.

"Where have you been?" she chided. "I was worried sick!"

"We've been to see Tandy's boyfriend," I told her even before I'd gotten out of the car. "We went to his house and talked with him."

"Boyfriend?" Phil asked, stopping all forward motion.

Gloria appeared on the other side of my car and waved. "Hi. It was weird."

"Tandy had a boyfriend?" Phil asked, still frozen.

"Come on in and we'll tell you about our adventure," I said.

Phil nodded. "I have *got* to hear about this."

"And by the way," I went on, keys in hand headed for my front door, "what are you doing sitting on the porch in the dark at this time of night?"

"I have news too," she said. "It's not quite as interesting

as yours, but I didn't feel it could wait until morning, never-theless. So."

At that we all fell silent as we adjourned into the house.

"Kitchen?" Gloria proposed. "I could use another beer if you've got one."

"I wouldn't mind some herbal tea," Phil chimed in.

"I'm too keyed up to sit down," I told them. "I have at least three plays going on in my head, and none of them are making any sense."

So they followed me through the kitchen, Bud in the fridge for Gloria, electric kettle on for Philomena, and a sudden re-alization for me.

"I haven't opened Rose's liquor cabinet since I've been back in town," I said, mostly to myself.

Phil and Gloria stared without comment.

I went into the dining-room mystery section of the shop whence resided the record player and the object of my affec-tion: the aforementioned liquor cabinet.

I couldn't believe I hadn't explored it since I'd been back. It was such an icon for me when I was younger.

First, watching Rose make a martini or a gin and tonic had been like watching an alchemist turn simple ingredients into mystical elixir. Elixir that unlocked Rose's endless sto-ries. The time she was in the musical version of *Animal Farm* and one of the horse's eyeballs fell out, bounced across the stage and into the orchestra pit, landing *boom* on one of the tympani drums. The time she was in the musical *Strider*, for-got a lyric, and sang "There Is Nothin' Like a Dame" instead. The time she got in an elevator with Alec Guinness. She told him she loved his work in *A Walk in the Woods*; she'd seen it in London's West End. He was so happy that she didn't know him from *Star Wars* that he took her out to lunch.

Later, when I was in high school, I'd sneak into the forbidden cabinet and poach a little Glenfiddich, which Rose had always told me was the only good single malt scotch she could get in South Georgia, and she had to drive to Tifton to get it.

Going to the cabinet was like approaching the altar for communion. I opened the creaky doors, and there, along with the gin and the vermouth and the tequila and the cordials was a half-empty bottle of Glenfiddich. I sighed, grabbed it, and cradled it like a baby walking back to the kitchen.

"Ladies and gentlemen, we have achieved scotch," I announced solemnly, returning to the kitchen. "Rose's favorite. Seems appropriate for a night like this."

"That wasn't her favorite," Philomena said. "It's just what she could easily get."

I stopped. "Right. She used to tell me that. What was her favorite, then?"

"She liked Macallan," Phil told me, but for some reason it was hard for her to say. "It's expensive, though."

I didn't feel like pursuing that particular conversation. "Okay, but I've got this."

I held the bottle aloft for a second, then went to the cupboard and fetched a glass. No water, no ice, I wanted the first taste to be pure.

"Could we just get outside for a minute?" I went on, headed for the back door. "I think I have to wander aimlessly around in the backyard until a few things come together in my head."

I was out the door before they could answer. The night was a little chilly, the sky was a little dark, and I was a little distracted.

"So what's your news?" Gloria asked Philomena as they both came out the back door.

"Oh." Phil went toward the ruins of the gazebo. "Well. I found out something a little unsettling about Tandy's brother, Frank Fletcher. He was . . . apparently, he hated Rose."

"Wow," Gloria said.

"Why?" I asked.

"Well," Phil began, unsettled by her own information, "Frank did not care for Rose's influence on little Tandy. And I'm putting it mildly. He thought it was Rose's fault that Tandy wasn't living at home, wasn't interested in staying put in Enigma; wasn't looking to settle down with some local boy."

"Well, to be fair, he was probably right about that," I said. "At least a little."

Phil had arrived at the charred remains of the gazebo and stared down at the wreckage like she was looking into a pool of water.

"Frank came here to the shop on several occasions," Phil went on, "to give Rose a piece of his mind."

I sipped my scotch. "Well, *that* didn't go well for Frank is my guess."

"It did not." Phil stepped lightly around the ruins. "On the final such occasion Frank was drunk, and he grabbed Rose by the arm, so she broke his nose!"

"What?" Gloria shook her head.

She'd wandered a little away from us, drawn by the scent of the last of the lavender and the impossible display of asters still blooming.

"Broke his nose," Phil repeated, nodding once. "That's why it looks funny. He never went to the doctor about it."

"Who told you all this?" I asked, pouring.

Phil lowered her voice. "David Madison."

I looked up from my glass. "Really?"

"Frank works for David sometimes, as I think you know," Phil said. "When he came in with that funny nose one day, David asked him about it, and Frank said it was a farm accident."

We waited, and when Philomena didn't explain, I had to ask.

"So what made David think that Rose had done it?"

"Oh, Rose told him the next day when he was over here fixing some of the roof tiles," Phil answered, shaking her head. "Do you think he can really restore this gazebo?"

That was Philomena Waldrop, it all came back to me then. You could never get a straight story out of her. She was always a little disconnected, a little tangential. And God help her, she could *never* get a joke right.

"How funny is his nose?" Gloria asked, wandering back in our general direction.

"It's like a boxer's nose, I think," Phil answered vaguely. "It's not ugly, really. Just, you know, funny looking. In a general sort of way."

Gloria chose not to pursue that topic in favor of another glug of beer. I hoisted my glass and sipped. The first sip of scotch is always the best, but the rest are evocative. The fire and the smoke fill up your mouth and just for a second, you're on some moor in Scotland or in some tiny cottage next to a peat fire, content and complete.

"Okay," I said, impatient to get to my news, "but you're not going to believe what we found out."

"Tandy had a boyfriend," Phil whispered, like it was a secret.

"She did," I went on, "and that was a surprise, but the weird part is: he and Tandy lived here in this house after Rose died!"

Philomena's face went pale. "What?"

She turned and stared back at the house.

"How about *that!*" Gloria declared, finishing her beer.

"B-b-but," Phil began, stuttering, "I came over here a lot. I never saw them."

"Yeah," I allowed, "but you said you just drove by. You wouldn't have seen them. And they were here at night. You told me you drove by here on your way to the college in the morning."

Phil swallowed. "Yes. All right."

She took the news about Tandy's trysts oddly. She was unsettled in a way I couldn't quite interpret.

We could hear the electric kettle beeping in the kitchen then.

"Chamomile? I asked Phil, headed back inside.

"Did you get your mind settled yet?" Gloria asked me.

I stopped where I was, staring down at the grass.

"Bo said he was in love with Tandy," I said. "He told me that they were saving up money to leave Enigma. Tandy wanted to get a degree in psychology, to be a therapist. And Bo was going to be a pharmacologist."

"Bo's a drug dealer," Phil mumbled. "Everybody knows that."

"Yes, but that's how he was getting up enough money to leave town." I turned to look at them both. "Or at least that's his story."

Phil shook her head. "They stayed *here*? In this house?"

"I know," I said. "Weird, huh?"

"I'll tell you what I think," Phil said slowly. "Bo's a liar. He killed Tandy."

Her voice had changed. She was talking to herself, not to us. She began to rock back and forth just a little, it was barely perceptible. She was staring at empty space in front of her. Gloria came over and put her hand on Phil's arm.

"Philomena?" she said.

"Bo came here that night," Phil continued, ignoring Gloria. "Tandy ran to the door because she had a crush on a wild boy. But what if Bo was only here to say he was breaking up with her? Let's say they argued. Bo was jacked up on his drugs. The argument escalated. Bo pulled out his pocketknife. He stabbed Tandy. Then he set this house on fire and he got in his truck and drove away."

Then she fell silent.

"That's quite a story," Gloria said calmly. "But you didn't see Bo when he was talking about Tandy. You didn't see his face. That boy was in love with Tandy. He wouldn't do anything like what you just said."

Philomena's head turned slowly toward Gloria, and they locked eyes with each other.

"I told you," Philomena said firmly. "Bo Whitaker is a liar and a drug dealer."

"Maybe," I chimed in. "But he's not an actor, not good enough to fake his feelings like that. Gloria's right. He was in love with Tandy. You could sense it in the room with him."

Philomena turned her gaze my way.

"You don't know anything," she told me, and her words were made entirely out of ice. "Everybody is capable of telling a lie that anybody else will believe. And everybody is capable of hiding a truth that no one else will be able to see. This world is made mostly of illusion and deception, only occasionally interrupted by a good meal."

Again there was a long moment of silence.

But Gloria came to the rescue. "As an official minister in the church—and I've got a degree and a certificate and a funny collar and everything—I would have to say you're wrong, Doctor I'm-a-psychologist-so-I-know-human-nature. The world is made mostly of living things trying to stay alive. We eat, we sleep, and we fall in love just to stay alive, to propagate the species, and to enjoy the time we have. Everything *else* is an illusion."

"Don't be ridiculous," I said, joining in the spirit of things. "The world is a play. The play in God's mind."

"Shakespeare," Gloria sang out. "'All the world's a stage.'"

"Sanskrit," I responded. "The word *Lila* in Sanskrit literally means 'the play in God's mind' but it generally translates as *life*, this world, all of our experiences."

"I thought you didn't believe in God," Philomena said accusingly. "When you were a little girl—"

"Doctor Waldrop," I said, stopping her. "I was only pointing out what's obvious about the three of us. You see the world from your psychological point of view, Gloria's perspective is more religious, and mine comes almost completely from the wide, wide world of theatre. Combine the three of us, and we've got all the bases covered, I think. Didn't we already decide that? So let's work together here. Together we'll figure out what really happened to Tandy—I don't think Bo killed her and neither does Gloria. Disagreement amongst ourselves is the devil, prevents us from discovering the truth. Now let's go back inside and get you some chamomile tea."

My soliloquy had the desired effect. Gloria laughed. Phil relaxed. And I took another drink. Because that scotch was really good.

"You should talk to Bo," Gloria suggested as we headed back inside. "Then you'd see what we saw."

"And I'll go talk to Frank Fletcher," I said. "See what's up with that guy. Because Bo also told us that Frank can get mean when he's drinking, and your story about him and Rose seems to confirm that."

"He wouldn't kill his *sister*," Phil said instantly.

I nodded. "Probably not."

Gloria looked around. "Well. This has all certainly been a weird little conversational divergence."

Phil laughed a little. "I don't think I've been quite myself since Rose died. And when I come to this house, I think I feel that sadness, you know? More deeply, I mean. Sadness that she's not here."

"I was just thinking something like that," I told her, "on the drive back from Bo's house. But it provoked some questions that are messing with me."

Phil looked at me hard. "Such as?"

"Seriously, why did Rose leave this place to me?" I stared at the back of the house. "And why did she do that thing of making me stay in the house, live here, for six months before I can do anything with it? I mean, when I first got the news, I grabbed at it like it was my rescue rope. But now, given a moment's reflection: what the hell is going on?"

"Mm-hmm," she mumbled, "I've been wondering about all that myself."

Gloria stepped up between us. "Have we wandered a little bit away from the subject at hand?"

Phil grimaced, deliberately trying to change her mood. "It was really brave of you to go to that boy's house. What was it like? Where is it?"

I stared at her. When I was a kid, I'd just taken her weirdness for granted. But at that moment, it seemed to be more pronounced than ever, and it concerned me. But I took another sip of scotch and forged foolishly ahead.

"It was out on 82," I said. "Past the apparently fabled

'stone bear' and a little past the Dillards' place on the other side of the road."

"Really?" Her brow furrowed. "What did it look like?"

"Umm," I began, "Little square box with gray asbestos tiles and a tin roof, bunch of wild boxwoods around it. Pretty nondescript, really."

"Had a rickety tin chimney sticking out the top," Gloria added.

"Huh." Phil looked off into space.

"What is it?" I asked her.

"Probably nothing," she answered. "I'm probably wrong about this. But that location and description sounds a little like a rental property that your parents owned."

"Oh." I couldn't think of what else to say.

My parents. They'd been gone for years, and if I was to be completely honest about the subject, I'd have to admit that I never thought much about them. They'd had me late in life. I was a surprise. I was an accident. They weren't bad people, but they weren't especially interested in taking care of a child.

My father was an old-style turpentine farmer. Which meant that he grew loblolly pines to tap for their sap. When I was very little, I watched him hack into the trees to remove the pine bark. After that, the tree would secrete the crude turpentine. That secretion was the way the pine tree had of trying to heal the wound that my father had made in it, to seal the scar. The cuts were made in V shapes that he called "cat faces" down the length of the tree. That way the crude turpentine could run into the buckets that my father used to collect it. In the old days, before I was born, he would take the buckets to a factory where the crude was evaporated by steam distillation in a copper still, just like moonshine. But he had a still of his own in an open shed behind our house, and after I was born, he distilled it himself. He was, I later learned, the last such turpentine farmer in Georgia, last of a long-dying breed.

I was always horrified, as a little kid, by what seemed like his cruelty to the pine trees. I never said anything to my father about it, though. I didn't really know the guy. I couldn't ever remember a single conversation we ever had. He rarely spoke at all, and when he did it was strictly informational. His back was sore. It was too hot. The fried chicken was good. All short sentences to which my mother would respond with a nod or a sigh. She never talked much either, but she was kind in her actions toward me. Brushing my hair. Kissing me at bedtime. And taking me to Rose's bookshop.

My mother did not approve of her sister, Rose. Rose was everything that my mother was not: garrulous, worldly, educated. But my mother, thank God, understood that I had more in common with Rose than I ever would with my mother. I was outgoing. I loved being in the school plays. I had a longing to escape Enigma that was nearly burning me up. Just like Rose.

So, forced to think about my parents for a moment, all I could come up with in response to the idea that Bo's house might have been owned by them, was disbelief.

"No," I said. "That would be *way* too strange a coincidence."

Except for the fact, as I slowly remembered, that I'd had a solid burst of déjà vu when I'd been going down Bo's driveway. Had I gone there when I was little? Was that possible?

"I know," Phil went on, oblivious to my unsettled state, "but your daddy had several rental properties, and one of them was like that. He wasn't rich or anything, your father, but he did quite well."

"He made turpentine in his backyard," I objected. "How much money could there be in *that*?"

Phil laughed a little too heartily.

"Oh, sugar," she said. "At one time your daddy owned half the land in this county!"

"What?" I shook my head. "No."

She nodded. "Sold some of it for Rose, to pay for her schooling. And later on he sold more and gave the money to Rose for *your* university education too."

"Wait a minute," I objected. "Why would he give the money to Rose? Why wouldn't he just . . ."

But I had no hope of finishing that sentence, so I started another one, one filled with more melancholy than I would have thought.

"So there's a little bit of cruel irony," I said. "I finally want to talk with my father, and here he is, more than ten years dead. How do you know he gave Rose that money?"

"Rose told me," Phil said.

I looked at Gloria for some reason. "All these questions I want to ask, and anybody who could answer them is dead. So, that's funny."

"God's got a weird sense of humor," Gloria agreed.

"I really want to know why my father gave money to Rose for me," I insisted.

"Well, I'm sorry, sweetheart," Phil said, head tilted in sympathy. "Your daddy was an only child, your mama only had one sister, and you know how closemouthed both your parents could be. I don't believe there's any way you could ever find that out. That I know of."

"Yeah." I sighed. "I know. But."

"I didn't mean to upset you," Phil said.

"You didn't upset me," I told her. "It just feels strange, wanting to talk with my parents. After all this time."

And what I was really afraid of was the floodgates that might open, all the things I wish I'd said to them, all the questions I wish I'd asked. I was afraid I might drown. Not to mention the nagging questions about "Rose's secrets" and her possible financial difficulties and wondering if all that had anything to do with my father.

So I steered myself toward the kitchen door and back to the more immediate tragedy.

"Whether or not my parents once owned the house that Bo Whitaker is living in now doesn't really matter, does it?" I finished my scotch. "I'm going to visit Frank Fletcher tomorrow, see if I can suss him out."

"I'd talk to him at work if he's working for David tomorrow," Philomena advised following me inside. "He's less likely to be drunk."

"Good thought," I said.

"Okay." Gloria sniffed. "I've had enough excitement for today. But I'll leave you both with this thought. When I was in the kitchen at Bo's house, Elbert told me something interesting."

We all made our way into the kitchen.

"You still want your tea?" I asked Phil.

"Who's Elbert?" Phil answered.

"Bo's roommate," Gloria said. "Anyway—"

"Not Elbert Mooney," Phil interrupted again.

"Didn't get his last name," I said. "Why do you ask?"

"Shaved head, full beard, drives a hopped-up Volkswagen?" Phil asked in response.

"That's the guy," Gloria said. "Why are you asking? You know him?"

Philomena sat back, and the look on her face was alarming. "I should have known he was Bo's roommate."

"Who is he?" I asked. "What's going on, Phil?"

Philomena looked back and forth between us both for what seemed like a very long time.

"He just got out of Central State Prison," she said at last.

I knew about the place. It was up near Macon, a medium-security prison. Billy Sanders's father used to threaten Billy with it. When I would babysit Billy, his father would say, "If you don't behave for Miss Madeline, I will carry you over to *Central State!*"

It wasn't a real threat. But Billy never did anything wrong. Ever.

"That surprises me," Gloria said. "He seemed like a nice kid. What was he in for?"

Philomena looked back and forth between Gloria and me.

"See, that's the thing," she told us. "He almost killed Frank Fletcher in some drunken roadhouse brawl. He was up at Macon for attempted murder."

17

THE NEXT MORNING came just a little too early for me, and a lot louder than I might have hoped for. I woke up to the sound of a band saw in the backyard.

I sat up, stumbled out of bed, and tore the curtains aside to see David and another man working around the place where the gazebo used to be.

The day was bright, and the house was chilly. I groaned. I got out of my pajamas and into a pair of jeans and a sweatshirt that had "Nick's Flamingo Grill" written on it. I tried to pull my hair together for ten minutes, gave up, and put on a baseball cap that I'd worn—backward, embarrassingly enough—when I was a teenager. Put it on frontways that morning.

I knew I couldn't face David, or even muster a coherent sentence, until I'd had a little coffee, so I lumbered uneasily down the stairs gazing down at my bright blue Skechers.

But to my surprise, I found the electric kettle on, the French press filled with coffee and waiting for hot water, and Cannonball chowing down on the freshly poured cat food in his bowl. Had Dr. Waldrop come over? Gloria? I didn't see either one of them. But at that particular moment I didn't really care how it had happened, I just poured from the kettle to the press and went to fetch a big mug.

It wasn't the single glass of scotch so much as the previous day's odd experiences and revelations that made me a little fuzzy. I sat down at the kitchen table, closed my eyes and rubbed my face. The sound of the saw in the backyard ripped through my brain almost as much as the fact that my father had actually paid for my college education. Or the concept that I might have to add good old Elbert to my list of suspects for Tandy's murder. Or the idea that Tandy had a sleep-in boyfriend.

I was startled from the maelstrom of my thoughts by a very cheery "Hi!" and I jumped like somebody had jabbed me with a live wire.

David Madison was standing just inside the back door: black jeans, work gloves stuffed in a back pocket, pale blue T-shirt, well-used work boots, and a ten-thousand-watt smile.

"Sorry," he went on, smiling. "Didn't mean to scare you. Just wanted you to know that we're out back working on the gazebo."

I caught my breath, running my hand through my hair. "Yeah. I heard."

He came in. "Are you okay?"

"I was . . . I think I'm not quite awake. You didn't scare me. I was lost in thought."

He glanced at the French press, plunger still up. "And you haven't had your coffee yet, looks like."

I took a deep breath. "I haven't."

"I'll get it," he said before I could manage to stand up.

"Did you put the kettle on and fill up the press just for me?" I asked.

"Yeah," he said.

"And feed the cat?" I continued.

"He looked hungry," David said.

He went to the press, pushed the plunger down, found a coffee mug, and brought them both to the table. All I could do was watch him.

"Join me?" I finally croaked.

He glanced out the back door for a second and then said, "Sure. For a minute."

He took a seat across the table from me.

"I had a weird day yesterday," I told him, pouring myself a cup. "Gloria Coleman and I went to talk with a guy named Bo Whitaker yesterday, and he turned out to be Tandy's boyfriend who, unbeknownst to me, was shacking up with Tandy here in the bookshop until I arrived in town."

And then I drank down half a mug of the life-saving elixir.

He smiled and nodded. "You don't hear the word *unbeknownst* much in these parts."

"Teasing me?" I shook my head. "That's your response? Sweet little innocent Tandy Fletcher had a sleep-in *boyfriend*!"

"Okay, but don't say that so loud," he whispered. "That's Frank Fletcher out there in the gray coveralls. And he's working with the power tools."

I had to crane my neck to take a look. I could see a large man in coveralls standing over the band saw.

"That's a convenient coincidence," I said. "I want to speak with him. You told Doctor Waldrop that he wrestled with my aunt Rose once when he was drunk."

David looked down at the tabletop. "You want to talk with him about that? That was over a year ago."

"But Tandy's boyfriend Bo also told us that Frank has a temper when he's drunk. And I understand that Frank didn't like Tandy coming here to the bookshop. What if Frank found out about Tandy and Bo, came here to talk to her about it, and things got out of hand?"

David shook his head emphatically. "That guy would never hurt his little sister."

"You told Philomena that he grabbed Rose and Rose had to bust him in the nose."

He shrugged. "But he didn't much like Rose, and he loved Tandy. He's been in a really bad place since she died."

"Since she was *murdered*, you mean." There. I could say it. Tandy was murdered. Where was Father Coleman when I needed to prove to her that I could do it?

"This isn't some Greek play," David said calmly. "Frank didn't kill his sister."

"Greek play?" I stared.

"Well, for example," he explained in a very professorial tone, "Medea killed her own children. Oedipus killed his father. Electra killed her mother. That sort of thing. Doesn't happen very much in Enigma, Georgia. These days."

"You're just talking about that kind of theatre stuff to impress me."

He grinned. "It's that obvious?"

So he *was* trying to impress me. Very nice. Very, very nice. But all I said was, "Yeah, but I still want to talk with Frank."

"All right, I'll introduce you," he said. "But first, take a look at what I found out there in the dirt where the gazebo used to be. They weren't, like, buried or anything. And they're not very dirty. I think these were lost out there quite recently."

He leaned sideways for a minute, digging down into one of his pockets, then straightened, opened his fist, and set a single earring and a vintage lighter down on the tabletop.

I peered down at them. "Huh."

"Given how much activity there usually was out there,"

he went on, "I guess I would have expected to find more stuff like this out there. But this is it. Either one of these things yours?"

I examined them a little more closely. "No."

"Maybe they're clues," he said, only half seriously. "Left by the person who set the gazebo on fire."

I shook my head. "That earring looks familiar. Maybe it was one of Rose's. But the thing is that I haven't been back here in a couple of years, so I don't see how I would remember her earrings." I sipped. "I have seen this one, though. I'm pretty sure."

It was an odd piece of jewelry. Three little silver monkeys were holding hands, trailing downward. Hanging from the ear, they would swing against one another, and I was sure that I remembered seeing them when I was younger.

"I really think I've seen this before," I said. "I'm just not sure how or why."

"Not the lighter?" he asked.

It was tall, slim, and looked like gold.

"It's an old one," David went on. "I think it's a Swiss Dunhill."

I looked up at him. "How in the world would you know that?"

He locked eyes with me and said very seriously, "I know *lots* of things. I'm a Johannes Factotum, remember?"

Which made me smile, obviously. "That's right, you *are*."

"All right, I'm glad that's settled." He finished his coffee and stood up. "So you want to go meet Frank Fletcher?"

I nodded, downed my coffee, and followed David outside. The day was bright but there were October clouds on the horizon, flat and charcoal against the hard, blue sky. As I got closer to the awful noise of the band saw I could see that its work had been useful. Dozens of wooden panels sat propped up on the back side of its table.

"Frank!" David called out.

The saw stopped. Frank turned. He had kind of a baby face. His hair was vaguely blond like Tandy's. His eyes looked like hers too, and it pierced my heart to see the sadness in them. What some had said about him was almost certainly true: this kid couldn't have killed his sister. Maybe he got wild when he got drunk, maybe he had some anger in him. But one look at that face convinced me he would never even consider killing anyone. And then he opened his mouth.

"You that Madeline Brimley?" he growled.

I stopped where I was, ten feet away from him. "I am."

"You was with my sister when she was killed."

"Yes."

He took one step my way. "What the hell was she doing here?"

David moved imperceptibly my way.

"She asked me if she could spend the night here," I told Frank.

"What'd she want to do that for?" he demanded, his voice rising. "She's got a dorm room at the college and a bedroom in her home."

I took a deep breath to stay calm against his obvious ire. "She told me that she wanted a little independence from her home, and she had a little spat with her roommate, so she didn't really feel comfortable going to either one of those places that night."

Frank's shoulders sank. "Rae Tucker."

He made the name sound like curse words.

"She ain't a thing but trash," he went on.

I leveled a look his way. "That seems a little harsh. Rae

lost both of her parents. And she loved coming to your house, spending the night there. She was Tandy's best friend."

"I never liked her," Frank snapped. "She was too wild."

"Okay, I don't really know anything about that," I said, "but I do know that Tandy was one of the sweetest people I ever met. I'm not family and I just met her, but I loved her too."

"This damn place ain't never done my sister a lick of good," he told me, looking past me at the house. "Your aunt Rose was a bad influence on her and looks like to me that you got her killed here. So, excuse me, but I don't believe I'd care to talk with you no more."

And with that he turned back to the band saw and re-sumed his labors; the mind-numbing sound of the saw killed the air all around us.

I glanced over at David.

"That went well," I told him cheerfully over the noise.

"Actually went better than I thought it was going to," he said. "He told me he wouldn't work in the house, but he was willing to help replace the gazebo. He and his girlfriend used to make out in the old one."

"I'm going back inside now," I said.

"All the time you used to spend here with Rose," he said, "you must have made out there too."

I shook my head. "I never found anybody that interested me in that way until I went to college, so, no. I never did."

"You missed something, then," he said. "It was an almost mystical experience. For one thing, you felt like you were getting away with something, sneaking into the yard behind an old house after dark. For another, the place had a signifi-cant . . . you could *feel* all the other couples who ever sat there and kissed and talked and made promises they knew they wouldn't keep. It was powerful."

"You clearly speak from experience," I said.

"I do." He looked down at the ground and smiled; lowered his voice. "I'll tell you about Faye sometime."

"Oh." I folded my arms. "Okay."

With that he returned to his work, and I went back into the kitchen.

So. Faye. There's a Faye. Well.

I sat down at the table and poured myself another mug of coffee. I had mixed feelings about my encounter with Frank, and I didn't know what to think about David at that point. So I just drank my coffee and stared at the silver monkey earring, distracted and diffused.

After a while, I had no idea how long, I heard noise at the front door. I moved a little more cautiously than I probably needed to. But when I got to the den, I realized that there were customers at the front door.

I went to let them in. There were six or seven people on the porch, all college students, I thought.

"Is it okay to come in?" one of them asked.

I looked at her and realized it was the owl-glasses girl I'd spoken with on the Barnsley campus, the one with the braids. And *then* I realized in a flash that she had Tandy's look, the glasses and braids. Physically they weren't anything alike, but the style was enough, and she was suddenly the ghost of a dead girl standing at the front door.

I shivered. Then I managed to say, "Yes, it's okay. Come on in."

They all did, slowly, taking deep notice of the burnt wood around the door frame and the floor. But I didn't feel up to engaging.

"If you need anything, I'll be in the other room," I announced. "Just holler."

I turned around and hurried back into the kitchen. I sat back down at the table feeling entirely unsettled. The strange events and revelations of the previous day moved in on me, and I realized how the harsh conversation with Frank Fletcher had unnerved me. And even though I knew it wasn't really any of my business, I didn't like the idea that David had a Faye. Didn't like it at all.

And it was in that state of mind that I glanced down at the earring on the table and realized where I'd seen it before. I'd admired it when I was a teenager.

I was almost certain that it belonged to Philomena Waldrop.

18

THE MORNING WORE on. I didn't sell much. Idell Glassie came in and I was able to tell her that Tandy had ordered a couple of newer Joe Grey mysteries for her. And then we both made sad small talk about how great Tandy was. But mostly it was clear that David had been right about the gawkers, there were plenty of them. I spent most of my time brooding, head on the desk. Every so often I got up to glance out the back door at David and Frank as they began to piece together the bones of a new gazebo. A few students came in and I made listless small talk. No one brought up the subject of the murder or even the fire. And no one except Idell said Tandy's name. Thank God.

I guess it was around noon when David popped his head in from the kitchen.

"We're going for lunch," he said. "You want anything?"

I realized then how hungry I was.

"I'd love something," I said. "Wherever you're going, get me one."

"Frank wants to go over to Mona and Memaw's," he told me. "You feel like barbecue?"

"Yes, I do," I said. "Get me one of everything. I'm *starving*."

He laughed. "Okay. Back in a while."

And he was gone.

The shop had cleared out too, and the coffee was gone. I went to the kitchen, swished out the kettle; washed out the press and the mugs.

I ambled back in the direction of the desk; I had it in mind to straighten out the morning's transactions, but just as I sat down, I heard the front door open.

"Knock-knock," said a deep and weirdly familiar voice.

I got up from the desk and peered around the wall. There was a short, stubby little man in a very cheap business suit standing in the open doorway. He had a tragically receding hairline and a sweaty face. His shoes were a little muddy and his tie was ten years out of fashion. He was carrying a faux-leather briefcase.

"Hi," I ventured.

"Oh," he said, turning on an obviously practiced smile. "Hello, Miss Brimley. I'm Speck Dixon."

Of course he was. That's why he looked familiar. The light was different from when I'd seen him before, and he was better dressed, but he was the same guy who'd screamed at Gloria and tried to burn the plywood saints.

He must have read the expression on my face.

"I have to apologize for the other night over at the Episcopal church," he told me, sticking out his hand and heading my way. "It got *way* out of line, ma'am."

I took a few steps in his direction and took his hand. It was clammy.

"Listen," he went on earnestly, "do you have just a minute? I need to talk at you about something real important."

He had the exact demeanor of a door-to-door insurance salesman.

"I was just working on today's accounts," I said, gesturing toward the desk.

"Uh-huh," he said, moving farther into the room. "And I truly do admire you keeping your place of business open after everything that's happened. This won't take but a minute, and, like I said, it's awful important."

Without further ado, he went and sat on the green sofa, flashed the smile, and waited.

I sighed. "Sure."

I sat on the sofa as far away from him as I could get, and he began his spiel instantly.

"Now I know you're new to the world of business," he said, looking around the shop. "I believe you used to be an actress, is that right?"

"Okay," I said.

"Like your aunt Rose," he went on. "She was quite a firecracker. I don't believe there was anybody like her anywhere else in the world."

"I agree." What was he doing?

"So, let me tell you what's happening here."

He set his briefcase on his lap and opened it, retrieved several large pieces of paper, closed the case again and presented me with what looked like architectural drawings.

"I represent a group of local businessmen who have a proposal before the town council to build a great big old outlet mall right here in Enigma." He lowered his voice. "See, I got wind of a very exciting possibility. There's talk about the land beside the train tracks that runs just out back of your house. They might be about to start building on what they call a *scenic highway*. Supposed to run right through Enigma, here, and on into the Okefenokee National Wildlife Refuge, then all the way down to Fernandina Beach. Can you imagine that?"

"No," I said slowly. "I can't imagine that."

"Yes, ma'am," he snapped, voice back at top volume. "Very exciting. So what we're proposing is that we build this outlet mall. It would be right there on the highway there. Biggest one in this part of the state! See?"

"Wait a minute." I just that second remembered Gloria telling me that this guy wanted to buy the land that the church was on. Was that why he was offering me his grubby little story? "Why are you telling me about this?"

"I'm very glad you asked me that," he fired back. "That's why I brought these drawings along with me. Take a look here."

He scooted a little closer to me. I stared down at the drawings. The one on top was nothing but squares and rectangles to me, but a lot of the squares had recognizable names: Adidas, Banana Republic, Calvin Klein, Crocs, Disney, GAP, J.Crew—so many stores.

"This looks huge," I said.

"Yes, ma'am." He beamed. "Stores alone is three hundred and eighty thousand square feet!"

My head drew back. "That's almost nine acres."

"Well," he drawled, "we expect we need over forty acres total, what with your access roads and your parking lots and such."

"No, that's insane." I objected. "That's nearly a quarter of the town."

He settled in.

"Right," he said. "You may have noticed that there ain't a whole lot of business on this end of town anymore. All these buildings next to this house, they're all closed up. Folks go up to Tifton for near about everything nowadays. Fact is—this little bookshop is the only thing still open around here."

"You went to Gloria Coleman to try to buy the land that her church is on." I stood up. "You're here because you want to buy the land that this house is on."

His face clouded over a little.

"Well, yes," he admitted, a little of the bonhomie gone from his voice. "I don't figure you'd care to permanently saddle yourself with a failing enterprise like this. And in a little bitty old place like Enigma. You're a New York kind of person. Like your aunt Rose was."

"You want me to sell this place to you," I said slowly, "so that you can build an outlet mall and a parking lot."

"You're the only thing left around here," he said, trying to sound reasonable.

"Me and the Episcopal church."

"And I'm working on that," he said firmly.

I looked around the room. Despite the fact that I had talked to Rusty Thompson just the other day about selling the place, I suddenly found myself very inexplicably attached to it. Maybe it was that I still sensed Rose's presence. Maybe it was that I didn't want to abandon Tandy's ghost to the well-meaning ineptitude of Billy Sanders's investigative pursuits. Maybe there was even an element of David Madison in my reluctance to leave the old place—even if he *did* have a Faye. But the most important ingredient in my refusal to sell to the little weasel on my lovely green sofa was the insurmountable codicil in Rose's will.

"The thing is, Mister Dixon," I said in my best attempt at an apologetic voice, "I'm legally bound by my aunt's will to live in this house for six months before I can do anything at all with the property. I was just speaking with Rusty Thompson, the lawyer who handled the will, and he told me all about it. I was shocked, I can tell you. But I don't legally own this place yet. So I can't legally sell it."

He twitched just a little and had to work up to speech.

"What?" he managed to croak.

"Rusty Thompson," I repeated. "Up in Tifton. Do you want his number?"

He looked down at his drawings and mumbled, "I've got his number."

"Oh," I carried on, mostly because it seemed to bother him. "You know him? He seems like a very nice person."

His head snapped up. "He's a lawyer! That is the *opposite* of a nice person."

He began packing up.

"I'm so sorry," I said, and I almost sounded like I meant it.

He didn't look up. "This ain't the end of the matter. I got me a lawyer too. We'll just see about this thing."

"Okay," I said, still hoping that I sounded at least a little sympathetic. "But really, if you could just wait out the six months . . ."

"I got to know about this inside of ten days!" He clicked his briefcase closed. "You don't know the first thing about *business*."

"I know this bookstore makes money," I said instantly. "Against all odds. The thing is, most of the college students buy their textbooks here, and their reading assignment books here. Also there's no house note, no mortgage on the place. The utilities and the taxes and even the upkeep are all paid for out of a trust that Rose set up. So I have no real overhead and I sell most of these books for almost twice what they cost me. That's what I know about business. Rose stayed in business until she died; I think I could probably do the same thing."

Sure I was exaggerating just a little, and I said most of that just to make Speck Dixon twitch again.

Speck stood up. His face was redder, and his eyes were hot coals.

"I guess you could *try* to do the same thing," he said in a low growl. "But it's a lot going on with this old house right now. A whole lot. I'd hate to think what else might happen."

With that he headed for the front door.

"Hey, *Speck*?" I called out, deliberately making fun of his name.

He stopped, turned around, and glared. "What?"

"Your voice doesn't sound that much different on the phone. You didn't do a very good job of disguising it."

I'd said it mainly to see what his reaction would be. And his reaction was spectacularly revealing. He blinked. His head twitched once more, just a little. And then his eyes widened.

"What you mean?" he asked after a moment. "We—we ain't never talked on the phone."

I shook my head and mustered a laugh. "Oh yes we have."

That was it for Speck. He sputtered, turned, and fled.

Which convinced me that Speck Dixon was the man on the phone, the one who burned down the gazebo, who threatened me—the man who killed Tandy Fletcher.

I sat around for a while trying to decide which person to call first: Philomena, Gloria, or Billy Sanders. But I was hesitant to call anybody, really, because of everything that was running around in my brain.

For one thing, I only *thought* the guy on the phone sounded like Speck. I didn't have any actual proof. For another thing, Speck seemed more like a moron than a murderer. For a third thing, I slowly realized that I had now catalogued at least three other people who might have killed Tandy: Bo, Frank, and maybe even Elbert.

I was still sitting at my desk sorting out my thoughts as much as the day's accounts when David sang out from the back door.

"Barbecue!"

I jumped up. I was only a little embarrassed to realize that I was actually salivating.

David poked his head in through the kitchen door.

"You want to come eat outside; see what we've done on the gazebo?" he asked. "It's kind of nice outside."

I nodded, he vanished. By the time I locked the front door of the shop and made it into the garden, David was taking item after item out of several take-out bags and setting them on a drop cloth beside the beginnings of the rehabilitated gazebo. Frank was nowhere in sight.

Besides the pork plate there was potato salad, coleslaw, baked beans, Brunswick stew, and what may have been an entire sweet potato pie. And a can of Diet Coke.

I started laughing. "Thanks for getting the Diet Coke, that'll probably make up for the rest of the fat I'll be eating."

"It just tastes better, to me," he said, finishing unpacking.

"Are you joining me?" I asked.

"I already ate," he told me. "And you said get you one of everything, so . . ."

"Is that a whole pie? I can't eat a whole—"

"Oh, I'll be having some of that."

I couldn't wait. I sat down and grabbed a white plastic spoon, dug into the potato salad, and filled my entire mouth.

"You'll never guess what happened to me while you were gone," I said with my mouth full.

He just laughed and sat down beside me.

"Speck Dixon paid a visit," I went on, despite his laughter.

"*That* idiot," he said. "What's he want?"

I went for a slice of pork with my fingers. "He wants to buy this place."

That made him sit down. "Buy the bookshop?"

"Uh-huh." A bite of coleslaw. "He wants to build a shopping mall."

"A what?"

"Sorry." I swallowed. "He's got some scheme about building an outlet mall near some new highway that's supposed to be going through Enigma."

"Oh, yeah," he said. "I heard about that. It's a terrible idea."

"Agreed." Baked beans. "I told him no."

"You told him you wouldn't sell," he clarified.

I nodded. "Plus, I actually can't sell even if I wanted to, not for six months. Rose put a codicil in her will."

I reached for another slice of pork and dipped it into the small plastic tub of sauce next to the plate.

"Sorry?" He tilted his head.

"I have to live here—here in the house—for six months before I can do anything with the property."

"That's interesting."

"That's Rose," I said. "I think she was probably afraid that I wouldn't want to come down here—although there might be something more to it than that. The thing is, for me, Enigma was a great place to get away from, not a great place to go back to. Rose knew that."

"But she came back," he said.

He popped open the Diet Coke and slid it toward me. I nodded and grabbed it.

"For a long while I couldn't understand that," I said,

swallowing. "But then I hit a certain stage of my so-called career in the wonderful world of theatre, and it got a little clearer."

He nodded sagely. "Parts for women who are no longer in their twenties."

I stopped eating. "First, how would you know that? Second, thanks for saying *twenties*."

He held up his thumb. "First, Johannes Factotum." Index finger. "Second, what else would I have said?"

I didn't want to just come right out and *say* I loved him for that, but I hoped that my expression conveyed it.

"*Anyway*," I said, going back to the meal, "you guessed it, kind of. And also, what's the Robert Frost line?"

"'Home is the place where,'" he said immediately, "'when you have to go there, they have to take you in.'"

I stopped eating again and looked up.

"Man," I said. "You really are the complete item."

"I don't know what that means," he said. "But, thanks, I think."

"You are *absolutely* welcome." And back to the food.

I wasn't sure if I wanted to tell him my suspicion about Speck Dixon or not. It was really just more guessing on my part, although it did seem to be informed guessing at least. So I shifted subjects.

I lowered my voice. "Did Frank say anything else?"

"About what?"

"You know," I said. "About me. Or Rose."

"Frank isn't really the talkative type."

I nodded. "Right."

He glanced up at the sky and smiled.

"Did you give that stuff any further thought?" he asked. "The stuff I found out here, the earring and all?"

"I did, as a matter of fact," I told him. "I think the earring belongs to Philomena."

"Really?" He was clearly surprised. "What would she have been doing out there?"

"Well," I began, reaching for what was left of the cole-slaw, "she and Rose planted all the juniper around the gazebo, didn't they?"

"Umm, yes, that's my understanding," he allowed, "but that was years ago. These things haven't been out there for years. More like days."

I smiled. "And you don't really figure Doctor Waldrop to be in the gazebo making out with some attentive beau."

"No, I do not," he agreed.

I shrugged. "Well, I'll ask her about it when I see her. She's come over here every day after classes, so I'll probably see her later today."

"All right." He leaned forward and got to his feet. "I guess I better get back to work."

I looked up at him. "Yeah, David, thanks for doing that, making this new gazebo. And thanks for getting me lunch. I don't know which I'm happier about, really. Sure, the gazebo is an iconic and historic structure, but this barbecue saved my life. And now I'm stuffed."

"So maybe we'll save that sweet potato pie for my after-noon break now," he said. "If you don't eat *all* of it."

"Ha-ha," I answered deadpan. "I'll save you at least one piece."

He was back at work almost immediately. I gathered up everything from the drop cloth, mindful of the pie, and went back inside to clean up. And while I did, I tried not to think so much about David Madison. It wasn't easy. He was making a new gazebo for free. He brought me barbecue. He knew about the scarcity of roles for women my age. And he quoted Robert Frost at the drop of a hat. I mean, the *only* thing stopping me from asking him to dinner was the barely mentioned hint of a *Faye*. So I tried to put my mind on other things.

Like was that really Speck Dixon's voice on the phone? Was that really Philomena's earring? And if it was, what was it doing out there where the gazebo used to be? Which was the real Bo Whitaker, the sweet heartbroken kid I'd met or the callous drug dealer that other people described? What were Rose's so-called secrets that Tandy had mentioned? And what about Elbert?

I had no idea how long I'd dithered in Question Land before I heard that familiar call from the front door.

"Yoo-hoo," Philomena sang. "It's only me!"

I looked down. I'd been standing at the kitchen sink with the water running.

"Hey, Phil," I answered. "I'm in the kitchen!"

I turned the water off, dried my hands, and turned around just in time to see Philomena's new dress.

I was stunned. It came slightly below the knee, and it was sleeveless, a deep blue background with dabs of lighter blue and green and white, subtle, impressionistic almost-flowers.

"What are you wearing?" I said, coming toward her. "Where's your usual dress du jour? I hardly recognize you!"

She set her purse down in one of the kitchen chairs. "I'm turning over a new leaf! And, to change the subject, it looks like someone went to Mona and Memaw's."

She was staring at the empty take-out bags that overflowed the trash container, and there was the matter of the whole pie I'd set on the kitchen table. It made a delectable centerpiece.

"Well," I told her, rolling my eyes. "This feast was hand delivered by none other than David Madison."

Phil stopped mid-motion. "No."

I nodded, grinning like an idiot. "And I'm saving the pie so we can share!"

She sang again. "I *told* you. You *like* him."

"Yeah, but there's a fly in the ointment," I said, coming to the table.

"What do you mean?" She sat.

"There's someone named Faye."

"Oh, yes." She sat beside me. "Faye. He told you about her?"

"Not really, he just mentioned her. In conjunction with the previous gazebo and its mystical influence on things like kissing. You know about her?"

"Mm-hmm." She nodded.

"Okay, so tell me what's going on with her."

She shifted in her seat. "I think that's something he should tell you about, don't you?"

She wouldn't make eye contact and her voice had gone all quiet. After a short but uncomfortable silence it was evident that she'd finished with the subject, so I moved on. What else could I do?

"So good old Speck Dixon paid me a visit a while ago."

"No!" Phil's voice came back to its full volume. "What did he want?"

"He wanted me to sell him this place," I told her. "Which you know I can't do for legal reasons."

"And wouldn't do for other reasons," she prompted.

"Right. But the thing is, he also went to Gloria and tried to make her sell the land that the church is on."

"Why in the world does he want to buy . . . wait. Is this about that awful outlet mall people are talking about?"

"Exactly," I confirmed. "Apparently some new highway is supposed to be coming through Enigma, and he's got this big scheme."

"Speck Dixon always has some kind of grand plan," Phil said disdainfully. "But it never works out. He's a joke. A nasty joke."

"I agree," I said, "and there's more. Talking with him face-to-face, I think I recognized his voice. I think it's the same one who made the threatening phone calls."

Her eyes popped. "Really?"

"I think so."

"Good Lord." She sat back. "I mean, I suspected, of course, but if you recognized his voice . . ."

"I was just trying to decide what to do about it."

"Call Billy Sanders!" she insisted.

"I thought about that. But I'm not positive about it, and I don't really have anything remotely like proof. All I have is an opinion."

"Yes, but, if I may extrapolate," she guessed, "your opinion includes the idea that he's the one who killed Tandy."

"Yes."

She folded her arms and shook her head. "I've been thinking all day about Bo Whitaker. You and Gloria seemed so charmed by him. I asked around. Everyone else is afraid of him. I don't think you got the real picture."

"Just yesterday you were fuming about how Speck Dixon was the culprit," I argued. "And now that I'm agreeing with you—for a couple of very solid reasons—you want me to look at Bo again?"

"Speck Dixon is a worm," she said. "But he's a coward too, I think. I don't know that he could muster what it takes to stab someone face-to-face. Over the phone he'd be brave. In person, not so much."

"I don't get it. You really wanted to hang the guy the other night after what happened at the church."

"I know," she hedged, "but after what I heard about Bo today . . ."

"Okay." I gave up. "What did you hear?"

She leaned in, about to deliver juicy gossip. "Well. When some boy in one of the fraternities tried to get drugs from him without paying, Bo beat the boy up so badly that the boy ended up in the hospital. Broken jaw. Broken leg. They said there was a baseball bat involved."

"Who said?"

"Oh," she said, straightening up. "Some of these girls."

"Okay, but I had a direct experience of the guy," I objected. "Not gossip. And I'm telling you he was all broken up about Tandy. He didn't do it. Whereas this guy Speck . . . let's say he came here that night to make good on his threat to burn down the house. He came in the front room not expecting to see anybody, thinking I was upstairs asleep, and suddenly there's Tandy. She freaks out, they tussle. Maybe he doesn't mean to, but he kills her. Now he's got to cover his tracks, and since he came to torch the place anyway, he douses the door, sets the fire, and scrams."

She made a face. "'Torch the place'? 'Scrams'? Are you writing a Philip Marlowe?"

I had to laugh because she was right. I'd clearly gotten carried away.

"All right," I conceded.

"But you really ought to call Billy," she went on, "and at

least tell him about your suspicions, or at the *very* least tell him about Speck's visit."

"I guess I should," I admitted.

"Oh!" She suddenly thrust her hand to her mouth.

I followed her gaze. She'd discovered the earring and the lighter amid the take-out mess.

"Right," I said. "Look what David found in the rubble out back. One of your monkey earrings. I remember those."

"Yes," she said weakly. "You used to love them when you were younger."

"I did." I looked at it. "What about the lighter? Does it look familiar?"

She sighed like something had quite unexpectedly broken. "Yes. It belonged to my father."

Her voice was hollow, and her face was pale. She just kept staring at the lighter.

"Phil?" I tried to get her to look at me.

"Mm?" She wouldn't look.

"Are you okay? What's wrong?"

She just kept staring at the lighter and the earring.

"Phil," I began tentatively, "what were those doing out there in the ruins of the gazebo?"

Her eyes welled up.

"Oh. Oh, sweetheart." She couldn't quite get anything else out.

I put my hand on hers. "What is it, Phil. You're scaring me."

She pulled her hand away. She wiped her eyes. She began to shiver just a little. She took a deep breath, started to talk, then exhaled and kept silent.

I had no idea what to say, or what was wrong with her.

She tried again. Words formed but would not come out. She swallowed. She settled. She took another breath.

"Maddy," she sobbed at last.

The last time she'd called me that I'd been nine.

"Philomena," I said sternly, "you *have* to tell me what's going on."

She finally looked at me, and I wished she hadn't. Her eyes were filled with such overwhelming pain and sorrow, a despair, in fact, that threatened to sweep her away.

She was lost.

"I did it, Maddy," she moaned. "I burned down the gazebo."

19

THEY SAY THAT the fall of the Roman Empire was a pretty significant event. Hurricane Katrina was horrible on all counts. The bombing of Pearl Harbor, the wreck of the *Hesperus*, World War I—all hideous beyond imagining. If you'd put them all together and dropped them on my head, I couldn't have felt any more devastated than I was by Philomena Waldrop's single sentence.

We just sat there for a very long time. She tried and failed to contain her crying. I tried and failed to say something. Anything.

After an eternity, Philomena dried her eyes, sat up straight, nodded, and told me her story.

"I'll begin here," she said softly. "Rose and I were more than friends. We began courting almost as soon as she arrived back to Enigma from her Broadway days. We'd known each other before she'd left. We always felt fondly toward each other. We wrote letters. I couldn't say the exact moment when my fondness grew into love. It was before she came home. In the letters. I think it be may hard for a person your age, or anyone in this part of the twenty-first century, to understand the power of a letter. A letter in the mail. You write something down with a pen on a piece of paper, something that you might not be willing or able to say in person. You fold it up and put it in an envelope. You put a stamp on it, and you take it to the post office. And then you wait. Sometimes it's a week, sometimes more, before you get any kind of a response. But when you see that envelope in your mailbox, the one from the person to whom you have written, your heart beats faster, and you can't wait to tear open the envelope and read what that person has written to you. Do you understand why I'm telling you this, in this slow and deliberate manner? It's because that is a fraction of the inebriating, agonizing time it takes between letters. You spend days, sometimes, just thinking about what you said, and what the other person might say in response. And then when you read the response, your heart lifts up and your pulse quickens, and you clutch the letter to your breast and sigh. Very few people know that experience anymore. An email or a text is so immediate, so fractured, so . . . typed. I would sometimes write to Rose in a spiral pattern. The first word would be in the middle of the page and the sentences would spiral outward until there was no more room on the paper. She would have to read it turning the page around and around. There's no way to do that in a text. Nowadays people get frustrated or worried or even angry if an email or a text isn't answered immediately. They don't have any idea what it is to wait a week. Two. Three. Or how ecstatically overjoyed you can feel when you see that letter in the mail after so long a time."

"Philomena . . ." I interrupted.

"Yes, yes, I'm getting to it," she said, reading my impatience. "My point is that by the time Rose came back to Enigma, I was already in love with her. In love through letters. I don't know when she began to feel the same way about me, but eventually it was clear that she did. And when we both knew, it seemed as if we'd always felt that way. As if it was inevitable."

She looked around the kitchen.

"We spent endless hours in here, in this kitchen, cooking and talking and eating and laughing." She cast a glance out the window to the backyard. "And even more time out there, in the garden. We planted everything. The juniper was my idea. Rose planted the verbena and the yarrow. Zinnia seeds every year. The black-eyed Susan and Shasta daisies are pe-rennials in this climate, of course. And when we were tired from a long day of garden work, we'd sit out there in that gazebo, reading or talking. I always thought of this line from Thomas Hardy: 'And at home by the fire, whenever you look up, there I shall be—and whenever I look up, there will be you.' And that was our life together for twenty years or more."

She fell silent then. Not because she didn't know what to say, but because there was really nothing more *to* say.

Except to end the story.

"And then she died," she said.

It wasn't a sad sentence; it was only a true one. She seemed reconciled to the transitory nature of all things, all life.

I was still absorbing the concept of their relationship when she went on.

"I confess that her death, and the loss of our life together, left me momentarily at sea," she said.

Her voice had taken on a disconcerting tone.

"And then Rusty Thompson informed me that *you* were inheriting the shop."

I studied her face. I was surprised to discover that it was as hard as stone and absolutely devoid of emotion.

"You thought that *you* would inherit the place," I realized.

"Yes." She didn't look at me. "Why did she do that? It was mine to inherit."

"So you burned down the gazebo the minute I came into town?" I hadn't meant for my voice to rise to such a loud volume, or such a high octave. "Why wouldn't you just write me one of your much vaunted letters and tell me that you wanted the place? I would have given it to you. God!"

Her voice grown much colder, she said, "Rusty Thompson assured me that Rose's wishes were quite clear. She wanted you to have the place."

"So go burn down *his* gazebo!" I roared.

"You have to understand," she said then, a break in her ice, "I wasn't myself. Really. I think a little something in me just broke in two and I didn't quite know *what* I was doing. I wasn't in my right mind. You have to believe that. Because when I saw you the next morning, I sort of came to, or something, and I realized what I'd done. I would . . . I would never do such a thing in my right mind." She exhaled loudly. "Lord. I'm so glad we're talking about this. I've been a wreck keeping all this inside."

I leveled what I hoped would be a killing look at her.

"*You've* been a wreck?" My voice was still as the grave; even gave me a chill.

"Someone's been threatening to burn down this house with me in it, and *you've* been a wreck?"

She blinked several times. "Well. Yes. But."

"Wait!" I shouted suddenly. "Did you get some man to call me on the phone and threaten me?"

She reared back. "God, no! I would never to such a thing."

"Yeah, okay," I fumed, "but you'd also never do such a thing as burn the gazebo either, but here we are! So you want me to believe that you set fire to the thing and somebody else thought, 'Hey! Good idea! I'll give Madeline a call and see can I toss a fright into her!'"

"Umm . . ."

"And this alleged other person took a cue from you, came here, killed Tandy, and lit up the door!"

"No, see—"

Then, at top volume, I was stunned to hear myself ask, "Did you kill Tandy Fletcher?"

The silence that followed was worse than a pit, worse than the dead, worse than any sound could have been.

And then, just barely above silence, she managed to whisper, "What kind of person do you think I am?"

I just shook my head. "I actually have no idea what kind of person you are. I don't really know you. And what I thought I knew, a long time ago, is *clearly* not the truth now."

"Maddy." Her voice was a whimper then.

Maybe if I'd been a Christian saint or a good Buddhist monk, I might have been able to see past my rage and understand her situation, her pain. But the terrifying image of Philomena Waldrop standing out in the backyard, dousing the gazebo with gas, and setting fire to it was too much to take. Especially given the rest of what had happened over the course of the previous few days.

"So, what did you do?" I continued. "You heard I was coming and waited in the backyard all day until I got here and then lit this stupid lighter?"

She glanced down at the lighter, then through the back door out to the garden.

"No." She was exhausted by the emotion of the moment. She was defeated by her own admissions. "I was at church. Gloria's church across the street. I just happened to see your car, that poor old beat-up car. I saw you pull up in front of this house. I watched you walk in. All the anger and, I guess, sorrow and pain—it just came welling up. Once you were in the house I snuck on over here, around the side, and sat out there just watching the house. I got madder and madder, or sadder and sadder, I really don't know which. The end result was that I was suddenly standing there with the lighter in my hand. I went to that shed where the lawn mower is and got the gas can. I poured the gas all over the thing. I lit the fire. But when it got going, I panicked. I tried to put it out. I—I ruined my dress, and I—my hair got singed just a little. That's why I've been wearing it up this way. Up like this. I guess that's when I knocked out my earring. Putting up my hair. Anyway, I ran back to the church and called the fire department. That's how they got here so quickly, you know."

"I don't care how quickly the fire department got here!" I barked. "That's not remotely the relevant part of this story! You burned that thing down!"

And she was back to tears.

"I know." She fiddled in a pocket of her new look dress and got a tissue. "I know."

She sniffed and wiped her eyes.

"I'm telling Billy," I assured her. "And that snooty fire guy what's-his-name too."

"Mike Jordon," she told me absently. "Yes. Go ahead. Tell them all."

More weeping.

"And you realize," I kept going, "that even if you didn't do anything else, you started all this other stuff. This whole awful mess started when you did that. You realize that, don't you? You enabled the threats, the fire in the house, and Tandy's murder!"

She looked up from her Kleenex, helpless. "I did?"

I stood up suddenly. "Get out."

My voice was calm, my stance was firm, my eyes were colder than Alaska. Northern Alaska.

"What do you mean?" she whimpered.

"I mean I want you to get out of this house," I said, still made almost entirely of ice. "And I don't want you to come back. Ever."

Her mouth went slack, and her eyes widened. "Never come back in this house?"

"You heard me."

She looked around the kitchen like it was the first time she'd ever seen it. "Never to be back in this kitchen? No. I don't think I could do that."

"You don't really have a choice," I explained. "If I have to file a thing. A restraining order. I'll do it. You can't ever come back in here. Jesus, Phil. Don't you understand what you've done?"

She fumbled with her tissue; she pushed the lighter around on the tabletop, staring down at her earring.

"I don't think I do," she said.

Her voice was made of glass—just about to break.

"And leave that stuff alone," I said, grabbing the lighter away from her hand. "That's evidence now. I'm not kidding. I'll see you to the door, and then I'm calling Billy Sanders. So. Come on."

For a second it looked like she didn't have the strength to stand. Then, in slow motion, she rose, turned away from me, and headed for the front door.

"I don't know who I am," she said to no one.

And *that* got to me. There she was, growing old, living alone, mourning the loss of someone she loved, and suddenly realizing what the culmination of her loneliness and grief had wrought. Someone like Philomena, whose life had been a pursuit of self-knowledge through psychology, might actually not know who she was anymore. Late in life, she was coming to grips with a stranger that lived inside her.

But that didn't soften me enough to relent. Maybe it should have, and maybe I could have been more generous or forgiving, but in that moment all I wanted to do was get her out of my house.

Huh. *My* house. There it was. All at once it was my house. Wasn't that just the funniest thing ever?

I saw her to the door. We did not have parting words. She didn't even look at me or look back at the house when she got into her car. She just drove away.

I went to my desk and snatched up the phone, found the card Billy had given me, and dialed.

"Uh-huh?" Billy answered.

"Hey, Billy, it's Madeline Brimley," I said just a little too quickly. "I've got news."

"All right then," he responded, and then it sounded like he switched the phone to his other ear. "About what, now?"

"Philomena Waldrop is the one who set my gazebo on fire!" And I instantly wished that I'd built up to it instead of just blurting it out like that.

"What?" Billy's voice betrayed his disbelief.

"She was just here," I insisted. "She *told* me she did it!"

"She—wait, she was there with you in the bookshop, just now, and she told you she set the fire in that thing?"

"Yes!" I sat down at the desk and sped on. "David Madison found a lighter and an earring out there when he was cleaning up to start making the new one. He brought them in to me. Then Philomena came in and saw them and admitted they were hers. Then she told me she set the fire."

I realized how fast I'd been talking, and how crazy I sounded.

"She *told* you that she did it," Billy repeated.

"Yes, she did," I confirmed.

"Huh." That was all.

"Well, aren't you going to arrest her? Or go question her, or something?"

There was a brief silence.

"I'm just trying to figure how this relates to the threats you got," he said carefully. "And, you know, to Tandy's murder."

"Right," I said, slowing down. "I wondered the same thing. Phil said she had nothing to do with all that, and, you know, she probably didn't."

"Well, it's a lot more to figure out about this, but—"

"Oh! Also, Speck Dixon came over before Phil got here. And while he was talking to me, I thought he sounded a lot like the person who—the voice of the threatening phone calls."

Another slight pause.

"You think Doctor Waldrop and Speck are in this together?"

"God, no. She hates Speck."

"That's what I know," he told me. "So . . . what are we saying here?"

My turn to be silent for a second. And then I gave up.

"Yeah, I don't know."

"What did Speck Dixon come over there for?" he asked.

"Well, that's a thing, too," I began. "He wanted to buy this place. And he already talked to Gloria Coleman about buying the church land. He wants to build an outlet mall."

"Good Lord." Billy laughed. "He's been going all over

town talking about that. I believe that will happen right after I get elected president. Of England."

It was unclear to me at that moment whether Billy was joking, or he really didn't understand the political systems of Great Britain, but I forged ahead.

"Okay, but if he did make the calls, maybe he was the one who came over that night, ready to confront me, and got surprised by Tandy . . ."

"And *he* killed her?" Billy said, finishing my thought. "Well, no, I don't think so. I've seen Speck drunk enough to shoot fish, but I don't believe he's got it in him to stab a person face-to-face."

So I said, "Billy?"

And he said, "What?"

And I said, "You never can tell. I have just recently come to understand that you never can tell what a person has inside them. Even somebody you thought you knew pretty well. You know?"

"I'll go talk to Doctor Waldrop," he assured me. "But I want you to think about whether or not you'll press charges. She's been all tore up about Rose's death. And, to tell the truth, she ain't all that happy a person to begin with. Not for all her life, you know?"

And of all things, that reminded me of Philomena's favorite childhood story.

Philomena was born and raised on Koinonia Farm, a Christian commune in our part of Georgia dedicated to pacifism, racial equality, and communal living. Founded in 1942, it was a wild, wonderful anomaly in the South, welcome to everyone. Everyone. As a result of *that*, the surrounding community shunned the farm almost completely.

So much so that when Phil was a little girl in 1969 and

got rheumatic fever, no doctor in the area would come onto the commune to help her. She might have died, except for the fact that Rosalynn Carter heard about the problem and sent to Atlanta for a doctor she knew there, someone who would make a house call to Koinonia. Without any hubbub, any publicity, any notice, Rosalynn and the doctor came to Phil's house with a combination of penicillin and kindness, and Philomena was healed.

"That's what a *real* Christian does," Philomena would always say when she repeated the story. "Not like these Sunday morning Christians who act like they don't know who Jesus is for the rest of the week. Rosalynn Carter was a saint, and I mean it. I would be dead right now had it not been for her."

When Jimmy Carter was elected president there was a celebration in her house that lasted two weeks.

As a result of her illness, though, she suffered a host of long-term ailments. She had permanent scarring on her heart valves, irregular heartbeats, frequent chest pains, and chronic anemia. And apparently adding to her cardiac difficulties since Rose died, a broken heart as well.

All of which gained her exactly zero sympathy in my book at that moment.

So I said to Billy, "I don't really care how unhappy Philomena is. She started all this mess and it ended with Tandy's murder, you get that, right?"

With the heaviest of sighs, Billy admitted it. "Right."

"Look, also," I forged ahead, "do you have any idea how I can get in touch with that guy Mike Jordon? I want to tell him who actually burned down the gazebo."

"Why?"

"Because he thought that I did it!" I railed. "And I want to show him that I didn't!"

"I don't think he seriously believed—"

"Do you have his number or not?" I snapped.

"Yeah," he groaned. "Okay."

He gave me the phone number and I hung up before I completely realized what a state I was in. I stared down at the phone and was about to dial the fireman's number when Cannonball intervened. He leapt up onto the desk—a remarkably agile move for someone of his girth—and sat down next to the phone, looking up at me.

"What?" I asked him.

He did not immediately respond. But I got the impression he wanted me to take a beat before I called Mike the fireman.

"What do you suggest?" I asked him.

With that, he hopped off the desk and went into the dining room. I followed and watched. With almost as little effort as he'd used to ascend the desk, he leapt up onto the sideboard where the record player lived.

"Music?" I asked him.

He rolled his head, eyes wide, and began licking his shoulder.

"So," I said. "Bath time music."

It didn't take me long to find the right record, an album called *Coltrane's Sound*. The tune I wanted was "Central Park West." It was calm, sophisticated, urban—everything Enigma was not. It put me back in New York on a Sunday morning, sitting in bed reading the *Times* and sipping espresso.

And as the music continued, I contemplated the joyous anachronism of listening to Coltrane's jazz in the land of serious country music. That joy was only compounded by the knowledge that someone like Bo Whitaker enjoyed listening to Miles Davis. Or did he? Was he only listening to jazz because Tandy listened to it? And was Tandy only listening to it because Rose made her do it? The way Rose had made me.

And with that thought, Cannonball stopped his bath and looked over at the worn leather chair in the corner of the room. Because that's where Rose would sit, sometimes for hours, listening to music, telling me details about this bass player or that pianist. And the overwhelming love she felt for that music seemed to fill the room as much as the music did. And it filled me up too.

Cannonball took a moment to get down from the sideboard, then wandered over to the chair, hopped up, turned around several times, and lay down there, eyes wide open.

"Yeah," I told him. "I miss her too."

The song ended and I took the needle up. I didn't want to listen to anything else. But it was a lonesome silence that replaced the music in the room. In the house. In the world.

"Rose." I sighed. "What have you gotten me into?"

The only answer that I got was the sudden grating resumption of the band saw in the backyard. But it was good because it reminded me that I had to call Rusty Thompson and have a very mundane conversation about insurance. At that moment, the boring specificity of such an enterprise seemed like the perfect antidote to the current atmosphere of melancholy and betrayal.

So, without further thought, I sauntered back into the other room, sat at the desk, and called up a lawyer.

"Thompson and Associates," the voice said. "How may I help you?"

"Hey, it's Madeline Brimley," I told her. "I really have to speak to Rusty. It's about Rose's house here in Enigma."

She brightened. "Oh, surely. Just a moment, hon."

And I was on hold. The Muzak that came on was only

meant to be calming but it would have put an elevator to sleep. After about a month, Rusty finally picked up the phone.

"Madeline!" He was only marginally less harried than in our previous conversation. "What's cooking?"

"Hey, Rusty," I said, doing my best to not be caught up in his jolly agitation. "I need to ask you just a quick question about insurance, and getting these repairs done on the house—"

"From the fires and all," he interrupted. "Yeah, I got the statement from Mike Jordon, and I already filed the paperwork. You're completely covered. There should be a claims adjuster over there to your place this week but it's just a formality. The papers I got from Mike did the trick."

"Oh. That was easy. But what's this about Mike Jordon?"

"Yeah, that Mike Jordon," Rusty went on, laughing, "he says you already don't like him, so he asked me to put a little extra hustle on this thing here."

"I don't like him," I explained, "because he thinks I set my own gazebo on fire. Why were you talking to him?"

"Well, he wanted to make sure I got the proper paperwork to document—"

"Look," I said, my turn to interrupt him. "While I've got you, let me ask you a couple of other questions. You talked to Philomena Waldrop about Rose's will, about my getting the bookshop, right?"

"I did. How'd you know that?"

"She told me." I tried to keep the poison I had in my mind out of my voice. "Did she say anything to you about it?"

"Huh. Matter of fact, she did." He took a second. "She called me, you understand, to see about Rose's will. Day after Rose died. And she was very surprised to hear about you, and she asked me if there was anything about her in the will."

"Was there?"

"Oh, sure, sure," he said. "Doctor Waldrop got some money and some, uh, records, vinyl records, and some furniture, can't remember what. Some other stuff. Why do you ask?"

I was just about to tell Rusty the whole sordid story of Philomena's betrayal and arson when Cannonball came into the room and stared me down. So I thought better of it.

Instead I said, "Doesn't matter. But look, are there any more surprises coming my way from Rose's will—like the secret codicil that keeps me living in this haunted fun house?"

The pause was a little too long before he said, "I'm really not at liberty to . . ."

I waited. He never finished his sentence.

I was just about to hang up, but as an afterthought I told him, "Oh, I got a visit from a guy named Speck Dixon today, do you know him?"

Silence.

"Rusty?" I pressed.

"Uh-huh, why are you asking about him?"

"Because he came here today, and he wanted to buy this house!" I told him, a little more forcefully than I'd intended. "Which, you know, I can't do, and that seemed to upset him a whole lot. And I think he's the guy who made those threatening phone calls. To try to scare me into selling him this house!"

More silence.

"Okay." He sighed.

I could hear his chair squeak and I could hear him shuffling some papers on his desk.

"The thing is," he went on after a minute, "Speck Dixon is the reason my office is in such an uproar. You remember my saying we had us a real estate fraud deal we're working on, and it had everybody up all hours like crazy?"

"I do remember that," I assured him. "You told me I had to give you a couple of days to deal with that; it's why you couldn't help me figure out how to get out from under this death trap I seem to be living in."

"Uh-huh, so anyway," he continued, ignoring my increasing ire, "that particular case, see, it actually *involves* Speck Dixon."

That sobered me. "It *does*?"

"Yeah. He's been responsible for a fair number of underhanded real estate deals recently, mostly involving family farms in the immediate area. Oh, including the Fletchers. Tandy's family."

"This is unbelievable," I whispered.

"I know," he agreed heartily. "I mean, the man owes money all over the state, so he's been missing with farm loans. I can't tell you the details. And now he's banking everything on this outlet mall thing, which, I'm telling you, is *not* going to land his way. So, anyway, I probably shouldn't even be talking with you about any of this. But if you think it's Speck Dixon that's made those threatening phone calls to you, you have *got* to report him to the police. And I mean right now."

"I already did that," I mumbled. "But now I want to talk with him again because now I'm convinced that he killed Tandy."

"Hold on," Rusty said, suddenly much more serious. "If you really do think that, you can't confront him about it. That's something you need to get the police to do. Speck Dixon is a nasty little man, and I don't believe he did that, but you never can tell what a weasel might do if you got it cornered. You hear me, Madeline? You never know about people."

That sentence landed hard, right in the middle of my chest. Because how many times had people said something exactly like that to me? And I'd just said it to Billy. Clearly a message from the Universe. I could never have imagined in my wildest dreams that my aunt Rose would leave me the bookshop in her will. Or that I'd have a crush on a gardener who had a Faye. Or that Philomena Waldrop, someone I'd known and loved all my life, would turn out to be so danger- ously unstable. Or that I'd care for a small-town college girl so much that I believed it was my job to solve her murder.

"Rusty," I announced, "you said a mouthful. I was just thinking that same thing myself. You never can tell."

"All right then," he responded absently. "You're all set with this insurance deal, so go ahead and get everything fixed in the house. I'll holler at you in a few days, you know, check in."

"Thanks, Rusty."

And that was that. We hung up.

I sat there for a minute trying to decide how best to ap- proach Speck. If I called him on the phone, I might get a bet- ter perspective on his voice, a clearer sense of whether he was actually the guy behind the threatening phone calls. But if I confronted him in person, I would be able to read him better, and he couldn't just hang up on me when I accused him of killing Tandy. On the other hand, if he *had* killed Tandy, was it really smart to be in the same room with the guy?

The fact that I didn't have his phone number or know where I could find him in person only occurred to me as an afterthought.

So I dialed up Billy again.

"Hey, Madeline." He sighed heavily. "What now?"

It was an uncharacteristically blunt greeting for Billy Sanders.

"I need to talk to Speck Dixon," I said.

Another hefty sigh. "No, you don't."

"I just talked with Rusty Thompson, that lawyer, and I found out about Speck's underhanded land deals, and that one of them involved Tandy's family and their farm. See?"

"Madeline," he groaned, frustrated, "I know you still think of me as a little kid you used to babysit, but you're going to have to understand that I'm a policeman now, and I kind of know what I'm doing, hear? I'm in the squad car right now headed over to Mae Etta's diner to have a cup of coffee and a piece of pie with old Speck. Because I consider him a possible suspect in the murder of Tandy Fletcher."

I took a breath, because, once again, you never could tell about people.

"Okay. Okay." I was trying to gather my thoughts. "So who else is a suspect?"

"I'm going to hang up now," he told me.

"Wait—" I began.

But he was gone.

20

SO. MAE ETTA'S diner. I hadn't been there since I was five. My parents didn't believe in eating meals outside the home. Rose had taken me there once because she wanted me to have key lime pie. All I could remember was that the diner smelled funny, and the key lime pie was heaven. When I told my parents about it, they got mad and told me I was never allowed to go there again. Considering how long ago that had been, and how many other places had gone out of business since then, I couldn't believe the place was still there.

But unless they'd moved it, which seemed doubtful, I did know where the diner was.

I hadn't had any customers in the shop since midmorning. David and Frank seemed to be getting along just fine without me in the backyard. Cannonball was probably asleep in Rose's chair. So all I had to do was nip upstairs, make myself a little more presentable to the general public, and then I could go see if Mae Etta's key lime pie was as good as it had been all those years ago.

Half an hour later, with my hair at least partially contained and clad in a smart and age-appropriate slate gray sweater, rust-colored jeans, and slate ballet flats, I locked the front door to the house and cranked up old Igor.

Only after I'd backed out onto the street did I consider that I should have told David I was leaving. But I was already on my way. No turning back.

Mae Etta's diner had always been on a corner across from the hardware store, not five minutes from the bookshop. Driving there was only a little depressing. All the stores and businesses I remembered from my childhood were changed or were gone. And my belief in the transitory nature of all things did not insulate me from a longing for the good old *temps perdus*.

Thank God the diner was still there, right where it should have been.

A little like a cheerful Edward Hopper painting—if there was such a thing—it was exactly what you'd use as a dictionary definition of the word *diner*. I had no idea how old the building was, but it looked like a thirties enterprise, squat, with large glass windows all around and a big neon sign on the roof, long since out of commission, that only said EAT.

Even at that time of the day, it was doing a fair business. I pulled into one of only three empty parking spaces. I hadn't even turned the engine off when I saw Billy and Speck in a booth near the front door. I checked myself in the rearview mirror for exactly one second, and then launched myself out of the car and toward the door.

Billy and Speck were in such an intense conversation that they didn't see me coming, which I considered lucky.

I pulled the glass door open and was assaulted by the exact smell I remembered from childhood. Only when I was five, I didn't understand that it was the smell of hot oil, French fries, grilled hamburgers and chicken livers, cooked onions and burnt coffee. And even though I'd had enough barbecue for three people, that smell made me hungry again.

I only had a split second to think about that before Billy caught sight of me. The look on his face was enough to stop me in my tracks.

But not for long.

"Billy!" I sang out.

Speck craned around, saw me, and groaned.

I slid into the booth next to Billy without asking, and he begrudgingly moved himself over toward the window. I looked around the place then. Seven booths, a counter with red vinyl swivel stools, a display case of pies, an ancient woman behind the cash register.

"Yup," I said happily. "Just exactly like I remembered it! Hey, Speck."

"Look—" Speck began.

But I forged ahead. "I guess Officer Sanders here has told you that I've identified you as the man who's been making threatening phone calls to me. I think I'll have some key lime pie!"

I settled into my seat and smiled at the only server I could see. She was a high school kid in a soft pink uniform and starched white apron, hair up, heavy on the dark blue eye shadow. The name tag said MARSHA.

"Yes, ma'am?" she piped even before she got to the booth.

"Any key lime pie over there?" I asked.

"Best in town," she assured me.

The fact that it was probably the *only* key lime pie in town made her statement irrefutable.

"I'd better have some then," I told her. "And a cup of coffee?"

"Right away," she said, turning to go.

"So," I continued, staring Speck down, "I'm prepared to file charges now, Officer Sanders."

Speck shook his head, mouth slack, eyes blinking. "Billy . . ."

I could actually hear the gears in Billy's brain as he was trying to decide how to handle the situation. But I couldn't stop there.

"The thing is," I went on, eyes still on Speck, "I'm now convinced that it was you who came to the bookshop the other night to make good on those threats. You came in, you splashed a little gas around, and you started a fire at my front door. But then Tandy Fletcher caught you at it. You didn't know she was staying there. She caught you and you tried to keep her quiet and before you knew it, you'd stabbed her dead."

I thought Speck's eyes would shoot out of his head. His mouth fell open even more and he sat back.

"Absolutely not," he whispered, struggling for breath.

"You already cheated the Fletchers anyway," I pressed. "Messed with their bank loan to try to get their land, right?"

He struggled. "Billy. You got to believe me. I ain't killed Tandy Fletcher."

"Madeline—" Billy began.

"Okay, sure, all right," Speck stammered at me. "I saw the fire the other day in back of the bookshop, that thing out there in the garden, and it looked like . . . I thought it would scare you if you thought it was somebody deliberately trying to . . . I took advantage of an opportunity, you understand, and, okay, I did call you a couple of times. But that's all! I did not set any fires, and I very much did not kill Tandy Fletcher!"

His voice had risen to such a volume that the rest of the diner had fallen silent. My key lime pie was frozen in the hand of the motionless server. The ancient woman behind the register was staring wide-eyed. The several men on stools at the counter had swiveled entirely around. People in the other booths stretched their necks to see over the torn vinyl seats.

Billy cleared his throat and said in a very soft voice, "So you admit to making threatening phone calls to Miss Brimley then, Speck?"

He sat back. "Uh. Yeah. I guess I do. But, look—"

"And Miss Brimley, are you prepared to make an official complaint about these phone calls?" he went on.

"Why, yes I am, Officer Sanders," I told him. "Thank you for asking."

Billy nodded once. "Okay, then."

"And, just so you know, Mister Dixon?" I added. "I don't believe you about Tandy. I think you killed her."

"Wait—" Speck began, his voice hoarse.

I turned to Billy. "Man. This went down a *lot* faster than I thought it was going to."

And after only the merest additional pause, the diner returned to its ordinary noise and my key lime pie arrived.

Speck was sweating and licking his lips. It was disgusting. I couldn't look. I focused on the pie; took a bite. It was every bit as delicious as I remembered it.

Speck cleared his throat and said, "Look, Billy, am I under arrest?"

"Well, no, not yet," Billy said slowly. "But don't leave town, hear?"

"Don't leave town? I got important stuff in Fernandina Beach, Billy."

"It can wait," Billy told him firmly.

Speck muttered under his breath getting out of the booth

and all the way to the door. I watched out the window as he climbed into his truck and drove away. And then I finished my pie.

"You think *that* person killed Tandy?" Billy said after a minute. "I believe I knew her pretty well. She was sweet as can be, but she was a farm girl. She would have kicked the stuffing out of poor old Speck if he even looked at her sideways."

I didn't want to hear it. "Uh-huh. What are you doing about Doctor Waldrop?"

He grunted. "She actually admitted to you that she set that fire out back of the house?"

"She absolutely did. I should have called Captain Fire Guy. He seems like he'd be a little more aggressive in his pursuit of a confessed arsonist."

"Mike Jordon? He'd come right to me. Because it's a matter for the law, not the fire department."

"I never got my coffee."

"You're in a weird mood," he told me.

"I probably am," I admitted. "It's been a weird couple of days. I'm feeling all amped up."

"You're *acting* all amped up," he confirmed. "You sure you want that coffee?"

I nodded and tried to catch the eye of the kid who brought the pie, but she was flirting with someone at the counter. Not even real flirting. Server flirting.

"Marsha?" Billy called. "Did you forget somebody's coffee?"

She jumped. "Lord. Sorry. Coming right up."

"Speck Dixon is desperate because of his real estate deals," I said. "Desperation makes a person do things they might not ordinarily do."

"Let me stop you right there," Billy said. "I am no longer considering Speck for the murder."

"Billy," I complained.

"I do have other suspects," he told me solidly.

I turned in the booth to face him. "Such as?"

"Such as none of your business!"

"None of my business?" I looked around. "I was the intended victim! And Speck is the only person who had what you policemen like to call a *motive*."

"That's not true," he said, working to stay calm. "There are other people with better motives. Which is why I am looking at someone who *would* stand a chance in a fight with Tandy and who *works* for Speck."

That stopped me. "Oh. Okay." I lowered my voice. "Is it someone I know?"

My coffee arrived.

"Sorry, ma'am," the kid said. "It'll be on the house. How was the pie?"

"Best in town." I smiled at her.

"Told you so," she said in the same flirty tone she'd been using at the counter, flashing me her a smile of her own.

She was gone and I turned my full attention back to Officer Sanders.

"Come on, Billy. Who is it?"

Exasperated but giving up, he sank in his seat. "You do know him, or you met him anyway. It's Speck's cousin Bo."

"Bo is Speck's cousin?" I said a little too loudly.

"He does some of Speck's dirty work," Billy confirmed a little softer. "Intimidating people, sometimes beats them up. I've arrested Bo maybe seven or eight times on some of these small little charges."

I shook my head. "I don't believe it. He was so sweet to

me. He's devastated by Tandy's death. He was listening to Miles Davis!"

"What difference does that make, exactly?"

"Doesn't matter. Are you sure about—you've arrested Bo for beating people up?"

"Yes. A lot."

"Maybe it was Elbert, his roommate," I said. "He seems like a bruiser."

"Elbert's got his own arrest record," was all Billy said.

I glanced down at my coffee, remembering what Phil had told me about Elbert's incarceration, and then I sat back in my seat. "Bo is Speck's cousin."

So maybe I was wrong about Bo. I'd certainly been wrong about Philomena.

"Seems to me like Bo might have pulled one over on you and Father Coleman," Billy said, not looking at me.

I took a gulp of coffee and nodded. "You know, before Philomena confessed to me, I probably would have argued about Bo, because he seemed like such a sweet kid when I went to speak with him. But would you like to hear what I know about human nature now, Billy?"

He sighed and shook his head. "Okay."

"Exactly *nothing*." I drank another serious swallow of coffee. "I know absolutely nothing about human nature."

"That's probably not true," he said, tapping the tabletop. "Let me out, hear? I got to get on with my work."

I stood up instantly. "Yes, sir."

He went for his wallet, but I put my hand on his arm.

"This one's on me, Officer Sanders," I told him. "I want to support my local constabulary."

He stared me down. "You do, huh?"

Before I could respond, Marsha spoke up.

"It's all on the house," she announced. "Everything at that table."

"What?" I looked over at her. "Why?"

The ancient woman behind the register answered.

"Y'all put on the best show we had in here since your aunt Rose died, sugar," she said in a surprisingly strong voice.

Billy grinned. "Thanks, Mae Etta."

So that was Mae Etta. That face—she could have been a hundred years old. I didn't remember her from my only other visit when I was a kid. And I didn't even question how she knew who I was, or that she'd found Rose entertaining. Which made me realize I was maybe getting used to the small-town phenomena. Everybody knew everything; I just had to accept that.

Except that I didn't seem to know Bo Whitaker, or at least I didn't know him well enough. And shame on me, I thought, for making him out to be a one-dimensional character. If I'd been playing him onstage, I would have done a better job of figuring out his backstory, his subtext, his motivations. Obviously, he could have some bad behaviors and still be in love with Tandy.

Billy and I thanked Mae Etta a little too much on our way out but we finally quit the diner together. I walked Billy to his squad car.

"What made Doctor Waldrop confess herself to you?" he asked me, keys in hand. "It had to be something."

"Oh." I nodded enthusiastically. "David Madison found her earring and a lighter in the wreckage of the gazebo this morning."

Billy stopped, smiled, and made eye contact. "Listen at the way you said *David Madison*."

"Yeah," I said, looking away. "He's—I mean, Philomena

called him to come redo the gazebo out there. And. Umm. He was out there . . . and he found the thing, the earring. And the lighter. And, as it turned out, those things were sitting on my kitchen table when Philomena came to visit, and she saw them and claimed them before she realized where and how she'd lost them."

"I see." He opened his car door. "She say why she did it?"

"Yes. She was expecting that *she'd* inherit the bookshop and she set the fire to scare me away."

I figured I could leave out the part about her being in love with Rose. That didn't seem like anybody's business.

But Billy was already wise. "Given the nature of their relationship, I guess you could see why she might think that Rose would leave her the house."

"You knew about that?" I hadn't meant to ask that question. It just came out.

"Everybody knew." He looked down. "Most people just took it as two old spinster ladies being best friends, I reckon. That's not so unusual. And to tell the truth, maybe that's all it was."

I lowered my voice. "You know there was more to it than that."

"I *don't* know. And, frankly, I don't care. And maybe there was more to it from Doctor Waldrop than there was from Rose. Which is what it always looked like to me. But it don't matter now, does it?"

"Unless it's a motive for arson," I shot back.

"I see." He blew out a breath. "So is that something you also want to press charges on? Arson. On Doctor Waldrop."

"Yes!"

He shook his head. "I believe I'm going to let you take a day or two to think about that thing."

"Billy—" I began.

But I could tell he was done with me. He just slid into his squad car and drove away.

So I turned my attention to the next example of my general inability to read people correctly: Bo Whitaker. If he'd really been muscle for Speck, then maybe his yearning for Tandy had been a little more of a performance than a genuine pain. That thought only made me want to go and talk with him again, to see if I could reassess his character.

So, back into Igor and pointed south, I headed down Highway 82. Alone.

21

EVEN THOUGH I'D just been there, I drove a little slower than I needed to, making sure I didn't miss any of the roadside landmarks. It didn't even occur to me to stop by the church and see if Gloria would come with me. Or to tell anyone where I was going. Or to think twice about what I was doing.

I just drove. Past the stone bear, past the organic farm, past the unmarked road, and into the autumn woods down a gravel driveway, right up to the little house where they cooked up the region's finest meth.

Elbert's souped-up VW wasn't there, only the mud-splattered truck.

I put Igor into park, honked the horn twice, and waited.

After a second or two the curtains in the front room parted, then closed, followed shortly by Bo's appearance in the doorway, in T-shirt, jeans, and socks. He did not look happy.

I leaned out the window.

"Hey, Bo," I said as sweetly as I could. "I'm so sorry to bother you again, but I just remembered a couple of other things I wanted to ask you. Can I come in for just a second?"

He craned his neck around, looking in my car.

"Just you? No lady preacher?"

"Just me," I assured him.

He puffed his cheeks out exhaling. "Okay, I guess."

He turned and went back inside.

I shut off the engine and got out of the car. The air was colder than it had been in town, and the leaves were raining down in red and pumpkin colors. There was no music on in the house.

Wishing I'd brought a sweater, I headed inside, but once I was there, I found that the heat was turned on and it was actually pretty comfortable.

Bo was sitting on the sofa. There was a half-empty bottle of Jack Daniel's in front of him on the coffee table. I glanced at it.

"You want some?" he asked.

I smiled. "I'll join you, if you're having some."

He smiled back. "I done already had some, but I guess I could take a little more. Get you a glass in the kitchen, do you mind? I'm kind of settled here, and I'm just about half drunk. Wait. Could you get me one too? A glass? I been drinking from the bottle."

I headed for the kitchen, searched three cabinets to find two water glasses, and returned. He had his stockinged feet up on the coffee table and his eyes were closed.

"Tandy didn't like me to drink," he mumbled. "She said . . . don't matter. She was trying to be a good influence on me. It might have worked. But you know. She's dead now, so."

And I could see that wasn't an act. Bo was genuinely lamenting the loss.

"So does that make me a bad influence if I'm drinking with you?" I asked, setting the glasses down.

He laughed, but it lacked all joy.

I went into the dining room for a chair, I didn't feel right about sitting next to him on the sofa.

"So," he groaned, reaching for the bottle, "what more you want to talk about?"

Right. Now that I was there, what *was* it I wanted to talk about?

Start small. "Mostly I was just wondering if I could get Rose's records back."

"Sure." He sighed. "I was going to get them back to you anyway. But just so you know, I really do like that music."

"I do too."

"People are always surprised that I do, you know. People around here. You ever watch *The Andy Griffith Show*?"

I took the bottle and poured myself a glass, Bo a glass, and then sat down on the dining-room chair.

"I have a friend in Atlanta who believes that everything you need to know about life can be found in some episode of *The Andy Griffith Show*," I told him.

"I always liked one where Barney says, 'The quality of mercy is not strained. It droppeth as the gentle rain from heaven.' And Andy looks at him like he's never seen Barney before in his life, and Barney says, 'You're not talking to a jerk, you know.'"

"I remember that one," I said.

"That's Shakespeare that Barney was saying," Bo told me.

"I know."

"I looked it up." He drank a healthy portion of his glass.

"Why do you like that one?" I asked him.

"Because." He made an effort to sit up just a little bit. "People look at you once and they think they know who you are. I like when that gets turned around. I like it that Barney knows Shakespeare. I like when people just assume that all I know is country music, and I toss out Charlie Parker. I can be a dumb hick from a little bitty old town and still know about Charlie Parker, you know? I like turning it around."

"Because I'm not talking to a jerk," I told him.

"No, ma'am, you are not." He finished his glass. "I'll get you those records."

"In a minute," I said. "Another thing I wanted to ask you about was: you're Speck Dixon's cousin?"

I thought that might take him by surprise, and it did. He froze for a second, then looked me in the eye.

"So?"

"So nothing, I just didn't know that."

He shook his head and reached for the bottle again. "I wondered if you recognized me from the church parking lot the other night. Didn't seem like you did, but I guess you do now."

That's why he looked familiar when I first saw him standing in the doorway of his house. Not because he looked like Sam Shepard, but because I'd seen him before in the shadows of the church parking lot when Speck was setting fire to plywood.

"You work for him sometimes," I forged ahead. "You do stuff for Speck."

He grunted.

"Why?" I asked him.

He shrugged and looked away. "It pays pretty good."

I nodded and drank.

"Is that the real reason you were interested in Tandy?" I asked quietly.

I knew instantly that it was a question almost as bold as it was stupid.

"What, exactly, do you mean by that?" he asked. And his voice had hardened considerably.

"I mean that you helped Speck scare Tandy's family into selling Speck some of their land," I said evenly. "And you got next to Tandy when she was living at the bookshop after Rose died thinking that maybe you could leverage that relationship into somehow getting the bookshop land too."

Sure, everything I'd said was speculation, but it wasn't all that wild. It was kind of what Billy had hinted about, combined with what Rusty Thompson had told me about Speck.

I don't know how I expected Bo to react to my accusation, but what he did was quite the surprise.

He laughed, and it was an awful sound. And his face transformed completely, like a mask had fallen away.

"Tandy was nothing but a *stupid* little girl." He coughed. "Rae told me she had a crush on me. I knew she was staying at the bookshop. I thought it was because Rose asked her to take care of the place. I told Speck. He told me to play up to her, and I did."

I was praying that I didn't look as stunned as I felt. I tried to cover my expression by putting the glass in front of my face, then by taking another healthy sip of whiskey. I gathered my thoughts, and I launched.

"But then when I came into town," I said, "and it got around that I was the new owner of the shop, you thought you could get on my good side by pretending to care about Tandy because you knew that I did. You knew because this is a little bitty old town, and everybody knows everything."

He finished his glass and squinted my way. "Something like that."

"You didn't love Tandy," I said.

"She was a *little girl*," he insisted. "I didn't have any feeling about her one way or the other."

Man, I thought. *My powers of observation are just gone!*

"Well." I finished my glass and set it down on the table. "You had me fooled. I guess you had Tandy fooled too."

"I did." Not one iota of remorse.

"You know," I said, at least partially to myself, "I've been in the theatre for a long time, and I can tell you one thing: you're really good. You had me going."

He poured himself another glass. "People believe what they want to believe."

"I guess they do," I said.

"So." He sat back. "You get what you came for? The records are over there by the stereo. And just so you know, I really do like Dizzy Gillespie."

"Because you're a real human being, not a small-town cliché," I said. "You're as complex as any character from Shakespeare."

His face contorted. "That's an odd thing to say."

He was right. I was just trying to decide if I was going to ask him my real question. The big question. The only question. Did he kill Tandy?

"When you came to the bookshop the other night," I said slowly, "you knew I was upstairs asleep, right?"

He shifted on the sofa. "What?"

"That last night you came to my house," I said a little louder, "you didn't care that I was there. You came to see Tandy, to spend the night with her."

"I don't . . ." he sat up, trying to focus. "What are you talking about?"

"You went to my house to sleep with Tandy," I began.

"Hold on." He leaned forward, distressed. "I never slept with Tandy. Not the way you mean. We made out and stuff. We went to sleep on that big old sofa. We never had sex. What kind of person do you think I am?"

I took a second. "That's the second time in very recent history that someone has asked me that same question. I'm beginning to believe that I really don't know what kind of person *anybody* is."

"And plus which," he went on, louder, "I was never in that house when you were there. Not once."

His protestation was so strong that it seemed like a lie.

"See, the thing is," I said, "if you go around fooling people like Tandy about your intentions, and fooling me about your feelings, then it's really hard to convince anybody that you're ever telling the truth."

His voice rose up. "I don't care what you believe!"

"I'll tell you what I believe," I fired back. "You took advantage of a sweet kid like Tandy under the mistaken impression that it would help your grotesque cousin Speck get my bookshop."

"Nobody cares about a big old house full of books!" he roared. "Speck needs that land for the outlet mall. Do you have any idea how many jobs it'll be when that thing opens? How much money is going to come into this town?"

"So all that talk about being a pharmacologist and you and Tandy leaving Enigma," I said, "that was just to get Tandy."

He took a breath and he looked confused.

"Well, no. I really do want . . ."

He sat back.

I studied that look on his face. A better picture of Bo Whitaker came into focus, or at least a more accurate one.

Tandy had influenced him to like a new kind of music. El-bert had influenced him to make a certain kind of drug. His cousin Speck had convinced him that a particular scheme was the economic salvation of his hometown. But the person I saw sitting on that sofa was just a kid looking in every direction, trying to figure out which way to go.

"I didn't mean to hurt her." His voice was barely above a whisper.

My entire body tensed up. There was a slight ringing in my ears. Was that a confession? Was Bo admitting to the murder?

Suddenly the wisdom of my being in a little house a long way from town seemed dubious at best. Especially if there was a drunken murderer in the house with me. I glanced at the door. I readied myself to sprint. I swallowed.

"I know you didn't, Bo," I ventured, mustering a deep-sounding sympathy.

"Tandy was such a sweet little girl," he murmured.

I understood that I was watching a drunk. He'd gone through a battery of changes in the short time I'd been with him. The problem with that kind of drunk was that you could never tell which mood would take over at any given moment. And if it was the angry one, the best thing you could do was just to get out of the way. Because I was convinced that the angry version of Bo got into some kind of argument with Tandy and then that version of Bo stabbed her to death.

"Maybe you realized the other night that she didn't really have any control over the bookshop," I said soothingly, getting ready to bolt. "I can understand how that would be frustrating after all the effort you put into your relationship with her. To help your cousin."

He blinked hard and looked my way. "What are you saying? I don't—I don't understand what you're saying. I'm sorry. I have had a *lot* to drink."

"I'm just saying," I continued, just beginning to feel a little desperate, "that you didn't *mean* to hurt Tandy. Like you said. It was an accident. Sort of."

"An accident?" It was clear that the words were all running around in his brain.

Further complicated wordplay was interrupted by the overbearing sound of Elbert's Baja roaring up to the front door.

When it stopped, he started yelling.

"Is that my friend Madeline Brimley in the house?" It was a cheerful inquiry.

So I yelled back, mostly to break the mood between me and Bo.

"Is that my friend Elbert parked out there next to my car?"

In answer, he burst through the door, three brown paper grocery bags in his arms.

"Hey!" he sang out.

"Hey, Elbert," I said, standing up quickly. "You need some help with those groceries?"

He shifted the bags. "If you could get the one out front here."

I took one of the bags and we went together into the kitchen.

"That guy George is, like, a genius," Elbert told me setting his bags down on the counter. "He had this idea about the entire exhaust system like I ain't *never* heard of. Swear to God I'm thinking about driving to Canada to shake his hand."

For one thing I was relieved that someone else was in the

house, even if it was a friendly meth dealer. But for another thing it warmed my heart that Elbert and George had hit it off so well.

"I'm not surprised," I told him, setting down my bag. "His understanding of the internal combustion engine borders on the supernatural."

"It does, it does," he agreed. "So. What're you doing here?"

It wasn't a rude question. He only wanted information.

"I came to collect my aunt Rose's records," I told him.

"Praise the Lord!" he laughed. "Get that junk out of my house! Listen. Did you ever hear any *real* music?"

I smiled. "I guess that depends on your definition of real music."

I was beginning to realize just how tensed up I'd been about Bo's confession. I was shaking a little.

"You ever listen at David Allan Coe?" he asked, heading out of the kitchen. "That is classic music. You would *love* him! He's a biker and an outlaw, spent a lot of time in prison—long hair, earrings, wrote 'Take This Job and Shove It.'"

"Oh," I said, a little surprised. "I know that song. It's a hundred years old."

Elbert stopped his forward motion and turned to me, serious as a judge. "Like I said, it's a *classic*."

Bo called out, but his diction was sloppy. "She didn't come here to listen to country music, Elbert. She came to get those records."

Elbert's eyebrows raised. "Sounds like somebody's been drinking."

Bo was doing his best to get up from the sofa.

"Did you get maple syrup?" he asked Elbert. "I'm thinking about making pancakes."

Bo seemed to have completely forgotten our conversation.

"Okay, then," I said lightly. "Let me just gather up those records and I'll get out of your way."

Bo made no response to that. He just teetered off the sofa and weaved his way past us and into the kitchen.

"I believe that boy drinks too much," Elbert observed casually.

I went to the stereo and collected Rose's albums. I had it in mind to ask Elbert if Bo had been at home the night of Tandy's murder, but I wasn't sure how to say it without sounding suspicious. And even if Bo had been at home some time that night it wouldn't necessarily mean that he hadn't been at the bookshop earlier to stab Tandy. He could easily have killed the girl, lit the fire, and driven home.

Then I realized that I was a little jangled by what appeared to be Bo's confession. What I really wanted was to get out of that house as quickly as I could, go home, lock the doors, take a shower, and contemplate my next move. Like maybe to Portugal.

"Okay," I said to no one in particular. "Got the records. Thanks. I'm off."

Bo made no reply. But there was a considerable clattering of pots and pans in the kitchen. Elbert was a little more traditionally polite.

"You come back anytime, you hear?"

"Right," I said over my shoulder, hurrying through the door.

The day was wearing on. The wind was cold. The leaves were everywhere, swirling around me, around my car, around the house. As I opened my car door I heard from inside the

house, at top volume, the lonesome strains of a song that began, "Well, it was all that I could do to keep from crying."

It was only after I was down the drive and out onto the
highway that my shoulders began to relax and I actually took
a decent breath. I hadn't even gone half a mile before I realized
what a complete idiot I'd been.

22

WHEN I PULLED up in front of the bookshop, I was surprised by just how glad I was that it was my home. I hadn't fully examined my feelings of gratitude since I'd been back home. When I did, sitting in my car out in front of the old place, I found that they were quite significant. Quite something.

"Thanks, Rose," I said softly.

Then I saw the curtains open in the upstairs bedroom that used to be Rose's.

Maybe if I'd been more seriously inclined toward the spiritual world, I could have taken the phenomenon for Rose's ghost and been comforted, even welcomed. But after my encounter with Bo—or, really, my encounter with almost all of Enigma since I'd been back—my only thought was that there was an intruder in the house.

I sat motionless in the car for a moment. The curtains closed. Then they fluttered. Then they shook.

Then I cursed myself for being such a Luddite that I'd always refused to get a cell phone. A cell phone could have called Billy Sanders. A cell phone could at least have called Gloria and asked her to come over and sit with me. In my car. Because I wasn't about to go inside that house.

It was late in the afternoon, still light, but sunset wouldn't be far off. So I finally got the gumption to crank up old Igor and back slowly out of the driveway into the street and then over to the church. The parking lot was empty. I pulled up close to the door, turned off the car, and got out, glancing back at the house in the distance.

I hurried into the church. The door was unlocked, but the lights weren't on. I located a switch and the lobby thing lit up, the *vestibule*. The place was silent, the brand of silence that can't be found anywhere except in certain churches and cathedrals.

I ventured into the church part of the church. It was also dark. The autumn sun couldn't quite manage to completely enliven the thick stained glass. I couldn't find any light switch. It felt like a crime to start yelling in all that silence, but that's what I had to do.

"Gloria?" I called out. "Are you there?"

The silence pushed back, and combined with the darkness, drove me to return to the vestibule.

I realized that I didn't know what day of the week it was. But I considered just staying there until Sunday morning when people started coming in for services.

I hadn't even completed that thought when the lights came on in the church.

"Madeline?" Gloria said. "Is that you?"

I couldn't recall ever in my life being so glad to hear another person's voice. I presented myself in the doorway and saw Gloria coming toward me up the aisle with a concerned look on her face.

"Are you all right?" she asked, hurrying my way.

I seemed to be frozen in the doorway of the nave, unable to answer her very reasonable question.

She got to me, put a very comforting hand on my arm, and smiled.

"What is it?" she asked me gently.

"I think Bo Whitaker just confessed to me that he killed Tandy," I said like it was all one word, "and now there's someone in my house, upstairs, in Rose's bedroom."

As the syllables were leaving my mouth, I could hear how unstable they sounded.

"Oh." Gloria nodded. "Well. That's news. You want to come into the office and call Billy Sanders?"

All I could do was nod like a little kid.

"Okay," Gloria said gently. "Come on."

I followed her down the aisle, past the altar, and into a hallway that went to her office.

Gloria Coleman's office was something out of an old-time movie. A movie made in 1935. Dark wainscoting, exposed beams, a huge antique oak desk, amber lighting, one big window, and the faint smell of frankincense which I recognized only because of my infrequent spa treatments.

She sat behind the desk. I took one of the stuffed leather club chairs, still apparently unable to talk.

It occurred to me that I might be in some sort of shock. I hadn't felt so very scared when I was actually in the house with Bo. It was *remembering* being in the house with Bo that threw me into a panic. And when I'd thought about the curtains moving in that old house, I was done for.

I heard Gloria say into the phone, "Hi, it's Gloria Coleman over at St. Thomas Aquinas. Could I speak with Officer Sanders please?"

She waited.

"Say that it's about Bo," I encouraged.

But Gloria said, into the phone, "Okay, would you tell him that I called? It's important."

Another pause.

"Yes, it's pertaining to Tandy Fletcher's murder. We have new information."

Apparently, that got a bit more of the desired response.

"That would be great. Thank you." And she hung up.

"What?" I asked.

"They're going to call him, send him over here right away. Or so they said, anyway." She sat back in her chair and suddenly looked like my idea of the perfect Episcopal priest, concerned and judgmental at the same time.

"Now," she began, "tell me exactly what happened."

If I'd been a little more present, I might have realized what she was doing. She was making me focus, making me tell a story instead of letting my apprehensions get the better of me.

"I went to Bo's house again," I said, the agitation in my voice filling the large room. "I thought about coming here first, to get you to go with me, which I should have done."

"But you went to Bo's house," she prompted.

"Yes—did you know that Speck Dixon is his cousin?"

"I did."

"And did you know that he was here in your parking lot that night that Speck threatened you and was trying to set a fire?"

"Huh. No, I guess I didn't see him. Was he the guy in the gray hoodie?"

"I don't know," I said, "but anyway he, Bo, was only coming on to Tandy because Speck thought she might have some control over what was happening at the bookshop—"

"Because she was living there," Gloria assumed, "and Speck wanted the place, the land, like he wants this land here where the church is."

"Right!" I confirmed. "But anyway as we drank, Bo and I—I mean, I kind of confronted him or something, and he said, 'I didn't mean to hurt her'!"

"Bo said that?" Gloria leaned forward, elbows on her desk.

"Yes!" My voice was just a little too loud. "'I didn't mean to hurt her'!"

"I guess that could be a confession," she said slowly.

"What else could it be?" I demanded even louder than before.

"You know," she answered reasonably, "maybe he was just sorry for his manipulation of a fairly innocent girl. Maybe he didn't mean to hurt her emotionally."

"Bo killed Tandy!" I stood up, hands on the desk, leaning into her.

Gloria remained calm. "Maybe. Maybe not. But I can tell, now, that you joined Bo in a little bit of whiskey. True?"

I took in a breath. "Umm . . ."

"And maybe the whiskey is skewing your perception just a little. Maybe?"

"I got spooked," I admitted. "That's for sure. And then when I came home and saw someone in Rose's room . . ."

"Right," she went on. "What did you see, exactly?"

"The curtains opened," I said, "and then they fluttered. Someone is in there, Gloria."

"Maybe the window was open," she suggested. "It's pretty breezy out there."

"The bedroom window was closed," I told her in no uncertain terms. But then I added, "I think."

She stood up. "You want to go over and we'll both check it out? Or would you rather wait here for Billy?"

My brain was all over the place. Bo's living room, Rose's bedroom, the darkened church, the drive home down 82, the fluttering curtains, Tandy's dead body on the floor in my house.

"I don't know," I confessed.

Gloria smiled. "Come on, let's walk over to your place. The cool air will probably do you good, and we can investigate the scary curtains together. And when Billy gets here, he'll see your car in my parking lot, then he'll see the lights on in your house, and he'll put two and two together. I mean, I know you think he's not the brightest guy in the world, but I'm positive he'll come up with *four* if he really puts his mind to it."

I could see that she was right. Cool air, reasonable thinking, a simple investigation of the house, probably just the wind parting the curtains. So I headed for the door. Gloria joined me.

We walked through the church. She turned off the overhead chandeliers. The dim glory of light through stained glass returned, and we left.

The air outside was indeed reviving, and I took a couple of really deep breaths, filled my lungs, relaxed my shoulders.

The sun was leaning into the horizon and the wind had died down. Everything was quiet, afternoon noise was finished, night noise had yet to begin. The day was slowly coming to an end.

We walked quickly; I think I set the pace. We were in front of the house in no time. It looked so calm that I felt a little ridiculous for thinking that there was someone in the house.

And then the curtains opened again.

"Did you see that?" I whispered to Gloria.

She nodded. "Let's check the front door."

"What?" I was still staring at the fluttering curtains.

"See if it's open," she went on.

We moved slowly toward the porch, up the steps, and tested the door. It was closed. It was locked.

"Back door," I whispered.

She nodded. "You go around that way, I'll go this way—see if there are any open windows, right?"

"Good idea." I took off.

No open windows on my side. I met Gloria at the back door.

"Nothing," she told me.

And the back door was also locked.

"The thing is," I said softly, "I think David and Frank were here when I left, and I probably left this door unlocked."

I turned to see the beginnings of a new gazebo in the slant of amber sunshine. Tools were gone.

"Maybe one of them locked up?" she asked.

I reached for my keys. "I guess. Ready?"

"Okay," she said, "but if I see Rose's ghost anywhere in there, I'm moving back to Savannah."

"Need a roommate?" I asked, unlocking the door.

The inside of the house was so quiet that every squeak of the door hinge and creak of the floorboards sounded like thunder. We were trying not to make any noise, but the house was talking to me again and everything we did was loud. There was no hiding the fact that we were moving toward the stairs.

The light and shadows in the downstairs rooms seemed

a little too calm, like they were trying too hard to give the illusion of peace.

And when we hit the first stairstep, it was so loud that we might as well have fired a cannon.

For some reason, that provoked me to suddenly and very foolishly announce our presence and our intention.

"We're here," I said, full voice, "and we're coming upstairs."

"All of us!" Gloria added.

I nodded and up we went.

The upstairs was darker. Doors were closed, curtains were pulled. The long thin rug in the hallway kept our footsteps a little quieter than the racket of the stairs. We moved together toward Rose's bedroom, slow but deliberate steps.

We made it to Rose's open doorway. We looked in. I gasped. Then I held my breath. The curtains were still moving but nobody was there. I could feel my heart pounding in my ears.

Until Gloria broke the mood.

"Oh for God's sake," she muttered.

A second later my eyes fell on Cannonball, on his back, paws tangled in the curtains, shaking them to beat the band.

I let out my breath. I felt like an idiot. I shook my head.

"I'm telling you," I began, "I would never in my life have been so spooked by this if I hadn't had my encounter with Bo. Never. Now I'm ridiculous."

"I think I understand." Gloria patted me on the arm. "You *inherited* a cat. You apparently didn't know one of the primary concepts of cat care. Classic rookie mistake."

"Which concept is that?" I asked, watching the cat wrangle with the hem of the curtain, chewing on a corner.

"*Everything* is a cat toy," she said. "Everything. Seriously. If you were a seasoned cat person, your first thought probably would have been that the curtains were moving because of this guy."

She turned a benevolent eye on Cannonball.

I closed my eyes. "I will pay you one hundred dollars to keep this particular little adventure to yourself."

"What do you mean?" she asked me.

"I would *genuinely* like to pretend that I didn't get all crazy over a cat playing with a curtain." I opened my eyes. "So could we just forget this whole thing? Especially when Billy gets here?"

"Sure," she said right away. "You want some coffee or something?"

"I didn't have that much whiskey at Bo's house," I said, "if that's what you're thinking. That didn't have any bearing on my behavior or my state of mind."

She patted my arm again. "That is exactly what someone who's had a little too much to drink would say. I'm going to make coffee."

And she was gone.

I took a few more steps into Rose's room. I'd stood at the doorway a thousand times when was a kid, but I'd never ventured in.

It was large, maybe the largest room in the house. The centerpiece was a huge antique mahogany Empire bed with a canopy. The four posts were spiral pillars, and they were topped with carvings that looked like lush bird feathers. The rugs were all handwoven, antiques as well. There was a crowded mahogany vanity to match the bed. The oil paintings hanging on the walls were all originals, she'd told me that. And, of course, one entire wall was a built-in floor-to-ceiling dark wood bookcase. The air was a little musty, but it was filled with the scent of lavender. And it also smelled like Rose.

I looked over at the continually cavorting Cannonball.

"You do realize that you made me look like an idiot," I told him in no uncertain terms. "That's what I thought to myself just a minute ago, and now I'm saying it out loud to you."

He appeared to be unmoved by my admonition. He continued his argument with fabric.

My eyes wandered. Everything about the room reminded me of Rose. The books on her bedside table, *The Dain Curse* was on top of the stack. The clothes on the back of the Queen Anne chair, her gray sweater with the leather patches crowned that pile. The slippers at the foot of the bed, the bottle of Joy on the vanity, the haphazard arrangement of books on their shelves.

I wandered over to them and was surprised to find an open book on a lower shelf that looked like a diary.

Then I remembered that Philomena had spent the night in the room recently. Was it her diary?

I picked it up and read the open page.

> I was out this morning, headed down the path toward the woods, when I noticed a single cumulus cloud overhead, standing still. I stopped to look at it, and when I did, I saw that it was actually moving very slowly, so I wondered if I'd been walking just right to match its speed. I started up again and found the perfect rhythm to make the cloud seem to stop moving, walking at the speed of cloud. And, as I did, a song came into my head to match the tempo of my feet. It was something

that the Episcopal church choir sang called "Strike Up
Your Instruments of Joy." So there we were, the three
of us, the cloud, the song, and I all in synchronicity.
And when I realized that, I had the overwhelming sensation that everything was like that. Everything was
moving at the same speed. Everything was one thing.
That feeling has passed now, of course, as I write this.
But it was there, and it was palpable. Proof enough for
me of some sort of grand, universal instruments of joy,
whose sounds are still ringing in my ears.

That was Rose. This was her diary. I held it motionless in
my hand for a moment. First, I wanted to sit down and read it
all. Then I wanted to close it up and put it in between some of
the other books on the shelf. I wondered if it had been open
like that because Philomena had been reading it and I had an
unwanted pang of sympathy for Philomena.

Then Gloria called me.

"Come on down, Madeline," she sang. "The kettle's on."

I closed the book and set it down. I went to Cannonball,
who ceased his activity just long enough to accept my scratch-
ing his chin. I left Rose's room trying hard not to admit to
any of the emotions that were swirling around me. Focus on
coffee. Focus on telling Billy who murdered Tandy. Better yet:
focus on David Madison. *There* was a focus worth focusing on.

Okay, maybe the whiskey had gotten to me just a little bit.

Down the stairs and into the kitchen. The smell of the
coffee in the press was more welcome than a day off. The
sight of *Father* Coleman's smile was more warming than a
Christmas fireplace. Or maybe I was just relieved that there
wasn't an intruder in my house.

And there it was again: *my* house.

"Grab a chair," Gloria told me just as the electric kettle beeped. "I'll do the honors."

I was still too keyed up to sit, so I paced while she poured the hot water into the press and brought the press to the table. There were already two pretty little hand-painted cups in evidence.

"Where did you find these?" I asked, examining the cups.

"They were behind the big Dutch oven down there, for some reason." She pointed to the lowest drawer in the dish cabinet next to the stove.

"Pretty," I said. "What made you look there?"

"I remembered Rose going there once," she answered, taking her seat. "I think it was my first or second time in this house, right after I got here, got to Enigma. She told me it was her secret hiding place, where she kept the best things, strictly for the most important visitors."

"Rose had a knack for flattery," I said.

"She did," Gloria agreed, "and I was flattered. But more than that, it was the first time I felt welcome here in Enigma. Made a real difference to me."

I sighed because Rose made that kind of real difference to so many people.

"Look," I said to Gloria, coming to a momentary standstill. "I'm sorry I got all weird and made you come over here for nothing."

"It wasn't nothing," she said, avoiding eye contact. "It was hilarious."

She tried and failed to stifle a laugh. And what could I do but join her?

"God, you must be a great priest," I said at length. "My jitters are almost gone, I'm laughing, I'm about to have some coffee."

"*That's* nothing," she insisted.

"No," I said. "*That's* a lifesaver after my close encounter with, you know, murder boy."

On cue the front door rattled and Billy called out, "Madeline?"

"In the kitchen," I answered.

Seconds later, there he was, a little red in the face and clearly agitated.

"What's going on?" he asked curtly. "What's your car doing at the church? And what's this about new information?"

"Coffee?" Gloria offered before I could respond.

He paused, sighed, and said, "I'd take a cup."

Then Billy looked at the cups on the table.

"Uh-oh, y'all in trouble now," he said. "That is Rose's secret personal china."

We both looked at him. He sat, so I joined him at the table.

"How would you know about that?" I asked him.

He laughed. "She hauled it out once, long time ago, when I was over here to introduce her to Cindy Perkins, my fiancée. Rose made a big fuss about it, made Cindy feel special. It's what they call Flora Danica. That's the pattern. All the way from Copenhagen. In Denmark."

"I know where Copenhagen is," I said. "I'm just impressed that you know about this china."

He sobered lightning fast. "See, that's the kind of thing that gets my goat. The assumption that just because I'm from a little town in South Georgia I wouldn't know about expensive china."

"Or where to find Copenhagen," I agreed.

"Or who Shakespeare is," he went on.

A startling coincidence, considering that I'd just had the

same conversation with Bo, but I knew I needed to stay focused.

"Sorry," I said contritely, choosing to bond with Billy.
"You're completely right. I *hated* when that happened to me
in New York. Which it did a lot. In fact it was among the main
reasons I went back to Atlanta after such a short time in New
York."

Gloria produced a third cup and pushed the plunger on
the French press.

"What happened to Cindy Perkins?" she asked Billy. "You
said she was your fiancée, but you're not married now, that I
know of."

"She got hitched to Bobby Barnett," he said right away.
"He's from over at Omega. Owns a feed store."

"Am I sorry to hear that?" I asked him.

"Not even a little bit." He smiled, but he didn't elaborate.
"So what's this new information you got? Apparently, Gloria
made it sound important on the phone."

"Oh, that," I said, feigning nonchalance. "It's just that Bo
Whitaker confessed to Tandy's murder."

Billy just stared. Gloria poured out three cups of coffee.
Seconds ticked by.

He finally said, "Say what, now?"

"Okay," I began, "after I saw you at the diner, I decided to
pay another visit to Bo—"

"*What?*" he interrupted. "Darn it, Madeline—"

"It was your idea! You said he was your suspect!"

"That don't mean you can go—"

"Just let me tell you what happened!" I insisted. "And, by
the way, it confirmed that you were right about him, and I
was wrong, because he really is kind of a rat."

"Madeline . . ."

He seethed. He sucked in a breath. I took the opening and told him everything. Then I held out my hands; I'd proved my case.

He looked at Gloria, then he looked at me.

"That's all he said?" He glared. "'I didn't mean to hurt her.'"

"Yes!" I told him.

"No." He shook his head. "That ain't hardly a confession, Madeline. That could mean at least ten other things."

"Like what?" I asked, irritated.

"Like maybe he was sorry he hurt her feelings," he snapped. "He might be a rat, but he's also a sensitive boy."

I looked at Gloria. "No. Tell him."

Gloria sipped her coffee. "Actually, I said the same thing as Billy, if you'll recall."

"What's the matter with you guys? Bo killed Tandy!"

"It's a possibility," Billy said slowly. "But drunken remorse for hurting a girl as sweet as Tandy ain't hardly a confession of murder."

"You weren't there," I raved. "You weren't in the room with him. He was dark. It was really scary."

"See," Billy posited sternly, "I like to have a little what we call *evidence* in a situation like this—murder situation. And the thing is, I never once came to Atlanta and told you what to do on the stage, so I'd appreciate it if you could leave off telling me what to do about a police matter here in Enigma."

"I'm not telling you what to do," I went on, unwilling to give up on my theory. "I'm just telling you what I heard. And it was cold and convincing."

Billy took a good slug of coffee and sat back in his chair.

"So what I've done," he said, deliberately controlling himself, "is I've checked out Bo's whereabouts on the night of the murder, for one thing. He told me that him and Elbert went up to Tifton, to that Terminal South place, it's a country music bar. Said they were there all night. So I'm checking on that. See, I talked with him, and he gave me an alibi, so I'm doing what they call my due diligence. You understand me?"

I could see how serious Billy was. I could see that his patience with me was at an end. And I could see that he really was working on the situation.

So I said, "I understand you, and I apologize. I won't go out to Bo's house again."

"Good," he continued in his severe demeanor, "because if Bo *did* kill Tandy, and you went to his house alone, I don't like your chances of getting out of there so easily as you did this time, you hear me?"

"Yes." I nodded enthusiastically. "I absolutely agree. One hundred percent."

But he still wasn't satisfied. "And Speck Dixon is a wild card too. It ain't no telling what he's liable to do if you corner him. You remember me telling you that?"

"I do," I told him. "I'll steer clear of Speck too. And if he comes here again, I won't let him in. Except, you know, if the store is open and he just comes in like a customer or something."

"Maddy," he began, more exasperated than ever.

"You know what I mean," I assured him.

What I didn't tell him was that I was a little touched that he'd called me Maddy.

He shook his head, finished his coffee, and stood. "Okay, whatever. I believe I'll go now and see can I solve this murder before you get yourself killed or give me a heart attack."

"Thank you for coming so quickly, Officer Sanders," Gloria told him, standing. "Sorry we wasted your time."

"Uh-huh." He wasn't quite willing to let us off the hook. "Also you don't seem to realize that we took fingerprint samples from all over this house, and we'll most likely get those identified by tomorrow morning."

"Fingerprints?" I shook my head. "You didn't take mine. And mine are all over the place, the crime scene . . . thing."

He blew out a breath. "You don't remember that you had to give your fingerprints when you got your cabaret license a while ago when you were doing some club work in New York?"

I blinked. "That's right. I forgot. How did you—"

"I'm a *policeman*, Madeline," he snapped. "I'm investigating a homicide in my hometown. I have access to the national fingerprint database. And I know what I'm doing."

His voice had risen considerably during his short speech.

"Billy," I said, hoping he could hear my contrition. "I sincerely apologize for making you feel that I haven't taken you seriously as a detective. That's my fault entirely. And completely. I can see that you know what you're doing and I'm sorry for being an idiot. Seriously."

He held his breath for a second, and then just shook his head, turned around, and left. We heard the front door close a couple of more seconds later.

"He didn't *quite* seem to believe me," I said to Gloria.

"No," she corrected. "He knew you weren't being honest."

I turned to her. "How do you mean?"

She lowered a priestly gaze my way. "If I could tell you had something up your sleeve, so could he. He's smarter than you give him credit for."

"I know he's smart," I said, only there was clearly an implied *but* in the sound of my voice. I could hear it.

"Are you going to stay away from Speck Dixon?"

"Yes," I assured her.

"And Bo Whitaker?"

"Umm, I don't plan to have any *direct* contact with him," I said.

"Madeline," she said. "What have you got in mind?"

"Well, Billy didn't mention Rae what's-her-name, Tandy's roommate," I told her. "I thought I might talk to her again tomorrow and see if I could get a little more information about Bo from her."

"Don't you think that would just stir things up?"

"Things are already stirred up, don't you think?" I countered.

I watched her make the decision to let it go.

"I'm going back to the church now," she said, already heading for the door.

I followed. "By the way, I noticed that you haven't put your plywood saints back up. All Saints' Day isn't far off. Did you give up on the idea?"

She turned my way but didn't stop walking. "Why do you ask?"

"Just trying to distract you from being upset with me that I'm going to talk to Rae tomorrow."

"You picked that up, did you?" she asked.

"Come on," I entreated her, "don't be mad."

"I'm not mad," she said as we arrived at the front door. "But you did kind of lie to Billy."

"I did not."

"You understood his admonition, that you were not to pursue any further investigation of Tandy's murder, and you deliberately misled him." She put her hand on the doorknob. "That's right next door to a lie."

"Man, I thought you were a fun priest," I said, "but you turn out to be kind of strict."

Her eye contact smacked me hard. "Madeline."

So I leveled with her. "I can't stand it, Gloria. I can't stand that Tandy is dead. I can't stand that it's my fault. Mine and Rose's."

"How is it your fault?"

"She wouldn't have been here in the first place," I answered softly, "if I hadn't agreed to let her stay. She'd still be alive if . . ."

I didn't even know how to finish that sentence.

Gloria took a second, then she changed the subject. "In answer to your question, Frank Fletcher is giving a little restorative attention to the plywood saints before I set them back up. One was burnt, as you know, and two others were broken in the fracas."

"Frank?"

She nodded. "He's the one who cut them out in the first place. He's handy with a jigsaw."

"You asked him to jigsaw saints for you and he agreed?"

"He volunteered. Tandy asked him to help me. She saw me out in back of the church a couple of weeks ago, making a mess of things. I outlined the guys with a Magic Marker just fine, but I turn out to be hopeless with power tools. So. Frank to the rescue."

"Huh."

"The good old saints, such as they are, will grace the front of the church sometime tomorrow, I hope." She opened the door.

"It's a weird idea, you know," I observed. "Plywood saints."

She turned around on the porch. "Rose's idea, actually. She stumbled across a gaggle of plywood santons in some church in Provence. I think they were originally crèche figures, but she gave me a couple of little saints when I first came to town and she told Tandy about them and—actually I'm not entirely certain whose idea it was, come to think of it, but there you are. I drew them, Frank cut them out, and the kids painted them. Oh, and by the way, going to talk to Rae is a really bad idea."

And that was it. She turned and walked off into the fading light.

23

THE NEXT MORNING was overcast, but I woke up in a cheery mood. I'd gone to bed early and gotten plenty of sleep. I was out of bed, dressed, and down the stairs before eight. I was actually looking forward to going over to the college campus and having another chat with Rae, finding out more about Bo. So that I could prove to Billy Sanders that what I knew to be true: Bo killed Tandy.

Bo killed Tandy. I marveled at the ease with which I'd thought those words. Six months earlier, winding up a terrible production of *August, Osage County*—so bad it actually got laughs in all the most serious places—I would never have imagined that I'd be trying to figure out who killed a sweet little farm girl in a bookshop that I owned.

Enigma didn't feel like home, exactly. It never had. The bookshop was comfortable, but it wasn't home either. Nowhere was. Maybe that's why I'd been so at ease on tour, skidding around the southeast in one show or another, sleeping in somebody's guest room with a cat tower and a disgruntled cat, or on somebody's sofa that smelled like cheese. If you don't have a sense of *home*, then you can't feel any discomfort at being away from home. All sofas were equal, all guest bed-rooms were the same.

Still, here I was in Enigma, forced into a sense of com-munity so strong that I'd taken Tandy's murder personally. And taken the idea of solving the murder so seriously that I'd done a fair number of foolhardy things. Was that what *home* was supposed to feel like—that things mattered to you? And was that, in fact, a part of Rose's grand scheme? Had she thought that making me live in the bookstore for six months would engender some kind of emotional attachment to . . . something? Was Rose still mentoring me from beyond the grave?

And because nature has a strange sense of humor, it chose that particular moment to offer me a rumble of thunder. *From Beyond the Grave.* Cue thunder. It just made me laugh.

So, coffee downed, cat bowl filled, back door locked, I was out of the house and into my car in a remarkably jolly frame of mind. As I drove past the church I saw Gloria, all by her-self, propping up life-sized two-dimensional children's draw-ings of saints for the approaching All Saints' Day. I stopped in the middle of the street and rolled down my window.

"Need a hand?" I called out.

She turned. "I think I'm okay. You're out early."

"Going over to the college," I said.

"You're really going to talk with Rae?" she asked.

"Yes."

"Okay." She turned back to her work. "Still think it's a bad idea."

"I'll fill you in when I come back," I told her.

The day was growing darker. It was going to rain. I wanted to get to the college and get inside before it did.

When I got to the campus, I was struck once again by the beauty of the landscaping, the carefully crafted plantings and the overall design of the place. There weren't very many students about, and I suddenly realized that I didn't know what day it was. That wasn't unusual. As an actor, my days always ran together. Every normal person's weekend off was always my busiest time, matinee and an evening show; Monday was my day off. So maybe it was Saturday.

But considering that it looked an awful lot like rain, maybe the students just had sense enough to come in out of the rain. Unlike me.

I parked in the lot closest to Rae's dorm. There were plenty of other cars there. As I was getting out of mine, I heard a welcome voice not far behind me.

"Hey! Student parking only!"

I turned to see David standing next to a row of newly planted young trees. His gloves were dirty, and the knees of his jeans were muddy. His hair was trying hard to go in every possible direction at once. His smile made the world forget all about the overcast sky. And everything else.

Frank was just behind him. He was down on his knees and packing in soil on top of the nearest tree. He didn't look up.

"What are you planting there?" I asked David.

"Pomegranates," he said. "Wonderful pomegranates."

I looked at the bare and scrawny seedlings. "They don't look all that wonderful at the moment, though."

His smile grew. "That's the varietal name. Wonderful. And it wasn't my idea to plant them, exactly. I'm doing this for the president of the college. He's from Maharashtra. India. They grow a lot of pomegranates there. He told me he missed seeing them. I thought maybe it would make him feel a little more at home here in Enigma when he sees them in bloom come spring."

"Oh." There it was again, the question of home. "I get that."

"They'll be really pretty, even these little guys. Nice red flowers, and, you know, the fruit."

Frank stood up then.

"Miss Brimley," he said, not looking at me. "I'd like to apologize for speaking at you the way I done the other day. David's been telling me all what you're doing to try to find out who killed my sister. And I know now how much you cared for her."

"I really did Frank," I told him earnestly. "That's why I'm here, in fact. I'm going to talk with her roommate Rae again."

Frank nodded, still not looking at me. "Okay, then."

And he returned to his work.

David sauntered my way. "You look bright and shiny this morning."

"Thanks," I said, and then I looked down at myself. I'd been so preoccupied when I got dressed that I didn't quite remember what I'd put on. Turned out to be a bright white mock turtleneck under a dark orange cashmere sweater, black jeans, and low-heeled ankle boots. Not bad.

As he drew closer, he lowered his voice. "You got something new?"

"What do you mean?"

"Last time we spoke," he said, "you were telling Frank about Rae, so I figure if you're back to talk with her again, there's something new going on. Also, you just took off without locking the house yesterday. Or, you know, saying goodbye."

"Yeah, sorry about that," I said quickly, "but, see, I was kind of in a huff, or whatever. You know Speck Dixon, right?"

"Yes," he told me tersely.

"He came to talk with me after I talked with you," I went on, rapid-fire. "He wanted to buy the bookshop, and then I went to talk with Billy to tell him that Speck was the one who threatened me on the phone, and Billy said that Bo was Speck's cousin and did dirty work for Speck, so I went to talk with Bo and he told me he killed Tandy but Billy won't believe me so I'm going to talk with Rae now to see if I can find out more about Bo so I can convince Billy to arrest him for murder."

I stopped to take in a breath.

"And also," I went on, "Philomena burned down the gazebo."

David nodded slowly. "That's a lot of information all at once. But I believe that the headline is this: Bo *told* you he killed Tandy?"

"Not in those words, exactly," he said. "He said, 'I didn't mean to hurt her.'"

More nodding. "Do *not* say any of this to Frank."

"Obviously," I said.

"And it all sounds just a little bit . . ."

When he didn't go on after too long a pause, I interjected. "Crazy?"

"Not exactly *crazy*, but it does sound like parts of it are just a little bit half-baked," he said.

"Well, that's why I'm here," I told him. "So I can fully bake . . . things."

"And Rae's going to help with that?" He sounded skeptical.

"Yes." I tried to sound more certain about it than I actually was. Who knew what Rae was going to say?

But before we could say anything more, Frank hollered, "Pine straw or nuggets?"

David turned his way, then back to me. "Gotta go."

"The siren call of mulch," I said.

That got another smile. "Exactly."

"I'll find you after I talk with Rae. Could you grab a coffee with me or something?"

"I think I could swing that," he said.

"Bye, Frank," I called out.

"Miss Brimley," he said, not looking up.

David returned to his work, and I made my way to the North Hall dorm in the chilly wind.

The inside of the building was a little too quiet. I tried to move up the stairs as silently as I could. When I got to the top, I could see that Rae's door was open.

I approached carefully. There was no sound coming from the room. I stood to the side of the door and peeked in.

There was Rae, wrapped in a quilt, leaning over her desk, squinting.

"Hi," I ventured.

She looked up, startled.

"It's only me," I continued, waving.

She tossed off her quilt and stood. She was bundled in gray sweats and shod in high-top tennis shoes.

"What do *you* want?" she growled. Honestly. Growled like a big old hunting dog.

"I just wanted to talk with you a little bit more," I said quickly.

But she stopped me. "You stay away from Bo, you hear me? He said you was out at his house yesterday. What are you doing?"

"I was just—"

"You're too old for him," she snapped. "Don't you know that?"

I tilted my head, just like another dog would. "I do know that, and I'm not interested in him not one little bit. Not in that way."

"That's what you *say*," she huffed. "But you been out to his place twice just since you pestered me!"

"I want to know about Tandy!" I said, matching her volume, if not her ire. "That's all. That's why I'm here now. To talk with you about Tandy. I can't get her out of my mind."

She let go a breath, and a fair amount of her irritation. "Yeah. Well, join the club. I can't get shed of her either."

She shifted her weight to one leg and for a second, she looked like she might cry.

"I was thinking I'd have some kind of memorial service for her at the bookshop," I said, making it up as I went along. "And since you knew her . . . and, sorry, according to what you told me, Bo knew her too, I thought I'd ask you both to tell me a little more about her. So I could do it right, you know?"

"Tandy." Rae sat down, staring off into space. But her voice wasn't sad. She was still angry, only not at me.

"She thought she was really something," she continued. "We been friends since grade school. Or anyway we were kind of *like* friends."

I took a second and stepped inside the door. "I don't know what that means."

"We were always in competition with one another, I guess you'd say." She was slowing down, maybe running out of steam. "Every year at the county fair, for an example. *Every* year. She beat me every time. Best peach pie. Best fried okra. Best biscuit."

I started to offer my two cents on the glory of Tandy's biscuits but immediately realized it would only make the situation worse.

"Then when I was eleven," Rae went on, "I raised this little baby pig, cutest thing you ever saw. I just knew she was going to win the piglet contest. I got all dressed like it was Sunday. I mean I *knew* my pig would win. I called her Baby Bee."

She stopped, lost in an old and obviously tired memory, often repeated, always regretted.

"But Tandy had a pig too?" I prodded. "She won?"

"No." Rae's voice had turned hopeless. "I won. But nobody took no notice of it. Nobody saw."

"I don't understand. Why not?"

Rae heaved a sigh that could have broken the walls of Jericho.

"Tandy was sitting on the rail fence around the area where the piglet contest was. She was there to, you know, cheer me on or whatever. And then along come that big fat Elbert Mooney and sat down beside her on the fence. He was a big 'un even back then. And Tandy said, 'Look at how pretty Rae's little pig is.' And Elbert said, 'It ain't near as pretty as you, Tandy Fletcher.' Well. Tandy had never had such a compliment as that from a boy before, so she kissed him. Kissed him flat on the jaw. He was so surprised that he fell off the fence into the competition area and everybody run over to him right at the very *minute* they said I was the winner! Nobody paid me the slightest nevermind."

I did a fair job of holding back my laughter for a second or two, but the image of Elbert being so startled by Tandy's kiss that he fell into the pig contest was more than I could withstand, and I finally broke down. Belly laughing.

"It's not funny!" And Rae was instantly back to being

mad. "It happened every time! Tandy was always the *good* one. When I was lonesome, Tandy let me stay with her. When my grandma died, she took care of me. When I was afraid to come here to college, she told me she'd be my roommate. She thought she was such a saint. But let me tell you. Like, for another example, when we was in high school one day, she told me she'd *help* me to make biscuits. Like mine was no good! So we got into a fight. A fistfight. I mean I swung at her like a gate! But she cheated. She moved! I broke a display case in the front hall of the school. I got suspended! All they done to Tandy was to take her to the nurse."

"Why did they take her to the nurse?" I asked tentatively.

"She got cut by flying glass when I broke the case!" Rae continued. "Everybody was so worried about her, and they did not give me a second thought!"

I could see that she was set to rail about Tandy all day long, so I tried to ease her into a transition. Or, really, just get her to talk about what *I* wanted to talk about. "That's why you were so upset when you thought Bo was interested in Tandy. I get it now."

"He *was* interested in her!"

I shook my head. "I don't think so, Rae. I think he was just trying to get next to her to help out his cousin Speck."

"Bo just works for Speck to get money," she told me, still hot, "same way he cooks meth."

"I can understand that," I said, hoping to sound sympathetic.

"He needs him some money," Rae continued. "He wants to get a degree. Like I do. College takes money."

"I know." Pouring out more concern.

"I couldn't be here at Barnsley at all if it wasn't for my scholarship money."

I did my best not to sound surprised. "You're here on a scholarship?"

She nodded. "Georgia Foundation for Agriculture gives me some money to study veterinary, and Gilbert's gives me the rest."

"Gilbert's is . . . what?"

"Gilbert's Large Animal Veterinary Clinic up in Tifton." She said it like I was the stupidest person she'd ever met. *Everybody knows Gilbert's.*

"You're going to be a vet," I concluded.

"I'm good with animals," she said, calming down a little. "Matter of fact, I like animals better than most people."

I smiled. "I'm with you there. Although a lot of the people I know could technically be considered animals. Have you ever eaten with an actor?"

She didn't think that was as funny as I did. She seemed to think I was making a scientific point.

"Pigs have all of the same thoracic and abdominal organs as a human person does," she told me, dead serious.

"Oh. I didn't know that." I gathered my thoughts. "So you're going to be a vet. That's fantastic. What's Bo want to be?"

"Bo?" She settled a little bit more. "He just wants to settle down. Maybe he don't see that yet, and I know he's a little wild right now. But if he gets enough money, and I get me that job at Gilbert's, we can find us a nice little place. You know, some acreage, just enough for a kitchen garden and some stock and all. He'd be just fine after that."

Her voice had gone from bilious to dreamy in five seconds flat.

"You've talked about it with him?" I asked. "About getting a little farm?"

"Uh-huh." She was staring into space. Or, more likely, staring at her farm fields, and livestock, and all the little chickens in the garden.

It hurt my heart to watch her face. I had the impulse to tell her about all the hardship that could be packed into a dream like hers, and then I realized that I'd stifled the very same urge to tell Tandy not to get her hopes up about a grander life. Rae was just a version of Tandy: a small-town girl with big-time dreams. Only with Rae the dream was so much smaller, as sweet and achievable as it was impossible and heartbreaking. Not just because farm life was backbreakingly hard and economically perilous, but because Bo didn't really want that. I had seen it on his face. Bo wanted out.

I knew what that looked like. I'd seen it a million times when I'd been a teenager in Enigma. Right there in the mirror.

So I tried to go easy on Rae. "Are you sure that's what you want? If you're a vet in Tifton—"

"I know what I know," she assured me, still nestled in the contentment of her imagined future.

"Look. Bo has a temper," I pressed.

"No, he don't," she said. "I mean, does he get mad sometimes? Sure. But when he gets mad at me, I get mad right back and it don't ever amount to much, so what'd I care about that? I can handle myself!"

And she was ramping up again. That was my fault.

"No," I ventured, "I was just saying . . ."

A momentary silence pervaded the room.

She looked away. "So. Maybe I'm the one with the temper. And sometimes it comes out the wrong way. Especially if I had a drink or two. And then maybe I feel, you know, guilty about being mad at Tandy when she was never a thing in the world but nice to me. And now she's dead and I can't . . . I can't say nothing to her about it. And I miss her. Miss her like *fire*."

I tried commiserating. "I understand all that. I recently thought the same kind of thing about my parents. And I think I'm a little mad at Rose for dying, for being *so* gone, for making me miss her so much."

But she shook her head. "That ain't the same thing at all. You got used to missing your folks and your aunt from being away from Enigma for a hundred years. This is all *right now* for me. Me and Tandy."

"Okay, but we were talking about Bo," I said quietly, still trying to get her on track.

"Okay, now *that*, see," she began, her mood shifting again, "that was maybe more my problem than anything else. When I watched him flirt with Tandy, I could see that she'd never sleep with him. And I knew that I would. And if I did, he'd belong to me. You know how *boys* are."

I sighed. "I'm familiar."

"So." That was all she had to say on the subject.

It came to me then how many people had lied to me since I'd been back in Enigma. Or kept things from me. Rae hadn't been at all honest about Bo. Tandy hadn't told me about spending all those nights in the bookshop. Rose had a hidden codicil, Billy had a hidden investigation, and David had a hidden Faye. And worst of all, Philomena Waldrop burned down my gazebo and hid it from me!

On the surface, small towns can seem so simple, but they're not. Behind every smile there could be an unspoken resentment. Every kind word was a possible pretense. Every action had more than one motive. Everybody had secrets and lived with the dull fear that those secrets would be found out. That's what made Rose so odd. Her smile was just a smile.

Her kindness was genuine. Everything she did was spontaneous and without a drop of malice aforethought. And she revealed absolutely *everything* about herself. All the time. No matter how embarrassing it was for her to tell or me to hear.

Maybe it hadn't been any different in New York, or Atlanta, all the little daily lies. Maybe it was just that there was so much else going on, I hadn't had time to notice how many things people were hiding. Or maybe there was some law of physics that I didn't know about: when there's less to do there's more to hide. Or maybe it was just like what an actor told me about teaching part time at a university. The arguments were so fierce because the stakes were so small. I'd taken it as a laugh line when she'd told me. But in that moment, I could see the serious side of it. Maybe that was Enigma. The lies were so big because the town was so small.

That was the revelation: that I couldn't really take anything at face value. No matter what anyone told me, there was probably something else going on under the surface.

So I changed course with Rae again.

"How are your classes going?"

"Umm." Rae glanced down at the book she'd been studying when I'd come in. "I won't lie to you; they could be going better. I have been drunk a *lot* of this semester. But, see, I've had a lot going on."

"You have," I agreed, mostly to keep her talking.

"It's one thing dealing with an animal in person," she continued. "It's a whole other thing to read about it in a book and write it down on a test."

"That's true."

Rae looked up at me for the first time since I'd come into her room.

"Tandy told me that she was so good in school because she read so much. You reckon that's true?"

"Well." I smiled. "I own a bookshop. I kind of *have* to say that's true, don't I?"

She gave me a little upturn in the corners of her mouth. "Right."

"Rae?"

"Yes?"

"I'm not one bit interested in Bo," I told her softly. "Not one little bit. Swear."

She nodded. "I just—I get jealous. Can't seem to help it."

"But here's the thing," I heard myself say. "I think Bo might have killed Tandy."

I hadn't planned that. It just came out of my mouth. I couldn't seem to help it.

Rae looked like I'd hit her with a bowling ball. Her head thrust forward; her eyes clouded over. She looked like she was about to throw up.

"I'm only telling you that—" I began.

"You have to get out, now," she said, barely above a whisper.

"He told me he did it," I tried again.

"You better get out *right* now." It wasn't a warning. It was a threat.

She stood. I saw the look on her face. I understood the situation. I backed toward the door.

"Sorry," I said, holding up my hands. "Seriously, Rae—"

The wail that came out of her then cracked all the air in the room wide open. It was a primal eruption of sound. It was a mythological howling. It wasn't a human voice.

It was also very, very loud.

I took two quick steps into the hall. She came at me

preternaturally fast, and I backed away some more, but she slammed the door right when she got to it. Slammed it with such force that the wall around it shook and the door frame cracked just a little.

Here and there a couple of heads poked out from other rooms on the hall.

I waved. "It's just Rae. She's okay."

Everyone nodded. Just Rae, most likely grieving Tandy. They all vanished as suddenly as they'd appeared, and I cursed myself for handling the interview so poorly. Cursed myself all the way down the stairs and up to the front door of the hall.

I stopped there because it was pouring down rain. There was no one outside. David and Frank were gone. The newly planted pomegranate trees stood shivering and forlorn in a row. The sky was slate, the wind was up, and the whole world suddenly looked very cold.

24

THE DRIVE HOME was hard. The rain was so heavy that I couldn't see. I had to pull over for a few minutes, blinkers on, and just wait. Wait and fret.

Fret about Rae's reaction to my visit, fret about Bo's confession that no one believed, fret about losing Philomena, who was family—all colliding in the big question. Why did Rose leave her bookshop to me, and why had I *ever* thought that moving back to Enigma would be a good idea? Sure, I wasn't getting cast as much as I used to in Atlanta, but, really, was a job in catering all that bad?

The rain didn't stop, but at least it let up a little, enough to be able to see more than three feet ahead. So I got back on the road and wended my weary way homeward, depressed that I had even considered catering.

As I drew nearer to Gloria's church what I *wanted* to do was go home, get into sweats, go back upstairs, get into bed with Cannonball, and stay there until spring. But I'd said I would stop by on my way home and given how little veracity there was in my life at that moment, I thought I really ought to keep my word.

So, right turn into the church parking lot, off with the

windshield wipers, off with the engine, I took hold of the door handle. It was still really coming down, though, and I had no intention of getting my cashmere wet. What to do?

I just sat there for a while, tried to make it stop raining just by repeating the magic words *come on* over and over again. Didn't work, not even a little bit. It may have even made things worse.

Just as it entered my mind to crank up Igor and go home, the bold red front door of the church popped open and Gloria emerged in her priest costume, a huge umbrella over her head. The thing had to have been six feet across.

She waved and scurried my way.

"Saw you sitting out here," she hollered over the rain. "Luckily, I have an umbrella big enough for a brass band."

She arrived at the car and held the umbrella over the driver's side door. I grabbed my key and slinked out of the car and into the elements. Gloria and I huddled together and made a dash for the open church door. Our feet and legs got wet, but my cashmere was saved.

Inside the vestibule, door closed, the roar of the rain shut out, I gave Gloria a wholehearted hug.

"Saved my life," I told her, "with this, the world's largest umbrella. It wasn't raining when I left."

"Man, it's really coming down now," she said, collapsing the umbrella and standing it in the nearest corner. "Coffee?"

I nodded. "I'd like a gallon, please. I had a very tense encounter with Rae."

"Your face—you *look* a little tense."

"And yet," I countered, "I must have coffee."

She smiled. "Yes, you must."

We hurried through the church and back to Gloria's office.

"Did you ever see that movie *The Bishop's Wife*?" I asked her.

"Sure," she answered, going to what appeared to be an ancient Mr. Coffee machine. "Cary Grant's an angel."

"Right." I sat in one of the leather club chairs. "Your office, this office, reminds me of the bishop's office in that movie."

"Huh." She looked around the room. "I can see that. It's all the dark wood, don't you think?"

"Probably."

"So, you talked to Rae even though a priest told you it would be a bad idea," she said, attending to the machine, "and look what happened: it started raining like it was the last days and you had a difficult encounter with a college girl. So it turned out to be a bad idea, see?"

I slumped down in the chair. "It wasn't *exactly* a bad idea. But it did not have the desired outcome."

"You wanted to learn more about Bo," she said.

"But instead I learned more about Rae," I told her. "And some interesting stuff about her relationship with Tandy."

"But it didn't get you any closer to proving that Bo killed Tandy," she assumed.

"Right." I shook my head. "All it really succeeded in doing was to get Rae all riled up. She made a sound that I would not care to hear again."

The coffee machine started making its own noises then, and Gloria came to sit next to me in the other club chair.

"What set her off?" she asked.

"Yeah. Okay. That was my fault entirely. I told her that I thought Bo killed Tandy."

"Uh-oh."

"And she turned into Godzilla," I went on.

"Lots of people have that kind of protective instinct when a loved one is threatened, I think." Gloria crossed her legs. "That's not so weird."

"You weren't there," I insisted. "She was, like, transformed. It was scary. And besides, I didn't threaten him, I called him a murderer."

"All right then, let's say you insulted someone she loved." Gloria gave the coffee machine a glance. "Rae's not entirely stable anyway, from everything I've learned about her. I think you kind of have to give her a break. That's why I didn't think it was such a hot idea for you to talk with her in the first place."

"What do you mean?"

"She lost both of her parents at a very early age," Gloria told me. "When she was in high school, she lost her grandmother, the person who raised her. And her best friend and college roommate just got murdered. She drinks too much, and she doesn't quite understand boys. Or college. Or life. So, as I was saying, I think you have to give her a break."

"You've been asking around about her," I assumed.

"I have." She stood.

"Why?"

"Because she strikes me as a lost soul, and, you know, that's kind of my job." She went to the coffee machine. "Because she seems to be someone in need."

I thought about it for only a minute before I concluded, "You've been talking to Philomena."

She had her back to me. "Yes."

"Philomena is the one who burned down the gazebo behind the bookstore," I said, cold as January midnight.

She stopped doing what she was doing for a second. Then: "I know."

"You *know*?"

"She told me yesterday," Gloria said, going back to her work. "You drink your coffee black, right?"

"She *told* you?"

"She came here, and she wanted to talk," Gloria said, "so I wanted to listen. She was completely undone. Shaking, crying—a real mess. I think she came here right after she told you what she'd done."

"Well," I grumbled, "she *should* be a mess. Look what she did!"

Gloria brought me my coffee in a gray mug that said "Jesus Saves, Moses Invests" on the side. She sat down and took a sip of her coffee. She leaned forward.

"Let's see." She set down her mug. "Philomena had a traumatic childhood and suffers the lasting physical effects of a disease that nearly killed her. She's a first-class mind teaching at a third-class college. She's getting old. She's all alone. And she just lost the love of her life. Or at the very least she just lost her best friend. That loss made her do a horrible thing out of grief and pain, and she did it to someone she also loves and has loved for a lot of years. She doesn't understand herself at all right now. She's currently lost in the wilderness of her troubled mind, and she doesn't think you'll ever forgive her, and she doesn't think she deserves forgiveness. And all of that, my good friend Madeline, is what we in the theology game call *hell*. Which is where Philomena is right now."

I didn't want to let all that into my heart. I didn't want to have sympathy for Philomena. I didn't want to forgive her.

"I guess it's good that she's got a priest to talk to, then," I said, and I could hear the petulance in my voice.

"Oh," she said, taking another sip of coffee. "I gave her the phone number of a counselor in Tifton. I'm glad she talked to me, but what she really needs is to get back in therapy."

I hesitated. "*Back* into therapy?"

"She's been in therapy most of her life; I thought you

knew that." Gloria slugged back more coffee. "Maybe there are a lot of things like that, things you don't know about her, I mean. She's really a remarkable woman."

"I don't want to talk about Philomena." I looked into my coffee mug. "I want to talk about how I can get Billy to take Bo's confession seriously. Did I tell you that Bo gave Billy some kind of phony-baloney alibi for the time of the murder? Something about a country music club in Tifton."

Gloria perked up. "Terminal South? It's great!"

"Not my point," I said. "His alibi partner is Elbert. Doesn't that sound a little made-up to you?"

She set her empty coffee mug down on the floor. "I don't know. My impression of Elbert is that he's a pretty forthright guy. And he told me the funniest joke. Jesus and Moses were playing golf—"

"Gloria!" I railed. "Is there any chance I could get you to talk with me about Bo's confession?"

She smiled patiently. "I've already told you what I think. I think Bo was sorry that he toyed with Tandy's affections. I think that he didn't mean to treat her badly. I think that when somebody you care about dies, you realize the irrevocable nature of death. You realize that you can't get that person back to tell them that you're sorry, or that you loved them, or that you wish they weren't dead. Maybe you have some of those same feelings about your aunt Rose."

I knew what she was doing. She was trying to get me to see things from Bo's perspective, from Rae's point of view, through Philomena's eyes.

But what I said was, "I reiterate my belief that you're a great priest, but not everybody can see things your way. It's just too hard."

She shook her head. "It's not hard at all. It's the easiest

thing in the world to do, to let go of a resentment, to get free from hurt feelings or angry responses—forgiveness is easy, really. It droppeth as the gentle rain from heaven."

"That's *mercy*," I corrected her. "If you're quoting Shakespeare to an actor, you have to at least get it right. The quality of *mercy* is what *droppeth*."

"Yeah," she acknowledged, "but you get my point."

"I get it intellectually," I admitted. "But I don't feel it."

"Okay," she said sweetly. "Then I'll give you a little more time. As to Billy, you told him that you trusted his abilities as a detective, didn't you?"

"But, as you so righteously believed at the time, I wasn't being entirely honest with him, was I?"

"I guess not." She picked up the mug and stood. "You need more coffee?"

"Seriously, Gloria," I said. "You didn't see the darkness on Bo's face when he said he didn't mean to hurt her. You didn't hear the sound of his voice. He did it. Bo killed Tandy."

"You also thought that Speck Dixon killed Tandy."

"And I also considered Elbert for a minute," I went on. "But—"

"You also thought that a ridiculously large cat was a dangerous home invader," she said. Sharply. "And your *first* impression of Bo was that he was in love with Tandy. And your first impression of Rae was that she was a harmless drunk, and now she's Godzilla. You're all over the map. Would you just consider a few things about your current perspective? You've been back home for less than a week, the home of your birth from which you escaped and to which you never expected to return. You're living in a strange house, dealing with the death of your beloved aunt and trying to decipher the weird behavior of your near-aunt Philomena. And while that's going on you're also trying to deal with at least three traumatic events in your life: a fire in your home, several death threats, and the murder of a sweet little kid on your brand-new doorstep."

I took a second to swallow all that and then tried to make light of her assessment. "Well, when you put it all together like that, it does seem like a lot to take, you know, for an out-of-work actor."

She nodded. "I've got the number of a really good therapist."

"You know," I said, looking away. "If I could, I'd unload that house and just beat it out of town—that would solve everything."

"The way you left Atlanta when things got difficult there." The sound of that sentence was a judge's gavel. *I sentence you to a minimum of five minutes of self-reflection.*

"That seems a little harsh," I said to Gloria.

She moved toward the coffee machine. "It also seems a little true, doesn't it?"

I said, "No." But I thought, *Yes.*

"Well," she said, "I told you that you ought to give Philomena a break, and give Rae the benefit of the doubt, so maybe I could let you off the hook too. Because you *have* had a lot to deal with here. In a very short amount of time."

"Yeah, but I guess I am kind of a mess at the moment," I admitted. "What am I doing here? And why am I running around like some cut-rate Nancy Drew? Isn't that what you said, something about Nancy Drew?"

"I guess I did mention her."

"And by the way, why would I ever need the number of a good therapist when I've got you to talk with?" I was hoping that she heard the warmth in my voice. "You really are something, Father Coleman."

She served herself some more coffee. "Yeah, I still can't quite figure out how to deal with that title. I mean, obviously *Father* isn't right. And neither is *Mother*. I believe that only belongs to Mother Maybelle Carter. And *Sister* seems a little too . . ."

"Too Baptist sounding?"

"Right." She turned my way.

"Reverend?" I suggested.

She shook her head. "Doesn't sound, you know, *Episcopal* enough."

"I get that. So what have you decided on so far?"

"Gloria," she said immediately. "I like to be on a first-name basis with everyone. I mean, how often does anybody use Jesus' last name?"

"Well," I answered, "I've had a couple of directors yell 'Jesus H. Christ!' at me."

"Did they happen to know what the *H* stood for?" she asked, returning to her chair.

"Holy?" I ventured.

She smiled. The room brightened a little and it was quieter outside.

"Rain's letting up," she said, glancing out of her one big window. "You want to go for an early lunch?"

I stood. "I think I'm going to go home now and indulge in a little good old-fashioned, down-home self-reflection. Isn't that what you were suggesting that I ought to do?"

"I probably was."

Without another word, we headed for her office door. Through the church and into the vestibule, I hesitated with my hand on the front door.

"Gloria," I said. "For the past twenty years—more than twenty—I've been used to a wayward life. Touring a show, or going from one part to another, it can make you feel rootless. You work on a show for three or four weeks, then you run it for however long it runs, and you get so close to the other people in the cast. You make best friends, you fall in love, you break up, you fight, you hug, you joke around. And then, when the show closes, it's very possible that you'll never see any of those people ever again. Ever again in your life. And it instills a sense of the *temporary* in your mind, and that doesn't go away. The downside of that is obvious: the depression of knowing that nothing will ever last. There's an upside, a kind of liberation that comes from realizing the transitory nature of *all* things. But that's really more of a philosophical realization than it is a comforting awareness."

"It sounds lonely," she said softly.

"It is," I agreed. "And it also makes it really hard to handle anything that isn't a three-week rehearsal period, or a five-week run."

"Well." She patted my arm. "Is it at least a little encouraging that your real life is now *way* more interesting than most of the plays you've been in?"

I smiled. "You don't know what plays I've been in."

"Name *one* that's more engrossing than the past couple of days in Enigma."

She had me there.

25

THE HOUSE WAS a little chilly and dark. When I first walked in, I thought about making a fire in one of the fireplaces, but I had no idea where there would be any wood. So I went to the kitchen and turned the front right burner on low and held my hands over it for a second or two.

Cannonball wandered in, deigned to give me a glance, and then wandered back out again.

"I'm retiring from the detective game," I told him as he left. "I'm no good at it."

He made no comment, but I was pretty sure he agreed with my assessment.

I stared out the kitchen window at the half-finished gazebo. For some reason I thought about an absolutely ridiculous show I'd been in called *Ashes*. I'd just gotten back to Atlanta from New York and landed the lead in a musical about the burning of Atlanta, a jolly premise for a song-and-dance show. Big budget, fantastic sets, I had seven costume changes, it was just the kind of theatre I hated, style over substance, spectacle over story. There was one number in particular called "A Brief History of Fire" that was especially objectionable. The soldiers sang it while they were torching Atlanta.

And then Sherman had a tap dance number.

The point of the play was supposed to be that Atlanta was a phoenix, risen from the ashes. The reviews were scathing. I, however, was singled out as "the one good thing about *Ashes*. Ms. Brimley, a New York transplant, steals the show." It only made me wish that someone had *actually* stolen the show way before it had gone into production. Because a review like that only served to alienate everyone else in the show from me, the "one good thing."

"Theatre stinks, Cannonball," I called out to him. "Theatre actually smells bad. The entire art form should be given a weeklong hot bath and then a one-way ticket out of town."

I guess I was thinking about that show because I was staring at the reborn gazebo, half-built, in the place where the old one had stood for a hundred years until my only living adult role model had torched it because she was crazy. I was picturing a very manic Dr. Waldrop singing, "Fire! Is! Good!"

I turned off the burner and looked around the kitchen, trying to come up with anything that would keep me from thinking about myself. Because even though I had told Gloria that I was up for a session of self-examination, it was by far the last thing I actually wanted to do.

So, go over the finances of my little bookshop!

I hastened into the other room and sat down at the desk. A little left-brain activity was just what I needed to wash away the deleterious effects of right-brain creative malarkey.

I sat. I opened the ledger. I looked down at the page. And there was Tandy's handwriting in a dozen little notes everywhere. "Madeline, we need three more copies of Janson's *History of Art*." And, "Who is Jorge Borges and why are students asking about him?" And farther down the page: "Dr. Waldrop just ordered thirty copies of *The Book of Sand* by Jorge Luis Borges. Where do we get that?"

I couldn't quite see the front door from the desk, but I could smell the lingering evidence of burnt wood. And all at once the only thing I could think about was Tandy's body lying there, and suddenly the house was colder than it had been a moment before.

Maybe Gloria had been right. Maybe I was in some kind of slow-motion shock, still dealing with Rose's death and leaving Atlanta on the run and having my life threatened and the murder of the sweetest kid I'd met in a long time.

Maybe, I thought, I should get the number of that therapist in Tifton.

And just as I thought that, there was a noise at the door.

"Hi," I said, standing. "We're not open at the moment."

I was just rounding the desk when Rae came into the room. She was in a soaking wet coat, and she was shivering. Her eyes were wild, and I could smell the alcohol on her breath even from seven feet away.

"I come to talk," she said in a dull voice.

"Geez, Rae," I said, coming to her. "Let me get you a towel. How'd you get so wet? You didn't walk here from the college."

"I went out in the rain after you left my room," she said, still sounding like a zombie. "I walked around there in the rain for a good bit. Thinking. Drinking and thinking. And then I decided to come see you. And I came in my car if it's any of your business."

"Come on in the kitchen," I said, taking her sodden arm. "I'll make you some coffee or some tea or something."

"Nuh-uh." She pulled away from me. "I come to *talk*!"

I stepped away from her a little. "Okay, I'll start. I'm sorry

I bothered you in your room. And I'm sorry I said that about Bo—"

"Don't talk about Bo!" she roared.

"Right. Okay." I backed away a little more. "Would you like to sit down?"

"You don't know," she said, slurring her words.

She began to pace. Not in any orderly way, just wandering around the room. Staggering, really. She was severely loaded.

"Bo loves *me*," she declared, trying her best to focus. "He was just messing with Tandy like you . . . like you said. It was a *job*. Job for that stump-jumper Speck Dixon. You know Speck came on to me one time over at Bo's house? Fat, greasy old man."

I felt I needed to clarify. "Stump-jumper?"

"Fat, greasy old man," she muttered again.

"He is unpleasant," I agreed.

"He's a gob of spit!"

"Okay," I said.

"He . . . he made Bo mess with Tandy. And Tandy, she's just too stupid to know what was going on. You know she wrote poems to Bo?"

"You told me," I said.

"Poems!" she snarled. "Who does that?"

"Tandy?" I suggested.

"Tandy had a home and a family and big brother who got a job at the college so he could watch out for her." Rae belched. "What did I have?"

It was clear this was going to be one of those drunken rants that started out in anger and would eventually deteriorate into sobbing self-pity and deeply sincere apologies—all of which would be completely forgotten the next day. I couldn't count the number of actors who had been in the

same condition, given me what amounted to the same mono-
logue, counted on me for some kind of solace. So I felt well-
prepared for this scene.

I said, "I'll tell you what you had. You had a good friend
like Tandy to help you. And now you're lonely and sad because she's gone. And the thing is, I am too. I really miss her
too."

That's exactly the kind of thing that would ordinarily
work. It just didn't work in this particular case.

"*You don't know!*" she repeated at twice her previous
volume.

"Rae—" I began.

"*Shut up!*" She spoke with such force that she almost fell
over. "I'll tell you about little Tandy Fletcher. Everybody
thought she was such a good-good girl. She was not."

Rae chose that moment to try to take off her raincoat. She
wrestled with it, shaking water all over the floor, but in the end,
the coat won. It was dangling from both arms, and she was
helplessly stuck.

"Come and sit down, Rae," I said. "Let me help you with
your coat."

She looked up at me. "I can't get it off me."

"I can see that. Can I help?"

She nodded, not looking at me.

I moved toward her very carefully. Experience told me
that this was a delicate moment. She could be calming down,
or she could just be taking a momentary breather. I didn't
want to get too close to her in case there was flailing. There
was often flailing in a situation like this.

I got as close as I thought was safe, took the right cuff of
her coat, and gave it a tug. Success. It dropped. I went for
the left sleeve, but she shook it hard, and the coat fell to the

floor by itself, defeated at last. She kicked it away to teach it a lesson. It skidded across the floor for a few feet, leaving a soggy trail behind. Her jeans were still soaked and even her oversized sweatshirt was a little damp.

"Good," I pronounced. "Now. You want to sit on the sofa and talk some more?

She glared at the sofa like it might give her some trouble too.

"The thing is," she said, heaving a sigh that was more of a sob, "it got to Bo, all that *Tandy* stuff. The poems and the— how sweet she was and all. You know?"

She made her way to the sofa. It wasn't easy. I sat down beside her.

"I can see how that happened," I said carefully. "Tandy kind of got to me too, and she didn't even write me a poem."

Rae stared at a spot on the floor. It wasn't any particular spot; it was just a place where she could focus on a memory.

"She wrote me poems too," she whispered.

I could hear the sadness in her voice, but there was also something else, something I couldn't quite decipher. She was slowing down, settling down—I assumed that the weeping was on its way.

She turned her unfocused gaze my way, head lowered, eyes red, and began to snarl.

"This is all your fault." There was gravel in her throat. "You and that Rose. You give them a place to meet up, Tandy and Bo. You let it happen. You *made* it happen."

I'd seen drunken actors almost that crazy. But this was different. Alarm bells went off in my head. I tried to gauge her, but I really had no idea what she'd do next.

So I moved away from her. "Rae, I don't know what you're talking about."

"Oh yes, you do." She suddenly had a dark clarity of vision. And of purpose, though I had no idea what that purpose would be.

I stood up. "I'm going to make you some coffee."

She grinned. It made her face a jack-o'-lantern in the hard slant of autumn sun.

"You know what they say about using coffee to sober up a drunk person," she growled. "It don't work. All you end up with is a wide-awake drunk."

She stood and took a step toward me.

I backed away. "Listen . . ."

But before I could form any kind of a coherent sentence, Rae shoved her hand in a back pocket of her jeans, and it came out holding a good-sized barlow knife. She snapped the blade open.

"You know what this is?" she asked me.

I took another step backward. "Looks a lot like a knife."

"See, here's what happened," she said, inching toward me. "Tandy didn't come home. I mean she didn't come to our dorm room for I don't know how many nights in a row. And when I seen her in class, I asked her about it. She said she was taking care of the bookstore because the owner died. She was living here. I bet you didn't know that!"

"I did know that," I said, "and I think you should put your knife away."

She looked down at the knife and her voice changed. "My grandma give me this knife when I was little. I used to chuck rocks at squirrels when she wanted to make Brunswick stew. It ain't really Brunswick stew unless it's got squirrel in it. She give me this knife so I could skin the things. You ever skin a squirrel?"

"No." Another careful step backward.

"It's easy. First you slit up the belly—"

"Listen, Rae," I interrupted, "you know Gloria Coleman?"

"That lady preacher?"

"Yes. She's coming over here any minute now. And I was thinking"—I backed toward the kitchen—"you might like to join us for a bite to eat or something."

"I followed him here." She ignored what I said and took another small step my way, holding the knife waist-high. "I followed Bo. He come to my dorm room to tell me to leave him be. Tell me he did not care for me. So I followed him when he left. I thought he was going back to his house, where I could give him a piece of my mind. But he came here."

I thought if I could get to the kitchen, I might find something in there to use as a weapon or some kind of defense. So I was backing away in that direction.

"Thing is," Rae went on, clearing the sofa and coming around to my left side, "Tandy already told me she was going to keep on living here, even with you in town. She said she was going to ask you and you were a nice person. Nice person. And you'd let her stay. And you did. You let Tandy stay here. And I followed Bo here."

Her sentences were beginning to run together. Her diction was increasingly slurred, and her gait was unsteady. But the blade of that knife was getting a little too close to me. Unfortunately, I had backed the wrong way and I ended up against one of the contemporary fiction bookshelves.

I had to move sideways away from the kitchen because Rae was in the way.

"Tandy told me," I said, "that she couldn't concentrate on her schoolwork in the dorm. Too much noise, too many distractions."

"Nuh-uh," Rae grunted. "She didn't stay in our room

because she was shacked up here with my Bo, sleeping together in this stupid old house!"

I took another step sideways. "That's not what Bo told
me. He said they just met here. They never slept together."

"And you believe that?" she shouted. "Is that how stupid
you are?"

"Well," I admitted, "it turns out that I'm *not* especially
bright, not about any of this."

"Huh?" She wavered.

"But like I said," I went on, "Gloria Coleman will be here
any minute now. So maybe you should put the knife away and
let's go into the kitchen and talk."

"I don't want to talk no more!"

And with that, she lunged, and the point of the knife came
toward my stomach.

I twisted around her lunge, and I twirled sideways. I'd
endured decades of stage combat training and, apparently, it
had locked itself into my muscle memory somehow.

Rae lowered her head and charged.

I swooped one step sideways and stuck my foot out just at
ankle level. She hit it, tripped, and tumbled to the floor, skidding into her wet coat.

I backed up, eyes on her. She scrambled to her feet almost
instantly, swiping her blade and making tiny little animal
noises.

I took a step her way, feinted right, and then jumped left.

She was momentarily confused, and I employed that confusion. I turned and ran for the front door.

But she was supernaturally fast, and she got to me, swiped
the blade across the back of my neck. It was a tiny cut, and it
didn't do much damage, but it stung.

I turned and popped my elbow hard into her jaw. There

was a sickening crunch and she howled. But the knife was still in her hand, and she jabbed it toward me again and cut my forearm. That hurt.

Then, without warning, I was momentarily divorced from all reality. What was happening to me was only a scene, the denouement, in fact. I only wondered, objectively, if it was the play where the killer was discovered and brought to justice, or the play where the lead got stabbed to death by a drunken college student.

I ducked low and her second swipe whooshed over my head, but I saw the dab of blood on my forearm, and that snapped me out of my theatrical stupor. I was low to the floor and very close to Rae, so I stiff-armed her flat in the stomach. She doubled over and I scrambled away.

I crashed into the dining-room area, the mystery section of the bookshop, but Rae threw herself forward, flying through the air, and tackled me. We rolled over and knocked into the sideboard where the record player was.

Her knife hand was too near my throat, so I did the only thing that seemed feasible in my panic. I bit her hand. Bit down as hard as I could.

Rae howled and I twisted away from her. I almost got away, but she grabbed my ankle. I dragged her with me for a step or two, but I couldn't keep my balance and I fell forward onto the floor again. I landed on my elbows and a pain shot up both arms.

I started kicking furiously, eyes squeezed shut, but then I forced my eyes open to see what she was doing.

Rae had managed to get herself into a sitting position and she raised her knife high above her head. She was about to come down hard. Time for my best stage trick.

I tucked, rolled into a backward somersault, landed on my feet, and stood up tall as a tree. Rae was baffled.

Unfortunately, she was also further enraged. She shrieked and launched herself toward me like a rocket. I did my best impersonation of a ballerina: the pirouette, the side step, the slide, and I found myself up against one of the bookcases.

Rae's face was red, a demon mask. She had me trapped and she knew it. She rose up slowly, wheezing like a broken accordion, and lumbered toward me.

At that exact moment Cannonball emerged from under the dining-room sideboard, awakened and frightened by all the noise, and made a dash for the next room. Rae was momentarily distracted by the streak of black. I used that moment to reach behind me and grab the fattest book I could find. I pulled it out of the shelf, held it fast in both hands, reared back, swung, and whomped Rae on the side of her head with all the strength in me, a total body effort.

I hit her so hard that she lifted off the floor, eyes rolled back. She landed down hard on the floor and the knife, at last, came free from her hand. She wasn't moving. She was out cold.

I kicked the knife away from her and then I kept kicking it all the way into the next room and under the desk.

I dropped the book there, grabbed the phone, eyes glued to the motionless form in the other room, and called Billy, called Gloria, called 911.

WHAT happened after that I couldn't have said. I know there was an interminable wait. Then Gloria showed up. Then Billy came in. Then, for no reason I could comprehend, Captain

Mike of the fire brigade—or was I just hallucinating at that point, because it was all beginning to take on the very convincing aspect of a dream.

The last thing I remembered was glancing down at the book I'd used as a weapon and laughing. It was something called *Encyclopedia of Murder and Violent Crime*.

26

THE NEXT THING I remembered was waking up in my bed with Gloria sitting in a chair at my bedside. For a second, I didn't know where I was. Then I didn't know what time it was. Then I tried to sit up.

"Oh," Gloria said. "You're awake."

"I am?" I wasn't sure.

"They said you'd probably sleep all night. And you did."

"They?"

"Well," she said, reaching for the full glass of water on the bedside table, "that nice Mike Jordon mainly."

"So he *was* here." I took the glass from Gloria and gulped. I was really thirsty. "Why was he here?"

"You called 911 and said you'd been stabbed," she said, taking the glass back. "The closest available medical unit was the one with the fire department, and he came along."

"What for?" I could hear the belligerence in my voice.

"He was worried about you." She smiled. "We all were."

I struggled a little to sit up. "Wait. So, I kind of remember that you got here first, but after that it's all kind of a blur."

"I'm not surprised," she said. "You had what they called

acute stress disorder. Your pupils were dilated, you had an irregular heartbeat, and a little difficulty moving; you said you
felt light-headed."

"Sounds about right," I said, blinking.

"Anyway, Mike also said you'd have a little cognitive fog
this morning," she added.

"Oh he did, did he?" I slumped down. "That guy *already*
thinks I have cognitive fog. What happened to Rae?"

"She was still unconscious when Billy got here," she answered. "You held up your cut arm, told him she tried to kill
you. And you also said that she was the one who killed Tandy."

"She was." I exhaled. "What happened then?"

"Billy got her up off the floor. She was *severely* drunk."

"Yes," I confirmed.

"And she was rambling. She said you bonked her in the
head."

"I did." I glanced down at my bandaged arm. "I guess
this isn't so bad, but she was about to stab me *real* good with
her—wait, did they get the knife?"

"They did," she assured me. "You made Billy get under
the desk and find it."

"I think it's the knife that killed Tandy."

"He's having it tested," Gloria said, "but that's really just
a detail, I think."

"Why do you say that?"

"Well, as I was saying, Rae babbled," she told me. "I didn't
get all of it, but the picture was pretty clear. She said that she
followed Bo here from her dorm room. They'd been fighting
and she thought she was following him home."

"But he pulled in here," I said.

"Right. Drink some more water. They said you had to
drink a lot of water."

"Hey, Gloria." I tried to sit up again. "I just realized—have you been here all night?"

"A lot of it," she said. "Drink."

I drank. Then I said, "Seriously, Gloria, I'm putting in the paperwork; you're on your way to sainthood."

She shook her head. "I'm not dead. Yet."

"You have to be dead to be a saint?"

"Do you want to hear what Rae said, or not?" she insisted.

"Yes." I slumped back down in bed.

"So she followed Bo here. They continued their argument in the yard. It must have gotten loud. The lights in the house came on. Bo said some not very nice things and then roared away in his big old truck. Tandy opened the door then. Rae was crying."

"And drunk," I assumed.

"And drunk," she affirmed. "She came in. Tandy was, well, *Tandy*: kind and consoling and caring. And so Rae stabbed her to death and set fire to the scene to 'destroy all the evidence,' she said. Something she'd seen on a television show."

"So she actually confessed to the murder?" I wanted to make sure.

Gloria nodded and sighed. "Uh-huh. A couple of times, actually. She was sobbing and shouting and—*really* in bad shape."

"That's what we call a *catharsis* in the theatre world," I said.

"Yeah, we call it that in the religion game too"—she laughed—"but I think we both stole it from Freud."

"I think you'll find it's in Aristotle's *Poetics*," I corrected her, "the original handbook of theatre, a couple of thousand years before Freud."

"Well, whatever its origin," she said, "it laid its heavy

hands on poor old Rae, and she made several very sincere murder confessions. In front of witnesses."

"She was jealous of Tandy," I said softly.

"Apparently," Gloria agreed.

"No, but I mean not just because of Bo. Bo was just the last straw. Rae had been working on it since she was a little girl."

"Okay."

"And speaking of which," I went on, "what *about* Bo?"

"Right," Gloria said. "When he heard that Tandy was dead, he *had* to have known—or at least very strongly suspected—that Rae did it. Which, according to Billy, might make him an accessory after the fact."

"And rightly so," I insisted.

"Okay, that's it." Gloria stood up. "Are you hungry? Mike said you'd probably be hungry this morning."

The second she said the word *hungry* I realized that I was starved. I tossed off the covers. I discovered I was still dressed in my clothes, which actually made me feel better about my circumstance, for some reason.

"Thanks for leaving me in my clothes," I said to Gloria.

She laughed again. "Wasn't my idea. You put up a considerable fight when I tried to get you into pajamas."

"I did?" No memory of that.

But at just the moment I realized that there was some kind of heavenly smell coming from downstairs.

"What is that I smell?" I went on, heading for the door in my stockinged feet.

"Wait!" Gloria commanded.

I stopped. I turned.

"That smell is chicken and biscuits," she said carefully, "and they're being prepared by Doctor Waldrop."

I sipped a breath and regarded the sudden war in my brain. I was still completely furious with Phil. But on the other hand, chicken and biscuits!

"I called her last night and told her what happened here," Gloria went on. "Even knowing how you felt, and what you said to her, she insisted on coming over. She sat up with you most of the night. I just came back here about an hour ago to relieve her and she went down to cook breakfast."

"Yeah." I looked down, trying to decide what to do.

And apparently Gloria could see my dilemma.

"Let me tell you your future," Gloria said. "Eventually you're going to forgive Philomena. You're going to realize that what she did, the fire thing, that was an aberration in her behavior. It's not who she really is. She's gone back to therapy now, like I said, and she's miserable about what she did. She'll get better and I don't think it will take that long. But no matter how long it takes, you're eventually going to forgive her, and I think you know that. She's the closest thing to a parent you've got left, and the closest thing to your aunt Rose that there is. So. You can take a lot of needless time and you can prolong her suffering with your righteous anger, or you can go have chicken and biscuits. My advice, as your spiritual advisor, is to take the chicken and biscuits! I mean, come on, don't you *smell* that?"

Spiritual persuasion is a mighty instrument indeed, but when it's backed up by a person's entire olfactory system, it's an irresistible force. What could I do? I was helpless.

I fairly floated down the stairs, across the floor, and into the kitchen.

And there, with her back to me, was Philomena. My beloved other aunt. My childhood refuge and the confidante of my teenage years. She was humming softly and turning shallow-fried chicken cutlets in the cast-iron skillet. She was dressed in a fancy pants suit, blue cotton, but it was protected by a fifties-style knee-length apron.

I stood there watching her, listening to her voice. She was humming "My Favorite Things" and it made me smile.

But all I could offer at that particular moment was a wan "Hello."

She spun around like a little red top. "Sweetheart!"

She ran to me, tongs still in hand, and threw her arms around me. I hesitated for one single breath, and then I burst into tears and flung my arms around her too.

Apparently, where Philomena was concerned, I'd held a billion-gallon reservoir of emotion in my belly, and it all came pouring out at once. I was the kid who fell out of the tree but didn't start crying until Mom came to have a look. I just sobbed. And all she did was hold me tighter. She didn't say a word. She just held me.

When I was done, I took a step back, wiped my face with my sleeve, and shook my head at her.

"I was so mad at you," I said.

"And I was so mad at myself," she countered.

"Well." I sniffled. "As the play says, 'There were friends, once divided; now we see them reunited.'"

From behind me I heard Gloria say, "Is that a prayer?"

"No." I turned her way. "It's a poem, Saint Ignoramus."

She shook her head and came into the kitchen. "It's not *much* of a poem."

"It's from a play I wrote when I was ten," I told Gloria.

"About Romeo and Juliet, only with an alternate ending," Philomena explained. "When Romeo gets to the crypt where Juliet is pretending to be dead, he kisses her, and she wakes up! Everyone lives happily ever after. It was a lovely play."

"I only learned, many years later," I said, taking a seat at the kitchen, "that dozens of productions of the play, especially in the nineteenth century, ended the story happily."

"Well." Gloria clapped her hands once, beaming at Philomena and me. "Who doesn't love a happy ending? Especially when there might be chicken and biscuits involved."

She took a seat next to me and stared up at Phil.

Phil took a beat, and then nodded. "All right, then."

She returned to her culinary labors.

Gloria, elbows on the table, leaned in close to me. "I'll tell you what I never saw coming."

"Rae Tucker trying to kill me?"

"Rae Tucker killing Tandy," Gloria said. "If I'd known *that*, I would have done anything to keep you from going to talk with her at the dorm yesterday."

"Yeah, but, I mean," I said, "are we a *little* stupid that we didn't know it was Rae all along?"

"I don't think anybody knew the depth of Rae's resentment, not the way she was babbling about it last night." Gloria sat back. "Who could have imagined that anyone would feel that way about Tandy."

"You know that Tandy reminded me a lot of you, sugar," Phil said over her shoulder, eye on the chicken in the skillet. "I mean when you were young. She had the same kind of get-me-out-of-this-place spirit that you had."

I looked at Gloria. "That's a kind of spirit a person can have?"

Gloria waggled her head. "I had it when I was in the swamp. The only difference between you and me is that I didn't have someone like Rose doing everything in her power to *get* me out."

"Yeah," I agreed. "I was lucky there."

Phil sighed at that, her back still to us.

Twenty minutes later the three of us were eating silently, all of our concentration on food.

I opened up my first biscuit, slathered a still-steaming chicken cutlet in honey and mustard, put it in the biscuit, and ate it like it was my last meal on earth.

Gloria chose ketchup, bread and butter pickles, and a dab of Duke's mayonnaise for her sandwich.

Only Philomena endowed our gathering with a modicum of dignity, eating biscuit—covered in butter and honey—and chicken separately, and both with a knife and fork.

And when we were done there wasn't a scrap of food left on the table. We three sat back in continued silence for a moment.

Then Philomena examined the table and shook her head. "Hours to prepare, moments to consume."

"That's your own fault," I told her. "If it hadn't been so delicious, it wouldn't have gone so quickly."

"Amen to that," Gloria mumbled.

"And in fact," I announced, "I make bold to say that these here biscuits, ma'am? They rival the sacred biscuits of the greatly sanctified Tandy Fletcher."

"Hallowed be her name," Gloria said, grinning.

Phil put her hand to her breastbone. "What a nice thing to say. And only a smidge sacrilegious."

"Which is far less than you've come to expect from the likes of me," Gloria volunteered.

"Exactly my point," Phil said, getting up to clear the dishes.

"Wait a second, Phil," I said. "Would you sit back down?"

She hesitated, then sat. "Yes?"

It was clear from the look on her face that she was expecting some sort of rebuke from me, or some harsh words at the very least.

"I was just thinking," I went on, "that I'd give our old pal Rusty the lawyer a call in a minute to see if we can make the bookshop . . . co-owned, or whatever. Put it in your name too. Your name and my name together. Would that be something—"

But I had to stop because Phil started crying, her left hand resting on the table, shaking, her right hand going for a tissue in the pocket of her apron.

"That would be . . ." she began. But she couldn't finish her thought.

"It only seems fair," I began.

"That would be . . ." she said again. But once again she couldn't quite manage to conclude her sentence.

"Okay, so just nod yes if it's okay for me to call Rusty about this," I said quickly.

"That would be wonderful!" And the waterworks came on full.

I put my hand on hers. She sniffled and just kept shaking her head. All we could do was sit there while Gloria cleared the table.

After a while I wanted to change the atmosphere in the room, so I got up and started washing dishes. Phil grabbed a towel and began to dry them. Gloria stood by for a minute, just watching us, before she announced her departure.

"Okay," she said, "I've got a church to run. It's Sunday morning, you know."

"It is?" I turned. "Look. Thanks for staying with me last night. Both of you."

"I'll just remind you that Mike Jordon said things would be a little weird today," Gloria said.

"Cognitive fog, like you said." I nodded. "I think I'm all right."

Gloria looked to Phil. "You'll watch her?"

Phil put her hand on my shoulder. "Of course I will."

I looked at both of them and I said, "I don't like being taken care of!"

But that was a lie. It felt really good.

"I'm gone," Gloria said, turning away from us. "Those plywood saints aren't going to set themselves up. At least I don't *think* they are."

"Yeah, but wouldn't that be something if they did?" I asked. "You'd get a lot of new customers."

She stopped and turned back around. "They're parishioners, not customers."

"'You say potato,'" I sang.

She just shook her head and left.

"It's fun joking around with a priest," Philomena observed. "Our previous one, Father Bott, he was no fun at all."

"Gloria's really something," I said, returning to my dishwashing duties.

"Isn't she." Phil sighed.

I stopped what I was doing and stared into the sink. "I'm sorry you lost Rose."

She took in a long, slow breath, and held on to it a second before letting it go. "I'm sorry *you* lost Rose."

"As luck would have it," I picked up again, "we still have her beloved bookshop to look out for."

I could see her smile out of the corner of my eye.

"Yes, we do," she whispered. "The good Old Juniper Bookshop."

"Long may it wave," I declared. "By the way, I've been meaning to tell you. I love that you're wearing Joy."

She looked my way. "What?"

"Rose's perfume," I said.

"I'm not wearing Joy, not today," she said slowly. "I thought you were."

"I haven't worn *any* perfume in fifteen years," I assured her.

And yet there it was, that unmistakable scent. We both knew it was there. But neither one of us said another word about it.

27

AFTER THAT, THE morning began in earnest. David and Frank arrived, and noisy work resumed on rebuilding Philomena's Folly, which was *definitely* what I was planning to call the new gazebo. College students began to wander in, mill around, some of them obviously looking for evidence of the rumors they'd doubtless already heard about the previous evening's adventures. It seemed like a lot of activity for a Sunday morning in Enigma, Georgia.

I recognized two of the students from my campus visit, the girl with the owl glasses, and the one who'd laughed at my "process server" line. That one was wearing another turtleneck sweater. Coulter Jennings came in, head down, eyes on the floor, and moved toward me sideways.

"Mary Oliver poems?" he whispered.

I nodded and went to the poetry section. I was very happy to see Idell Glassie kneeling in the corner to scratch Cannonball's chin.

After that, Philomena and I argued for a minute about leaving me alone in the shop. She wanted to go to church but she wasn't going to leave me. In the end, I prevailed by pointing out that David Madison was right there in my own backyard. She was reluctant, but she admitted that she didn't feel at all good missing church. So she took off and I settled down at the desk.

It was oddly soothing to watch the people idling about the shop. Even though no one seemed to be buying anything.

But I could only sit there doing nothing for so long before I got impatient. I didn't feel like looking at the shop's financial stuff, which is what I should have been doing, so I picked up the phone and called Rusty Thompson instead, see if he would be there on a Sunday morning.

His office phone rang nine times before someone answered, and it wasn't anyone who'd answered any other time I'd called.

They said, "Law offices of Russell Thompson."

Very businesslike.

"Hi," I said, "this is Madeline Brimley calling Rusty. Could I speak to him for just a second if he's there?"

"What is it regarding?"

I didn't know why the cold professional approach irritated me, but it did.

So my answer was, "Tell him a drunken college student stabbed me last night and I hit her in the head with a book."

There was a long pause.

"Excuse me?" the voice intoned.

"It's regarding the Old Juniper Bookshop in Enigma."

There was another shorter pause before a very perfunctory, "Hold please."

I held.

And while I was holding, the girl in the turtleneck sidled up to the desk.

"We heard about Rae and all that. Are you okay?"

I held up my bandaged arm. "I'm great. I'm going to have

a cool scar. I can't believe how fast gossip gets around in this town."

"Why did you think there were so many people here on Sunday?" She squinted. "I thought you were from here. Your aunt Rose was, like, the main topic of gossip in the entire county."

"She probably was," I agreed. "I was just blissfully unaware."

"And then you went to New York," she said.

"Well, college and *then* New York, yes."

"I love New York." She nodded sagely. "I'm going to London."

"You are?" I smiled.

"Uh-huh," she assured me. "I got an internship at the Tate Modern."

"You're kidding." I hadn't meant to sound so surprised. "That's my favorite art museum in the world!"

"You've been?" She sounded very adult, all of a sudden.

I nodded. "I was in a production of *Beowulf* at the National."

That got her. "The National Theatre in London?" She sounded like a kid again. "Cool!"

"What's your name?" I asked.

She held out her hand. "Jennifer Davis."

Just as I took her hand, Rusty came on the phone.

"Madeline!" he sang.

"Rusty," I said into the phone.

Jennifer Davis nodded and backed away.

"What's this about you being stabbed?" he asked.

"Yeah, I'll tell you all about that, but we should probably be drinking when I do. I have another reason for calling."

"Okey dokey."

He was a little too chipper for my post-traumatic sensibilities, but I soldiered on.

"I'll be brief. I was wondering if I could somehow make it so that Doctor Waldrop is a co-owner of Rose's bookshop. You know, along with me."

"Well, I'll be." He laughed. It sounded like a cough.

"What is it?" I asked him.

"Your aunt Rose. Man." I could hear him shuffling papers. "Yeah, I kept it here on my desk just in case."

"Kept *what* in case of *what*?"

"There's a second part to the codicil in her will about you having to live there for six months," he said. "I couldn't say anything about it unless and until you made an inquiry of this nature, but it says that if you ask anything about Doctor Waldrop, I'm supposed to allow you to—I mean, can you believe this? I'm supposed to allow you to put it in both your names."

I sat there for a second, struck dumb.

"How is that possible?" I asked finally.

"Yeah, I know." He laughed. "I guess she knew you—and Doctor Waldrop—pretty darn good, don't you think?"

"No, but I mean how could she possibly . . ."

I trailed off, trying to fathom Rose's grander scheme. All I could come up with was that she couldn't leave the shop just to me because it was really too complicated an enterprise for one person; and she couldn't just leave it to Philomena because she was a busy college professor who could not possibly have handled a business on top of her academic work.

"Madeline?" Rusty prompted after I was silent for too long.

"Yeah, sorry. Trying to figure this out."

"So can I go ahead and get you both to sign the papers? I already had them drawn up."

"Okay." I shook my head in continued disbelief. "I guess we'll come up to your office sometime in the next couple of days, then."

"Alrighty," he said.

"Hey, by the way," I said, "how come you're in the office on Sunday morning? Are you some kind of heathen?"

"Baptist," he said instantly. "Went to the eight o'clock service. We all had to come in today on account of we go to court bright and early tomorrow morning. That big case I was telling you about."

"The one about Speck Dixon?" I asked. "How's that going?"

"I'm afraid I can't comment on it," he said cautiously. "Except that I *will* tell you we're just about to whup his entire behind."

That made me smile. "I am very glad to hear that."

"Bye, then."

And he hung up.

After the merest pause, Jennifer Davis approached me again.

"Sorry," she said, "but I just wanted to ask if you needed any help here in the shop."

I looked up at her. My hand was still on the phone.

"What do you mean?" I asked her.

"Well," she said, "I know that Tandy used to help out here, and I was just thinking that you might need someone, you know."

I nodded. "And you need a little extra cash for London."

She looked away. "Well . . ."

I stood up. "As a matter of fact, Jennifer Davis, I just might be in the market for an elfin helper. Are you good with financials?"

She nodded with an enthusiasm that would have frightened a lesser person.

"That's one of the things I'll be doing at the Tate Modern," she said quickly. "And if I work here, that will give me a kind of head start."

"And are you familiar with the shop?" I asked. "Do you understand the organizational system here?"

She hesitated.

"I've been in this shop a lot," she said, slowing down, "but I don't think there's anybody on the planet who understands the organizational system here. I don't think there *is* one, not in the traditional sense of the words."

She was wearing the look of someone who'd just lost a job. I knew that look well, having worn it myself so many times.

I smiled. "It was kind of a trick question. You're absolutely right, there's not much of a plan to all of this. But you at least have to know what general sections are in which rooms."

She responded instantly. "The dining room is the mystery section, and two cases of poetry, plus one wall of records. This room here, which I guess was supposed to be the parlor, is for contemporary fiction and nonfiction. The study is history, biography, and older nonfiction. The most important room, from a financial point of view, is over there, the smaller parlor. That's where the college textbooks are."

She beamed. She knew she'd gotten it right.

I stood up. "Congratulations, you passed the audition. You can start immediately. Have a seat."

She stood there momentarily, adjusted, and then stuck out her hand.

"You won't regret it," she said.

I shook her hand. "I'm not big on regrets in general, so you're probably right. You want some coffee?"

She looked around the room for a second and then sat at the desk. "No, ma'am."

Ma'am. That's *just* what you want to hear when you get to a certain age. But there it was. *Ma'am*.

"Okay," I said, walking away. "I'll be in the kitchen."

She said something that I didn't hear but I just kept walking.

The light in the kitchen was autumn gold, the previous night's rain forgotten. There was still a little coffee in the dregs at the bottom of the French press, so I found a mug and poured. It was cold but I drank it anyway. While I was staring out the back window. At David.

I tossed back the last sip. There were a few bitter grounds. That seemed perfect for what I had in mind. Because I had in mind to go into the backyard and talk with David.

About this alleged *Faye*.

28

THE AIR OUTSIDE was crisp as a cold apple, and rain washed. Frank was on his knees doing something in the muddy ground and David was concentrating on a large piece of drafting paper, presumably the design of the new gazebo.

I was almost to where they were before I realized I was still wearing yesterday's clothes, slept in and wrinkled and probably dabbed, here and there, with a little of my own blood. Mangled dark orange cashmere sweater, rumpled black jeans all twisted around, and a pair of boiled-wool slippers that I didn't even remember putting on.

Just as I turned to run back inside, Frank saw me and stood up.

"Madeline." He was moving toward me.

David looked up from his paper. "Hey!"

Frank kept coming. "I heard you caught Tandy's killer last night."

I supposed that was one way of looking at it.

"Umm . . ." I began.

"Amazing work," David chimed in, also coming at me.

I was trying to put words together in my head that would disabuse them both of the idea that I'd done anything about

Tandy's killer. Except that I'd almost gotten killed by her myself.

But Frank arrived right in front of me, and he clearly had something on his mind.

"I need to apologize to you again," he began, softly and a little sheepishly. "I was not polite to you the other day, and that is *not* like me. I had a better upbringing than that. And plus, you almost got killed last night by that Rae Tucker, but you took her down instead. And she murdered my sister."

"I was just—"

"If it had been me in your place," he went on, "I'd be in the jailhouse right now, because I would have killed her."

"The thing is—"

"So I mean to say thank you for catching the person that took Tandy away from us," he concluded, "and for keeping me out of a life in prison."

He took one more second in silence, thinking, and then nodded, satisfied with his speech. Without another word or a glance my way, he returned to his work.

David smiled as he watched Frank go.

"I think he's been rehearsing that in his head all morning," David whispered.

"It was a good speech," I said. "Look. Have you got a second or two?"

He nodded. "Tell the truth, I've been dying to come in and talk with you. But since you are currently the town hero, I didn't know if you could spare me the time."

"Please shut up," I told him gently.

"I saw you talking with Doctor Waldrop in the kitchen earlier," he said. "I guess you've arrived at some kind of understanding about her pyromania."

I smiled. "I guess we have. You know, when it's someone

you really love, it probably doesn't matter what they've done, you have to forgive them, don't you?"

He looked down. "Most of the time."

"So, will you come sit on the front porch with me or not?" I asked him.

"Front porch?"

"It's the only place I can think of where I can keep an eye on things and still have a little privacy at the same time." I lowered my voice. "I don't want to ask you my question in front of Frank, and I don't want any of my so-called customers to overhear."

"There's a question?"

"Oh," I assured him, "there's a question."

Without further conversation we went back inside and through the kitchen into the parlor, where Jennifer waved at David.

"Hey, Mister Madison." She offered him a shy smile.

"Hello, Jennifer," he said.

I just kept moving. Through the house and onto the front porch. I took a rocking chair, he remained standing.

"You don't want to sit down?" I asked.

"Is this a question about the gazebo?"

"No."

"Oh." He seemed a little disconcerted by that answer. "Well. What is it about?"

I took a breath.

"It's about Faye." That's all I could say.

"Oh." He nodded and went for a chair; the color of his voice changed significantly. "What have you heard?"

"Nothing," I told him, "except that you said, 'I'll tell you about Faye sometime.' And I was hoping that *sometime* could be *now*."

"All right." He sat and stared into the front yard. "Maybe I told you that I studied organic gardening a while back."

I nodded. "With Wendell Berry. Actually Philomena told me, but you confirmed it. He's one of my heroes, you know."

"Same for Rose," he said. "You've got his books in the shop, here."

"So you went to Kentucky," I prompted.

"I went to Kentucky," he continued, "found Wendell Berry, worked on his farm, learned a bunch of stuff about compost and poetry, and it was all pretty great."

"And this relates to the aforementioned *Faye* in what way?"

"That's where I met her," he said. "At Wendell Berry's place. Are you familiar with the Dillard place, the organic farm out there?"

"I've driven past it on the highway," I said.

"Well, that's her family's place. Faye Dillard is the reason I came to Enigma in the first place."

"You came with her when she came back home from Wendell Berry's Kentucky home," I said.

"Yes." Heavy sigh. "So. Then I worked on their farm for a good while. She's the one who brought me to this place too. Rose's shop, the first time. And I can tell you that I fell for Rose like an avalanche. She was almighty fine."

"She was," I agreed impatiently. "But about this *Faye*."

"Right." He went on. "So, like I said, I was working on their farm, writing a little poetry, this and that, and it began to look like Faye and I would get married."

But before he could continue with his story, Bo's Dodge Ram and a huge tow truck pulled up in front of the house on either side of Igor.

I stood up.

"This might be uncomfortable," I mumbled to David. "Bo might be . . ."

But I didn't finish my sentence because Elbert emerged from the driver's side of Bo's pickup.

He waved and smiled. "Hey!"

"Hey, Elbert," I responded hesitantly.

"Hey, David," Elbert went on.

"Hey, Elbert." David smiled.

And then the biggest man I had ever seen in my life climbed out of the tow truck. He must have been six foot seven, easily two hundred and seventy-five pounds, and in his navy coveralls he looked like he might be made out of steel, crew cut, baby face, and all.

"This is my partner, Delmar," Elbert told me.

Delmar waved shyly.

"Hey, Delmar," I acknowledged.

"I hear you caught Tandy Fletcher's killer last night!" Elbert went on.

"Not really," I demurred. "How did you hear that?"

"Don't matter." Elbert walked my way. "The deal is, your friend George? He completely solved my exhaust system problems. Over the phone! The man is a genius."

"He's pretty great," I agreed.

"So, anyway, I ask him what I can do for him in return, and he says I got to look after your car since he's, you know, in Canada."

"Oh." I looked at Delmar, then back at Elbert. "That's not really necessary."

"Yes, ma'am, it is," Elbert said. "I promised George. He said first thing to do was bodywork on your vehicle."

I looked at poor Igor. He suffered a crumpled front

bumper, mangled passenger-side damage, and the headlight on that side hung out a little like an eye slightly out of socket. The scarred and peeling paint on the roof made it look like he was losing his hair. And his front hood was a little bunched up, like he had a broken nose.

"I'm not saying he doesn't need it—" I began.

"And it'll give me a chance to really look at that engine," Elbert went on enthusiastically. "Check out some of the parts George made. So, we'll get it up to Tifton—see, me and Delmar is about to open a garage and body shop up there in Tifton. We got all the equipment. Grand opening in a month or so. Anyway, we would either retool or replace them parts that need it, and even give it a whole new paint job. Delmar thinks he can match the original color exactly."

Delmar nodded once.

"So it would be more like a restoration project," Elbert concluded.

"This is really nice of you, Elbert," I said. "But it's too much. I couldn't possibly—"

"I promised George." Elbert was very, very serious.

Then Delmar spoke up. "It would be an honor to work on a classic such as this. It would add a certain air of distinction to our business if this were to be our first enterprise."

I'm a little ashamed to say that I gawked, eyes wide. Delmar's voice was infinitely smooth and deep, like Gerry Mulligan's baritone sax on a really beautiful ballad. And his diction was more Princeton than Enigma, more music than mechanic.

Elbert saw my face and grinned. "Delmar ain't from around here."

That was all, no further explanation.

I gathered myself. "The thing is, it sounds like this would

take a while, all that work, and I don't think I can be without a car for so long."

"That's why I brought Bo's pickup," Elbert said, then lowered his voice. "He won't need it for a while."

"What do you mean?" I matched his volume. "What happened?"

"Billy Sanders happened," Elbert said. "He come to our place late last night and took Bo in. Accessory to murder. That's how I heard what you done. About Rae."

"Yeah, about that—" I said.

"I have really *got* to do this, Miss Brimley," Elbert insisted. "It's a matter of honor."

I stood there for a second not knowing what to do or say.

So David said, "How long you think it'll take, Elbert?"

"Well," Elbert said, "since it ain't nothing else to do at the shop until we have the grand opening, I believe it won't take more than a week."

"Or two," Delmar added softly.

David turned to me. "I don't see how you can pass this up. I mean, *look* at your poor car."

I did. I gave Igor a serious looking-over. And I could have sworn he gave me a kind of pleading look back.

"Okay," I said. "I guess I really can't pass this up. And, Elbert? This is really great of you. You too, Delmar. Seriously. Free books in the shop. For life."

"Don't tell him that!" Elbert said, glancing at Delmar. "That boy reads ten or twelve books a week. You'd be out of business by next Christmas."

Delmar just laughed. It sounded like benevolent thunder.

"Well," David said, getting up. "That was fun, but I've got to get back to work."

"Wait," I snapped. "You're right in the middle of your story about Faye."

He nodded. "It'll keep. How about we go to dinner one of these days and I'll tell you all about it?"

Dinner. Yes. Dinner.

"Okay," I managed to say.

"Take care, Elbert," he said. "Delmar."

They waved but they were already busy trying to figure out how to hook Igor up to the tow truck. And David was already gone through the front door on his way to the backyard.

So I watched the boys work for a minute.

"What am I going to call him after you make him beautiful?" I asked Elbert. "I can't call him Igor anymore, can I?"

"A rose by any other name would smell as sweet," Delmar responded absently, not looking up from his work.

That made me decide to go back inside because I was already disoriented enough. I didn't even say thank you or goodbye to the boys. Maybe it was the cognitive fog.

Through the front door and a few steps inside, I noticed Cannonball lounging beside the stereo in the dining room. How he had managed to get his significant bulk up onto the sideboard was a mystery, but there he was, on his side, head nuzzling the stereo.

I approached.

"I owe you," I told him. "That was a nice bit of distraction last night, racing out from under this piece of furniture to distract Rae the way you did. It's possible that it saved my life."

Cannonball looked at me with his head upside down and clawed at the stereo.

"Okay," I told him. "What do you want to hear? Just tell me, and I'll play it."

But the answer was obvious, and we both knew it. I went to the wall of records and searched. Anomalous to all the rest of Rose's system, the records were alphabetized by artist. So it really didn't take much doing to find Georgie Fame's *Cool Cat Blues* album.

I put it on the stereo and set the volume just a little louder than it needed to be. Georgie started singing instantly. "It's early in mornin', soon be a new day dawnin' . . ."

And as the song filled up the shop, some of the students paused, listened, and nodded.

I sauntered into the parlor. Jennifer was just finishing up with a customer—a customer who was buying a whole stack, and not all of them were textbooks.

The customer gathered up her finds, nodded my way, and moved on.

"Who is this?" Jennifer asked me. "Who's singing? What kind of music is this? It's cool."

My face warmed and I smiled. "That, my friend, is jazz. Let me tell you about it."

And whether or not anyone in the shop recognized it at the moment, the entire place was filled up with Joy.

ACKNOWLEDGMENTS

Acknowledgment is made to the Georgia Council for the Arts, which placed the author in the position of writer-in-residence in smaller South Georgia towns for extended periods of time. Living between Enigma and Omega gave everything in life an odd air of mystery.

ABOUT THE AUTHOR

P. J. NELSON is the pseudonym of an award-winning actor, dramatist, professor, and novelist (among many other professions) who has done just about everything except run a bookstore. P. J. lives in Decatur, Georgia.